LADY IN THE BRIARS

LADY IN THE BRIARS

Carola Dunn

Walker and Company
New York

First published in the United States of America in 1990 by
Walker Publishing Company, Inc.
Published simultaneously in Canada by Thomas Allen & Son
Canada, Limited, Markham, Ontario

Library of Congress Cataloging-in-Publication Data

Dunn, Carola
Lady in the briars/Carola Dunn
ISBN 0-8027-1116-2
I. Title.
PR6054.U537L24   1990
813'.914—dc20   90-35567
CIP

Printed in the United States of America
2 4 6 8 10 9 7 5 3 1

Prologue

October 1819

PALE WRAITHS OF mist waltzed across the dew-drenched lawn as Rebecca slipped out through the side door of the manor. She set down her portmanteaux and turned to close the door behind her. Despite her care the click of the latch sounded loud in the dawn stillness.

She held her breath and listened. A rook cawed in a distant elm but there was no sound from the sleeping house.

To renew her courage she touched the letter in her pocket. Lady Parr was in need of a companion and would be happy to offer her young cousin a home in London. All the contrivances to keep the correspondence secret from her uncle were worthwhile since they had brought that response.

Rebecca pulled her hood close about her ears, picked up the bags and flitted across the wet grass to the shelter of the woods. Her grey cloak merged with the grey beech trunks, veiled by the mist. She did not look back.

New-fallen leaves crunched crisply beneath her half-boots. She trudged down the path, her luggage growing heavier at every step but her heart buoyed by the hope of freedom. When she reached the lane, Geoff Carter was waiting as he promised, with his wagonload of beechwood chairs for the fine furniture stores of London.

Geoff's son had been transported for poaching. He had

430734

no love for the squire and would never give her away.

"Marnin', Mistress Beckie." He stowed her bags among the chairs and helped her up onto the bench. With instinctive courtesy he kept his gaze from the bruise on her left cheek.

"Good morning, Geoff, and bless you."

The taciturn countryman nodded. He clucked at his team and the patient horses plodded on.

It would take fourteen hours to reach the city, but if Squire Exbridge searched at all he would check the stagecoach from Aylesbury. Nor would he start the search soon, for he always slept late after one of his violent drinking bouts while Rebecca and her aunt huddled in their rooms, away from the curious, commiserating eyes of the servants. She would not be missed for hours.

She touched her sore cheek and reminded herself that her uncle was no longer her legal guardian. Yesterday she had turned twenty-one. Though he controlled her fortune until her twenty-fifth birthday, he had no other power over her.

Never again would she allow any man power over her.

= 1 =

March 1820

LORD JOHN DANVILLE screwed up his aching eyes against the glare of the rising sun. The headband of his beaver was pressing unbearably on his forehead, so he took it off and let the light breeze ruffle his dark hair. He groaned.

"Why did this seem like such a good notion last night, Bev?" he enquired in a failing voice.

"There was no bearing old Worthington's sneers about the effete younger generation." His friend was a literal-minded gentleman. "When Rawley boasted about seeing Minette on the sly while she's under your protection, the only thing to do was to challenge him."

John groaned again.

"You're by far the better shot," Mr. Bevan hastened to assure him.

"I've no intention of shooting a man over the honour of a ladybird!"

He stepped down from the carriage, moving cautiously so as not to awaken the drummer in his head. The hoar-frosted grass of Paddington Green crackled beneath his Hessians. Bev, who had drunk at least as much of the Royal Saloon's brandy last night, jumped down after him with infuriating alacrity and walked over to talk to Rawley's seconds. He returned moments later, grinning, to offer his principal a choice of pistols.

1

"Rawley don't mean to aim for the heart either," he reported, "but we're agreed you'll have to go through the motions to show old Worthington."

John chose a gun at random and waited while the seconds measured out the distance. Reluctantly, he took his place. There was a crow perched on the branch of an oak not six feet beyond his opponent and slightly to one side. He would aim at that.

The handkerchief dropped. Raising the pistol, John turned towards the bird. As he squeezed the trigger, his foot slid on the slippery turf.

The two reports sounded almost simultaneously, ringing in the frosty air. The crow flapped away, croaking its disgust.

The Honourable Augustus Rawley slumped to the ground.

"He is not dead, thank God. I swear to you, sir, it was an accident."

"I believe it." Despite his words, the Duke of Stafford's sternness was unabated. "Whatever your faults, you are no liar, nor, I trust, so stupid as to fight over the favours of a Paphian. The fact remains, I have had enough of your irresponsibility. Your present way of life can lead only to disaster. You need an occupation."

"I begged to join the army ten years ago." John tried not to sound resentful.

"Perhaps I was wrong to let your mother persuade me not to allow it. It is too late now. My intention is to find you a post abroad."

"I had rather go into Parliament, sir."

His father raised his eyebrows. "Indeed? Prove yourself in the diplomatic service and I shall speak to Liverpool about finding you a government post."

"I'm afraid I'd prefer to sit on the opposition benches, sir. I've a mind to join the fight against slavery." John's voice grew enthusiastic. "I have thought of it on and off since Teresa told us about rescuing those slaves in the Indies, and the other day I was talking to Iverbrook . . . I beg your pardon, sir. I do not expect you to help me join the Whigs."

"I daresay you think my influence does not run so far. You are mistaken. However, that is beside the point at present. You must leave the country until this scandal blows over."

"Like Cousin Teresa's father. But he killed a marquis, did he not? And I have merely wounded the heir to a barony."

"There is no comparison with my brother Edward. Your grandfather exiled him for life. You will be taking a position in one of our embassies, and I sincerely hope you will exert yourself to be useful. Until I can make arrangements, you are to go down to Lincolnshire."

Though John grimaced, he knew better than to argue. His brother Tom was starchy and Muriel, Lady Danville, was a bore, but in truth it would not be so bad to leave town for a while. There might be some good hunting with the Fitzwilliam, and he could ride over for a day or two to join the Belvoir or the Cottesmore. Somewhat to his own surprise, he also found himself looking forward to seeing his nephew again—a game little fellow, young Ned.

As for the embassy post, even if he was set to scribing reports there would be a foreign land to explore at leisure and he was not be exiled forever.

He tactfully withheld a jaunty whistle until the duke's study door closed behind him.

After a fortnight as a guest in his house, Rebecca still found Lord Danville intimidating. She had never seen him lose his temper, and he was kind to her in his somewhat pompous way, but he was a man, and men were by defini-tion unpredictable and threatening.

In her nervousness at finding herself alone at the break-fast table with him, she spilled her tea. Without a pause in his disquisition on the state of the fields after last night's storm, his lordship raised a finger. The butler swiftly and silently removed the offending cup and saucer, laid a clean napkin over the spreading stain, and presented a fresh cup.

"Do you mean to walk this morning?" Lord Danville enquired. "There was great deal of rain in the night, but if the past week's north winds have not deterred you I daresay you will think nothing of a little mud."

"No, sir . . . I mean, yes, I shall go out."

"I don't blame you a bit." His tone was conspiratorial. His relationship with Lady Parr, his mother-in-law, was far from cordial. "Lucky thing the old dragon rises late. Muriel asked that you pop in for a moment before you go. I'm afraid she doesn't feel at all the thing. It always takes her this way, you know. Have another muffin, do."

Rebecca obediently took the toasted muffin the butler offered her and spread it with butter and jam, but she could not eat more than a few bites. Though Lady Parr was constantly admonishing her for being skinny, mealtimes were inextricably connected in her mind with her uncle's unavoidable presence. The very act of sitting down at table made her lose her appetite.

Lord Danville finished his methodical demolition of a plateful of devilled kidneys, washed it down with a glass of ale and took his leave. Rebecca thankfully abandoned her muffin and hurried above-stairs.

Muriel was in bed, a lacy nightcap crowning the golden curls above a pallid face. As Rebecca entered her chamber she put down the dry toast she was nibbling distastefully and waved to her maid to take the tray away.

"This wretched morning sickness," she wailed. "I always feel like death until noon for the first three months. Poor Tom is so patient with me."

Rebecca thought that it was entirely Tom's fault that his wife was increasing again, but she made soothing noises and patted Muriel's hand.

"Lord Danville—Cousin Tom—said that you wanted to see me?"

"Oh Beckie, I'm so sorry about Mama scolding you last night in front of the servants. I ought to have remonstrated with her, but I am so used to obeying her that even now I am married I cannot bring myself to confront her."

"It was nothing. I promise you it takes more than a reproof or two to overset me, and I had indeed forgotten to fetch her shawl. Pray do not worry about me, Muriel, for I am content with my position. I have been with Cousin Adelaide for nearly half a year and she has never raised a hand to me."

Muriel looked at her in astonishment.

"Mama beat you? Oh no, she would never do that, however sharp her tongue. Why, I don't believe she has ever so much has cuffed her abigail, and you are a relative."

Embarrassed, Rebecca changed the subject. "A very distant relative. It is kind in Lord Danville to insist that I call him cousin."

"Dear Tom has a very strong sense of family. Which reminds me, Nurse says little Mary was fretful in the night. Will you go and see her when you come in from your walk? She and Edward do love you so."

"I'll go up at once."

"No, take your walk first, before Mama rises. You remind me of Teresa, the way you walk in all weathers. We should never have been abducted if she had not insisted on tramping through the mud, and then I should have been married to Andrew instead of Tom and we'd all have been miserable forever."

Rebecca laughed. "I do not expected to be abducted, nor to find a husband! Shall I take Buttercup? She will get muddy."

"One of the stable boys can clean her before she comes in. She has been much better behaved in the house since you have been exercising her regularly. How glad I am that Mama brought you to visit! You are by far the nicest companion she has had."

As Rebecca left the house, with the little spaniel frisking ahead, she reflected on her predecessors in the post of companion to Lady Parr. In the four years since Muriel's marriage to the heir to the Duke of Stafford, her ladyship had gone through a round dozen. Most of them, according to Muriel, had left in tears or in a huff.

Rebecca saw no cause for either. A scolding unaccompanied by a blow was nothing. Muriel had been shocked at her comment, but experience had taught Rebecca to expect violence from those in authority. She knew Cousin Tom never raised a finger to Muriel, but then Muriel never crossed him, being a placid, obliging creature. She never crossed her mother either.

Though Lady Parr was easily irked, Rebecca did not fear her and she enjoyed being useful. She had time to herself, to walk and read, and since coming to Lincolnshire she had found in Muriel her first friend since childhood.

She enjoyed Muriel's little daughter and son. It was a pity that one could not have a family without first taking a husband. That precondition put it beyond her reach, but perhaps one day she might find employment caring for children.

Passing the row of tall, narrow poplars that sheltered the house and gardens, Rebecca and Buttercup left the gravel path and set out across the meadows. Only yesterday the flat green fields had been frozen hard; after the rain they were as muddy as Lord Danville had warned. Undeterred, Rebecca walked on, watching the last stormclouds drifting eastward. They crossed several wooden bridges over the frequent drainage dykes, and she saw that the water level had risen. Buttercup stayed close to her heels as they passed through a herd of Lincoln red cattle, staring incuriously, then they reached the river embankment and the little dog dashed ahead again.

Rebecca followed, up the steep, slippery grass slope. From this slight eminence she could see for miles across the levels. The church tower rose above the trees around the village, and she turned in that direction. The usually placid river was in full spate. Grey-brown water swirled almost to the raised banks, tugging at the skirts of the willows.

Rebecca picked her way carefully along the path towards the bridge that led to the village.

The spaniel rounded a twisted hawthorn and started to bark, her high yips sounding above the river's roar. Rebecca could see nothing but a stumpy tail, wagging madly. She hurried past the tree. A small boy, perhaps eight or nine, was perched on the edge of the bank, fishing in the turbulent stream with a stick and a bit of string.

"Hush, Buttercup! Come here."

"Thet's all roight, miss, Oi don't moind 'im." The child flashed an engaging gap-toothed grin, then turned back to the serious business of baiting the bent pin on the end of his line. Reaching for it, he lost his balance and slid feet first into the river.

Rebecca dropped to her knees and grabbed at his flailing hand. Her fingers closed over him as the current took him with a jerk. Feeling herself falling, she caught at a tuft of grass. It came loose in her fist and she gasped as the icy water closed over her.

Somehow she kept her grip on his hand. They were swept downstream, tossed and tumbled, to fetch up with a thud against one of the timber supports of the bridge. Clinging instinctively to the post and to each other, they gulped air into their starved lungs.

Buttercup was yelping from the bank. She ran onto the bridge and stopped above them, her black-and-tan rump in the air as she peered anxiously over the side.

Her worried eyes looked very far away. Rebecca cautiously freed one arm and stretched upward. Her fingertips curled over a cross-brace.

Her feet were touching the riverbed, she realized. If she managed to wriggle out of her heavy, sodden cloak she might just be able to pull herself up. But the boy could not reach, nor could she lift him. If she deserted him he would be torn away by the raging torrent.

Helpless, they hugged the post with numbing arms.

= 2 =

"DEVILISH DAMP PART of the country," observed Mr. Bevan critically as the horses' hooves drummed across yet another plank bridge.

"It was all marshland once," John informed him. "The Romans were the first to drain it."

"I say, old chap!" His friend sounded alarmed.

John grinned. "Not to worry, I shan't lecture you. The place has been in the family practically since the Conquest, and m'brother's liable to spout off about the history at the drop of a hat."

Bev clutched his hat. "Don't know Danville well, but now I come to think of it, I remember the bear-garden jaw he gave us when you had that shooting match with your cousin. Prosy sort, too, is he? Daresay I shan't stay long." Inspiration struck. "Bad for my rheumatism, you know, all this water."

"Coming it rather too thick and rare! Just tell my sister-in-law that your family is expecting you. Speak of the devil—that looks like Muriel's spaniel on the bridge there. Here, Buttercup. Here, girl."

"Buttercup!" Bev snorted in disgust. "What a name for an inoffensive creature."

The dog darted towards them, barking furiously, then backed away, refusing to leave the bridge. This one crossed not a drainage channel but a river, a raging torrent sweeping branches and other flotsam along in its rush towards the sea.

John saw half the sunken remains of a rowboat caught in a willow on the far side. Surely no one would have gone boating on a flood like that, yet the dog was behaving oddly. Frowning, he spurred forward. Buttercup raced to the middle of the bridge and stopped, yapping at something in the water.

With a gesture to Bev to halt behind him, John drew rein. As soon as the sound of hoofbeats died away, he heard a weak cry.

"Help!"

He swung down and knelt beside the little dog. Two white faces gazed up at him.

Tossing his hat aside and ripping off his greatcoat, he issued rapid orders to Bev. His boots followed his hat and he lowered himself over the side of the bridge. His feet found a cross-brace. He swivelled to sit astride it, half under the span, and saw with satisfaction that the unfortunate pair were within reach.

A girl and a freckle-faced child. She was holding fast to a post, the other arm about the boy so that he would not be swept away if he lost his grasp. The lad raised his arms. John leaned down and gripped his wrists. Muscles long strengthened in Gentleman Jackson's Boxing Saloon and in wild curricle races tautened. He was in an awkward position, with little leverage, but inch by slow inch the river unwilling yielded its prey.

Lying flat on the bridge above, Bev stretched down and took over the burden as soon as he could reach. As the lad rose above his head, John thanked heaven that he was travelling with his favourite sparring partner.

He looked down at the girl. He could not possibly lift her in the same way. He had reluctantly reached the conclusion that he would have to join her to help her when he saw that the derelict rowboat had broken free of the willow branches and was racing downstream towards her. Without hesitation he slithered down beside her, pressing her to the post.

The shock of the frigid water was instantly succeeded by

the shock of the boat hitting his back broadside. It hurt, but the pain was numbed by the coldness.

"A spectacular bruise, no doubt," he muttered, then shouted in her ear above the roar of the river, "Soon have you out of here!"

His feet were on firm silt, the cross-brace was within easy reach of his six foot plus. Moments later he was sitting on the planks beside the huddled figure of the rescued girl, shivering as he ruefully contemplated the duckweed that decorated one of Weston's best efforts.

He shrugged out of the ruined coat, his gaze moving to the girl. She lay very still, eyes closed, her lips bluish. He glanced at Bev.

"Be a good fellow and take the tyke home," he half requested, half commanded.

"My coat will never be the same again," Mr. Bevan mourned, but he picked up the dripping child, set him on his horse's withers and mounted behind him. "Sure you can manage?"

"I'll manage." John was already struggling with the fastenings of the girl's cloak.

Her eyes opened, filled with terror, and she made a feeble motion towards his hands.

"Keep still. I shan't harm you but you'll freeze to death if I don't get these wet things off you quickly."

Though she obeyed, he felt her frightened gaze on his face as he stripped off the cloak. It worried him that she was not shivering. He had to tear her dress to remove it, and as he did so he talked to her soothingly, as he would to a nervous horse. Her wet shift clung to her skin. She was skinny, her ribs showing clearly, the dark nipples of her small breasts visible through the thin linen.

"Where are you from?" he asked abruptly. He had nothing to dry her with, so he might as well leave her the minimal decency of her underclothing. He reached for his discarded greatcoat, wrapped it about her and fastened the buttons.

"V-visiting . . . Lord Danville," she whispered.

She must be a friend of Muriel's. He picked her up to lift her to his horse's back. She was light as a feather without the wet garments. As an afterthought he kicked their clothes into the river—no need to start any unnecessary rumours.

"We'll be home in ten minutes," he reassured her.

She managed to cling to the horse's mane while he swung up into the saddle. He pulled her back against his chest and resumed his interrupted journey to his brother's house, Buttercup prancing alongside.

The girl was shaking now, and a little colour had returned to her lips. On the other hand, John was frozen. He had not been so cold and wet since his cousin Teresa had doused him with a bucket of icy water.

She had soaked Andrew too, he remembered with a grin, in her successful effort to stop that dog fight. What a woman she was! If she had fallen into that river, as she well might with her talent for scrapes, she would doubtless have rescued both herself and the boy without a second thought. John sighed. Teresa had been Andrew's wife for years now, and he would never find another like her. The girl in his arms, for instance, seemed to be a fearful creature in need of protection, very different from his lively, independent cousin.

Not that he had any intention of marrying. He rather thought he should enjoy a life of bachelorhood, like his Uncle Cecil, though he'd be damned if he'd ever let himself grow so stout.

They cantered around the poplar windbreak and up the drive. Rebecca felt a flood of relief as the house grew nearer. The stranger really had brought her home. She was much warmer already, in control of her limbs, and she could not wait to escape his overpowering, masculine presence.

As soon as their mount came to a standstill at the front steps, she pulled away from his restraining arm and slid to the ground. To her dismay, her knees buckled. Grasping for support, she found herself clinging to a well-muscled leg clad in damp buckskin. The gentleman grinned down at her and an embarrassed flush swept her from top to toe.

She transferred her grip to the stirrup leather, still far too close to him for comfort. As a stableboy ran up to take the reins, her rescuer awkwardly dismounted on the horse's other side.

Whatever he thought of this strange manoeuvre, the patient, well-mannered beast merely snorted gently.

His master advanced on Rebecca. For the first time she realized how very large he was. Though her height was above average he topped her head and shoulders, making her feel small and helpless. The feeling was intensified when he picked her up without a by-your-leave and strode up the steps to the front door, shouting for service.

Lord Danville's footman had the door open when they reached it.

"Lord John!" he gasped. "Miss Nuthall!"

"Hot baths," ordered the gentleman, coming straight to the point. "A hot drink for the lady—Miss Nuthall?—and brandy for me."

"At once, my lord." The butler appeared. Unruffled by the commotion, he dismissed his underling about his business with a wave. "An accident, I take it, my lord. Perhaps your lordship will be so good as to carry Miss Nuthall into the parlour, where there is a good fire."

"No, I can walk," Rebecca protested. Lord John's arms tightened about her and, panicking, she began to struggle. At once he set her on her feet, steadying her with a hand at her elbow.

Lord Danville emerged from the library to one side of the vestibule, Muriel from the parlour on the other, the latter followed by Lady Parr.

"John, what . . . ?"

"Beckie, what . . . ?"

"Rebecca, what is the meaning of this disgraceful scene?" Lady Parr's enquiry cut through the babble.

"Pray hush, Mama, can you not see that she is unwell? Dear Beckie, come above-stairs at once. Tom will lend you his arm, will you not, my love?"

"To be sure," said Lord Danville, advancing. "My arm is at your cousin's disposal and my wardrobe at my brother's."

Of course, he was Tom's brother, thought Rebecca as her host and hostess helped her unsteady steps up the stairs. There had been something familiar about him, but she had been in no case to ponder it. She glanced back.

"I demand an explanation." Lady Parr's penetrating voice reached her. "What sort of scrape has that foolish child fallen into now?"

Lord John stood dripping on the flagstones, towering over the short, stout lady.

"I'm dashed if I know the details, ma'am," he said with indignation, "but I'll go bail Miss Nuthall had no intention of taking a swim. Sort of thing that could happen to anyone."

Rebecca heard Lady Parr's disbelieving snort as they reached the landing. Lord John's ingenuous defence warmed her.

The hot bath Muriel and her abigail hurried her into completed the thaw. She was ready to go down and make her excuses to Lady Parr, but Muriel insisted on putting her to bed with an extra eiderdown and a cup of broth.

The kindness made tears rise to Rebecca's eyes. A distant memory of a childhood illness returned: Mama and Grand-mère had cosseted her thus, and Papa had brought marzipan and a wooden monkey on a stick. She had long since discovered that it was best not to think of those happy days, for they made her life in her uncle's house the more unbearable by comparison. Yet now she was free of him, perhaps she dared allow herself to remember.

"If you are sure you feel well enough," Muriel was saying, "I shall bring Mary to see you in a while."

"Pray do. And then I must explain to Cousin Adelaide how it all happened."

"There is no need for explanations, Beckie dear. We are just glad that John was there to make himself useful for once. Now, I must go and see that he has been made comfortable. Try if you can sleep a little."

Rebecca watched her bustle out, smiling at her firmness. Timid as Lady Danville seemed in her mother's presence, she ran her household with the greatest aplomb, and would doubtless make an excellent duchess one day.

All the same, Cousin Adelaide must have an explanation sooner or later. Muriel and her abigail had delicately avoided commenting on Rebecca's lack of clothing under John's greatcoat. Doubtless they would not spread the word, but would John himself be equally reticent? His sister-in-law had commented more than once on his disgracefully rakish ways, his irresponsibility. Rebecca shuddered to think how utterly she had been at his mercy, and still she was not free of him. He might think it an amusing story, or even suppose that it gave him license to pester her with his attentions.

She resolved to avoid him as much as possible. That was not likely to prove difficult, for he would hardly seek out the company of Lady Parr!

If she had heard the conversation in the bedchamber just across the hall, it would have confirmed this supposition.

"Not even his grace's orders could have persuaded me to come within a mile of the place if I'd known you had that devilish woman visiting," grumbled Lord John, stretching carpet-slippered feet to the fire and sipping at his bumper of brandy and hot water.

"Family." His brother was apologetic. "She won't be here more than another fortnight, for even Muriel won't put up with her longer than that. I've developed a veritable plethora of ways to ensure her departure on time. But tell me just why we have been honoured with your presence. His grace's orders, you say?"

"I'll tell you when you have explained to me who Miss Nuthall is."

Thomas, Viscount Danville, heir to the Duke of Stafford, had never been known to refuse an invitation to speak.

"Rebecca Nuthall is a distant cousin of Muriel's. Lady Parr's maternal uncle was married to . . . "

"Cut line, Tom! I can do without the family tree. What is she doing here?"

"Acting as companion to Lady Parr; the thirteenth, I believe. She's lasted longer than the rest. A meek, nervous creature."

"Oh, a lady's companion." John's tone dismissed the occupation as beneath his notice, but he went on to ask, "Does the old dragon starve her? She's thin as a rail."

"Starve her? In my house? I trust you are joking! Rebecca has a delicate appetite, I daresay. What exactly happened this morning?"

"She fell into one of your devilish watercourses and I fished her out. There was a boy, too. I wonder what's become of Bev?"

"Mr. Bevan arrived a half hour since, while you were in your bath. He, too, was in need of a borrowed coat."

John jumped up and headed for the door. "Bev's less likely to split your seams than I am," he said over his shoulder, "and our traps should arrive at any minute. The carriage set out from Stamford at the same time we did."

"Where are you going? You cannot wander about the house in my dressing gown in broad daylight!"

"Tell me which chamber is Bev's and I shan't have to wander about. Or I could leave the dressing gown behind," offered John with a grin, his hand on the knob.

With a resigned sigh Tom went to fetch Mr. Bevan and moments later the three gentlemen were once more seated cosily about the fire.

"The lad was right as rain by the time I got him home," Bev reported. "One of your tenants' brats, Danville, and more like to get a hiding than sympathy by the look on his father's face."

"Did he tell you how the accident came about?" Tom asked.

15

"He swore up and down the young lady jumped in to save him, and that she could have climbed out but she wouldn't abandon him. Regular heroine, I collect."

"That doesn't sound like Rebecca." Tom shook his head. "She's a spiritless little thing, couldn't say boo to a goose."

John agreed. "She struck me as the timid sort. Delicate. I'll wager you it's all a hum."

"Regular heroine," his friend persisted. "You're on for ten guineas. The boy would have been washed away if she hadn't held him up. How is she? Looked to be in queer stirrups when you fished her out."

"Yes, I'd have sworn she was half dead, yet she managed to walk above-stairs after I carried her in. Insisted on it, in fact. Come to think of it, that showed some pluck."

"Told you so," Bev said triumphantly.

"How is she?" John turned to Tom.

"I'll go and ask Muriel. I've business to see to, can't sit about chatting all day. We'll talk later." With a dark glance at his brother, the viscount heaved himself out of his chair and departed.

"Not in the way, am I?" Bev lounged back with his boots on the gleaming brass fender, reaching for the glass of brandy on the table at his elbow.

"On the contrary. *Your* presence has postponed a painful explanation of *my* presence."

"Haven't told him about the duel yet, eh?"

"Of all the ill-considered, muttonheaded starts," John said gloomily, "that was the stupidest."

"It seemed like a good idea at the time. Tell me about the young lady you pulled out of the river. I gather she is staying here?"

"Tom's mother-in-law's companion, Miss Rebecca Nuthall."

"Not an heiress then. Pity."

"Don't tell me you're looking for an heiress! Under the hatches again?"

"Not at all! Well, I admit it's low tide with me till quarter day but that's not far off and I'm not about to let it drive me into parson's mousetrap. Never hurts to have an unknown heiress up one's sleeve though. Pretty, is she?" Bev asked.

"Don't be a clunch. If there's a woman on this earth who looks pretty when she's frozen and half-drowned, I'd like to meet her. Besides, pretty females have no need to become lady's companions."

"True." Mr. Bevan's sigh was philosophical. "And from what your brother said she's not even a lively 'un. Ah, well, daresay I ought to be on my way tomorrow."

"You can't mean to desert me so soon! And don't tell me the damp is bad for your rheumatism."

"My dear fellow, you can't expect me to stay in the middle of a family row without even a flirtation to amuse me."

"There won't be a row," said John optimistically. "Tom may be six years my senior but he ain't head of the family yet. At worst, he'll sermonize."

"In that case," Bev resolved, "I'll be gone at first light!"

When Tom cornered him later that afternoon, John's optimism proved well-founded. The viscount tut-tutted at the story of the duel, but agreed that the outcome had been an unfortunate accident.

"Rawley's not likely to die, is he? Barring a fever or putrefaction of the wound? So that's why his grace has sent you to rusticate."

"Worse than that. He's sending me abroad. I'll be leaving as soon as he's arranged a post for me in one of our embassies."

To John's indignation, his staid brother roared with laughter.

"You—a diplomat!" he spluttered. "This is too rich!"

"I daresay I can be as good a diplomat as the next man."

"Where are you going? I suppose he will not reward you with Paris or Vienna."

"More likely some godforsaken hellhole like Calcutta or Cairo. The sort of place Teresa and Andrew would love to visit."

"They are off to far more civilized parts on their next posting. I heard from them only this morning. They will be coming to stay for a few days next week on their way to Hull to take ship for St. Petersburg."

John brightened. "Coming here? Famous! I haven't seen Teresa since they stayed with us in London in the autumn, just after they arrived back in England."

"Muriel hopes to persuade Teresa to leave the little girl with us."

"She'll catch cold at that. The child was born in China, wasn't she? She has already travelled half round the world. I'll lay you a monkey Teresa will think nothing of taking her to Russia."

"That's one wager I'll not take you up on, though I don't say I approve. Our cousin may be an intrepid traveller but it is the outside of enough to endanger her daughter unnecessarily."

"Russia's not so very different from England. I met Prince Nikolai Volkov when the Tsar was here in '14, and I assure you he was up to every rig and row."

"That is hardly reassuring! However, it is certainly safer than China and I do not mean to pinch at Teresa about it. I beg you will not lead her into mischief while she is here."

"Come, Tom, she is a respectable matron now."

"If she has changed, you have not."

Foreseeing the expected lecture on his here-and-thereian ways, John made his escape.

= 3 =

"IS THAT MISS Nuthall? You had me expecting a muffin-faced drab!" Bev's whispered indignation was just audible above the crackle of the drawing-room fire.

John turned towards the door. He was pleasantly surprised by the slight figure poised there like a nervous doe. The hair he had seen in lank strands intertwined with duckweed turned out, when dry and wound in a coronet of braids about her head, to be a glossy bronze. Her brown eyes had a slight, attractive tilt, and her thinness was less obvious when her clothes were not damply revealing every inch of her figure.

Muriel bustled forward and took her hand.

"Beckie, dear, come and be introduced."

The gentlemen bowed and murmured, "Delighted," as the girl curtsied, a flush mantling her delicate features.

"Thank you, my lord, Mr. Bevan, for rescuing me." Her soft voice was composed, but before she lowered her gaze John noted the look of apprehension she cast at him.

"Our pleasure, Miss Nuthall." Eager to put her at ease, he continued, "Bev tells us you are a heroine."

"Heroine?" She seemed bewildered.

"The farmer's lad told me how you jumped into the river to save him," Mr. Bevan explained.

"Oh no, I did not jump in, I slipped."

John had never before met a female who would deny a story so much to her credit. It intrigued him.

"And you did not stay in the water to hold him up, when

19

you might have climbed out on your own?" he asked.

"I . . . I doubt I am strong enough to have climbed out unaided."

"Then you did not even attempt it? That qualifies you as a heroine in my book, ma'am. You must accept the title."

"Of course she is a heroine," said Muriel, "but pray do not bother her about it now, John. She is not yet quite recovered. Come and sit down, Beckie."

John had a distinct feeling that the girl was glad of an excuse to escape. Wealthy, titled and handsome, he was more used to being chased by hopeful maidens. He watched thoughtfully as she followed his sister-in-law across the room.

Bev dug him in the ribs with his elbow and muttered in his ear, "Ten guineas."

John scowled at his inoffensive friend. He had completely forgotten their wager and now it struck him that if Miss Nuthall came to hear of it she might think he had questioned her with the ulterior motive of disproving her heroism.

"Hush!" he hissed. "We'll be going in to dinner at any moment. I'll pay you tonight."

At that moment Lady Parr came in. With a regal nod to the young gentlemen, she sailed past them and plumped into a chair beside the sofa on which Miss Nuthall now reclined. Her piercing voice easily reached John's ears.

"Well, girl, where have you been hiding?"

"Cousin Muriel would not allow me to rise from my bed, ma'am. I hope my absence has not been troublesome."

"Of course it has been troublesome," said her ladyship testily. "I mislaid my spectacles and could neither read nor set a stitch without you to find them for me. What is this shocking tale I hear of you jumping into a river after a village urchin? I expect more decorum of my·companion."

The girl seemed not in the least discomposed by the combined interrogation and tongue-lashing but John found it acutely irritating.

"May I join you, ma'am?" He took a seat nearby before

any objection could be voiced. "I think you cannot have heard that Miss Nuthall is something of a heroine."

Lady Parr raised a quizzing glass that had quelled many an impertinent jackanapes. Lord John was made of sterner stuff and withstood the scrutiny with scarcely a blink. However, to his dismay he saw that his taking up arms in her behalf, far from pleasing the girl, had brought back the look of alarm to her pale face.

Why was she afraid of him? Surely she could not suppose him such a blackguard as to tell anyone how he had stripped her nearly naked on the bridge!

"Heroines are best left between the pages of a novel, or on the stage," Lady Parr was declaring. "It is, to say the least, indiscreet for a young woman to put herself forward in such a way."

John smiled at the girl, reassuringly he hoped. "They say discretion is the better part of valour, but since your valour saved a child from drowning, I cannot agree. Allow me to help you, Miss Nuthall," he added as the butler appeared to announce that dinner was served.

"Oh no, I can manage very well, my lord. Pray take in Cousin Adelaide."

He acquiesced, though with a bad grace. Doubtless had she accepted his aid it would have led to another scolding for putting herself forward and he wanted to spare her that.

Tom escorted Miss Nuthall into the dining room, but she did not take his arm, John noted. While bearing his part in the general conversation, he watched her. She scarcely spoke, seldom raising her eyes from her plate though she ate very little. To be sure her position was awkward, both companion and relative, yet such reticence seemed excessive. And she was too pretty to waste her life away jumping at the bidding of the old tartar.

John sensed a mystery.

It might be amusing to try to fathom her secret before the duke sent him off to the ends of the earth. In any case, he must seek her out privately to assure her that she need fear no scandalous revelation from his lips.

As it happened, his continued silence had already reassured Rebecca on that head. Neither by word nor by look had he so much as hinted at having seen her *en extreme déshabille*. She was grateful, but nonetheless embarrassed by his presence. She also found him even more intimidating than his brother.

She mused on this when she retired to her chamber, shortly after dinner and long before the gentlemen joined the ladies in the drawing-room. Lord John was taller than the viscount, to be sure, though not by much, and broader in the shoulders. Yet it was not so much his size that disturbed her: after all her uncle, who terrified her, was not a large man. It was his air of vitality, perhaps, the sense of boundless vigour barely held in check.

Muriel had intimated that her brother-in-law's energies were chiefly expended on such frivolous pursuits as gambling, drinking and wenching. However, Rebecca had seen no signs of the flabbiness of dissipation. On the contrary, Lord John possessed a splendidly muscular figure as well as a face certain to guarantee success with any number of wenches.

Taken one by one, his features were very like Cousin Tom's, but whereas Tom's expression in repose was definitely haughty, John's liveliness made a quite different impression. It attracted Rebecca even as she fled him.

She had just slipped into bed when there was a light knock on the door and Muriel came in.

"I just wanted to make sure you are all right, Beckie. You may make nothing of it but it must have been the horridest experience. John has been making us all laugh with his description of his valet's disgust at the condition of his clothes. It seems that Pierce made John promise that if he ever again jumps into a river he will not do so in a coat from Weston."

"Oh dear, I had not thought, his things must be quite spoiled. That is a poor reward for his gallantry in saving me."

"I assure you he does not regard it in the least. You must not suppose that because he is a younger son he is purse-pinched. His allowance from the duke is excessively generous. Besides, Tom says he is amazingly lucky in his gaming and wagering on horse-races and prize-fights and such. He may be a scapegrace, as Tom calls him, but he is very droll and always ready to laugh at himself. I wish you had stayed to hear his joking."

"I was a little tired."

"John asked if you were indisposed. How he defended you against Mama's reproaches! I do believe that having rescued you once he considers himself your champion."

"I hope not. I promise you I was in no need of his help with Cousin Adelaide. I ought to have gone down this afternoon, as she said."

"Nonsense, it was I who insisted that you stay abed, and Mama managed very well without you. Now I must let you sleep. Good-night, my dear."

Rebecca woke early the next morning, much refreshed. She dressed and went down, but as she approached the breakfast room she heard three masculine voices within: Lord Danville, Lord John and Mr. Bevan. Though she would have liked a cup of tea, she decided to wait until after her walk. She fetched Buttercup and set out in the opposite direction from the river.

The sun was shining and a breeze from the west carried a hint of spring warmth. The meadows were sprigged with clumps of pale pink lady's smock and golden kingcups spangled the banks of the dykes.

Rebecca felt she could walk to the end of the world. When she turned back, reluctantly, she had to hurry so as to be there when she was needed. She reached the house to find the gentlemen gone, their place in the breakfast room taken by Muriel and Cousin Adelaide.

She joined them. Her appetite sharpened by the exercise, she requested a slice of ham with her toast.

"I see you are quite recovered," observed Lady Parr with

rare approval. "If you ate thus more often you would soon lose that emaciated look. Though of course a lady must always be seen to eat like a bird." She delved into the mountain of food on her own plate and carefully raised a forkful of buttered eggs past a vast expanse of plump bosom to her mouth.

Muriel exchanged a smile with Rebecca.

"Mama and I have to pay some duty calls on my neighbours this morning," she said. "Do you care to go too?"

"There is not the least need for Rebecca to come with us." Cousin Adelaide's tone was firm. She enjoyed being introduced as the mother of the future duchess and saw no need to dilute the glory of the occasion with the presence of an indigent relative.

"You will not mind being alone?" Muriel asked Rebecca. "Tom has gone out with his bailiff and John rode up to Grantham to set Mr. Bevan on his way."

"Not at all. I shall go up and see the children, and then hide away in the library with a book."

The day nursery was a large, light room at the top of the house. The carpet was worn to a faded shadow of its blue-and-rose pattern, the furniture was somewhat battered, but bright chintz curtains hung at the sunny windows and Nurse was a large, motherly woman with a comfortable lap.

The children were eating their nuncheon when Rebecca arrived. Mary, a dark imp just over a year old, banged a welcome with her spoon, spattering something white and sticky across the table. Ned, with his mother's golden curls and something of his father's staidness, climbed down from his chair and bowed solemnly before running to catch Rebecca's hand.

"You want some bread-and-milk, Aunt Beckie?" he asked. "It's good. You can have some of mine."

She bent down and hugged him. "No, thank you, pet, I have just had my breakfast. Come and sit down and eat yours up, or Nurse will be cross."

"Did you have a egg for breakfas'? I did." He let her lift him into his chair and his next words were muffled by a spoonful of food. "Unc' John brung me a new book."

"Don't speak with your mouth full, Master Ned," said Nurse automatically.

"He brung me a drum too, but Papa said only play it outdoors."

Rebecca stayed long enough to read aloud the tale of Tom Thumb from the new book, and admire the rag doll Uncle John had presented to Mary. She was surprised and impressed that a Buck of the Ton should have remembered his little niece and nephew, let alone chosen such appropriate gifts. What was more, he seemed to have spent some time in the nursery. Ned chattered about Uncle John saying this and that, and having promised to take him up on his horse. Lord Danville was doubtless right to call his brother a scapegrace, but at least he was a kind scapegrace.

Some time later Rebecca made her way to the library. Tom's taste ran mostly to treatises on politics and agriculture, but he had gathered a collection of books on China since his cousin Teresa had gone there. Rebecca curled up in a chair by the fire with a new translation of the *Travels of Marco Polo*. She was half a world away in spirit when the butler came into the room.

"There's a Mr. Exbridge to see you, miss. Will you receive him?"

She had no time to deny herself before a short, sturdy man, beginning to run fat, pushed past the butler.

"Uncle!"

"Well, miss, what have you to say for yourself? A fine dance you've led me!"

Seeing that the visitor was a relative, the butler withdrew. He did not, however, shut the door completely behind him, and he was hovering anxiously outside it when John, returning from Grantham, strolled into the hall and spotted him.

"What the devil are you . . . " John stopped at the sound

of a raised voice—an angry male voice—in the library.

It was followed by a cry of pain. Once more the butler was brushed aside as John strode past him, slamming the door open. He paused on the threshold, his gaze drawn at once to the couple by the fireplace.

A man was standing over Miss Nuthall, shaking her.

"How dare you defy me!" he shouted, ignoring the crash of the door. "You'll do what I say or suffer the consequences." He raised his hand and hit the girl across the face.

John was upon him in a moment. He seized the back of his collar and swung him around to meet a right uppercut that stretched him dazed on the floor.

Miss Nuthall looked equally dazed. On her white face, the imprint of a hand stood out in painful red. There was a blank look in her eyes and she stood motionless, leaning against the chair to which she had reached for support when the man involuntarily released her.

John started towards her, then caught a movement on the floor. The man rose to one knee, stood up somewhat shakily, and glared at his assailant. He had bitten his lip and blood was trickling down his chin.

"Who the devil are you?" John demanded, putting into his tone all the haughtiness of generations of ducal ancestors.

"Joshua Exbridge." He pulled out a handkerchief and dabbed at his mouth. "And who the devil are you to interfere between a man and his niece? I'll thank you to keep your nose out of my business."

"Lord John Danville, at your service, sir." John's bow was a masterpiece of arrogant contempt. "An assault on my brother's guest is most certainly my business."

Mr. Exbridge seemed to wilt a little, though his truculence did not lessen. "Lord Danville won't thank you for this day's work, my lord. I've only come to fetch my ward home, as is my right and duty. The ungrateful chit ran off without a word to anyone and it's taken me half a year to track her down."

John glanced at Miss Nuthall. She had not stirred. The

red patch on her cheek had faded a little but the outline of a hand was still clearly visible. He clenched his fists, suddenly blazingly angry again.

"Get out." He stood over the smaller man, his voice soft with menace. "Get out, before I throw you out. And do not dare to set foot in this house again."

Exbridge backed away. "You haven't heard the last of this, my lord," he said shrilly, then turned and hurried from the room.

The girl had sunk into the chair. John hurried to her side. He reached out to touch her shoulder, to reassure, to comfort.

Flinching, she eluded his touch, started from the chair, and sped past him, wild terror in her eyes.

= 4 =

SHRIEKS OF LAUGHTER met Rebecca's ears as she opened the nursery door. An uncertain baritone was singing, "Ride a cock-horse to Banbury Cross."

Her refuge had been invaded by the enemy.

However, it was difficult to be afraid of a gentleman intent on bouncing a little girl on his knee. Lord John glanced up and flushed crimson but gamely continued:

". . . To see a fine lady upon a white horse.

"Rings on her fingers and bells on her toes,

"She shall have music wherever she goes."

Mary crowed with glee and demanded, "More, more."

"It's Mary's turn," explained Ned gloomily. He was sitting on the floor, very straight-backed, with his new book balanced on his knees. "I be good. Will you read to me, Aunt Beckie? *Tom Thumb*?"

"Please," said Lord John.

"Please," repeated Ned. "Please, Aunt Beckie, will you?"

"More!" insisted Mary.

"I don't know any more riding songs." Her uncle looked a trifle harassed.

Rebecca smiled at him. "Surely you remember 'To market, to market?' And then there's 'This is the way the farmer rides.'" She took a seat close to the fire for it was a raw morning. Beyond the windows, grey sleet was falling, which doubtless explained why Lord John was indoors being a horse instead of outdoors riding one.

It was vexatious. For the last two days she had, by

claiming indisposition, avoided seeing anyone but the children and their mother, and the latter only in the dim light of her curtained chamber. Still, the mark on her cheek was fading. She must soon resume her duties for Lady Parr, whose messages were growing increasingly querulous. Besides, she had little to hide from Lord John.

Very little.

She took Ned up onto her lap and began, " 'Once upon a time there was a teeny, tiny mannikin who went by the name of Tom Thumb.' "

As she read the familiar words, she listened to John's voice, quieter now so as not to interrupt her story.

"To market, to market to buy a fat pig.

"Home again, home again, jiggety-jig."

Mary giggled in delight as the horse speeded up for the second line.

"Miss Nuthall, what comes next?"

"Why because don't you call her Cousin 'Becca like Papa?" asked Ned.

"Because I have not received permission to do so, young man."

"Can he, Aunt Beckie?"

John's eyes dared her to say no. She felt her cheeks grow pink.

Ned was struggling with a problem. "And you can call him Cousin John," he announced triumphantly. " 'Cos he's not your uncle, is he?"

"No, he's not," Rebecca admitted.

"There then. Tell me about Tom Thumb now."

"More!" reminded Mary.

"Cousin Rebecca, you were about to refresh my memory of the verse." His eyes were laughing at her now.

"Why, Cousin John, how could you forget?" she said primly. "I doubt you are more than a quarter century out of the nursery; certainly not yet in your dotage. It goes:

"To market, to market to buy a fat hog.

"Home again, home again, jiggety-jog."

He laughed—whether at her, at her feeble joke, or at the nursery rhyme she could not guess—and resumed the game.

By the time Mary had twice been tumbled over backwards to demonstrate how the sailor rides, her squeals were growing overexcited. Nurse came in and said she must sit quietly for a few minutes before her morning nap. She ran over to Rebecca and squeezed into the chair beside her.

Rebecca continued reading, conscious that John was watching her. Between that and Mary's squirming it was difficult to concentrate, and she found herself repeating a line, to Ned's disgust. As she turned the page, Mary grabbed at it and it tore.

"My book!" Ned slid down to the floor and slapped his sister.

Rebecca put out a restraining hand and he kicked her leg. She froze. After a moment's startled silence, Mary broke into shrieks and wails. Nurse swooped down and bore her off to the next room.

John promptly picked up Ned and followed them towards the night nursery.

"I won't go to bed!" screamed the little boy, struggling. "Put me down! Put me down or I'll hit you too!"

"You can hit me all you want," John said calmly, "because I am big enough to hit you back. But don't you ever, ever . . ." The door swung shut behind them.

Rebecca shuddered.

Her impulse was to flee. She fought it down and, for something to do, took the book over to the window to examine the damage. Luckily none of the pictures was spoiled. She could glue a strip of paper over the tear and print the missing words on top of it. All the same, it would never again be the splendid new book Uncle John had given Ned. She understood the child's upset, yet slapping his sister was inexcusable.

She set the book on the table, sat down at it, and picked up some sewing that Nurse had left there. When John reappeared she was hemming a pink pinafore for Mary.

He sat down on the other side of the table and drew the book towards him. "I suppose this can be mended. Yes, it is not so bad. It is too much to suppose that Mary understands her offence, but Ned has kissed her and said he is sorry like a regular little gentleman. He will apologize to you when he is allowed out of his bed."

"Did you beat him?" Rebecca whispered, raising her eyes to his.

"Beat a child a tenth my size?" He looked half angry, half amused. "What a villain you must think me!"

"Oh no. But you . . . you struck my uncle."

"Would you rather I had let him continue to hit you?"

"You could have stopped him without knocking him down."

"I frightened you almost as much as he did, didn't I?" asked John gently. "I'm sorry, Rebecca. I didn't understand. Will you tell me about it?"

She shrugged helplessly. "It was a shock to see him. I hoped I was free of him at last."

"Did you always live with him, until you joined Lady Parr?"

"Sometimes it seemed like forever. But no, I was twelve when my parents died, and Grandmère too. It was some fever, I don't know what. I was very ill too, and I don't even remember being taken to my uncle's house." She spoke in a monotone, but she had dropped the sewing and her hands twisted restlessly on the table.

"He is married?"

"Yes, to Papa's sister. I think he must have restrained his brutality to my aunt as long as my father was alive. At least, she said he was never so bad before I went to live with them, and surely Papa would not have made him my guardian if he had known. She blamed me. Not that *she* was cruel, but perhaps we might have comforted each other!" Her voice broke in a cry of desolation.

John's large hand covered and stilled hers, though he did not interrupt. Rebecca took a deep breath and regained a shaky composure. Talking about it, even to so unlikely a confidant, seemed to ease the pain a little.

"He would strike out whenever he was irritated, but it was worst when he had been drinking. He lost all control then. Almost all. My aunt was confined to her bed for a fortnight once after a beating, but he never hurt me so badly. There was a lawyer, in London I think, who had some sort of joint responsibility for me, and perhaps Uncle Exbridge was afraid he might find out."

"Did you never try to contact the lawyer?"

"I did not know his name or direction. He came to the house once, about a year ago."

"And you did not tell him?" John was puzzled.

"I was afraid to. He could hardly have taken me away at once, and it would certainly have enraged my uncle. You cannot imagine what it was like!"

Her voice was trembling again. John's strong fingers tightened their grip on her hands, steadying her.

"But you did speak to him?"

"Yes, that was what he came for, to explain my situation before my birthday. It was then I learned that once I turned twenty-one I was no longer my uncle's legal ward. I began to lay plans that very day, and the day after my birthday I ran away to London."

"Good girl! However, I cannot see why the man should chase after you—if you will forgive me for suggested that anyone should need a reason for desiring your presence."

Rebecca managed to smile and was rewarded with a nod of approval.

"Since it cannot be for affection's sake, I must suppose it is because of the money Papa left me. The lawyer holds the principal, he told me, but Uncle Exbridge controls the income until I marry or reach the age of twenty-five."

John frowned. "There must surely be a legal way to put you in possession of the income, at least, since you are no longer living in Exbridge's house. I'd make enquiries for you but I'll be leaving the country soon."

"Muriel told me you are going abroad."

"Did she tell you about the duel? Of all the wretched, bungled affairs!" John stood up, running his hand through his hair, and began to pace restlessly.

Rebecca picked up her sewing and fixed her eyes on it. "She did not tell me, but I heard you . . . you shot a man. . . . "

"More incomprehensible male violence. But it was an accident, believe me. My foot slipped." He was earnest now, wanting to convince her. "It was all a joke originally, a stupid drunken joke that went wrong. His grace—my father, that is; Tom and I call him that—he decided that I must take up a useful occupation. I told him I wanted to go into Parliament, but he wants me out of the country for a while."

"Parliament!"

John stopped and looked at her. There was surprise on her pale, thin face, but he thought he saw interest too. He had not told even his brother of his ambition, for fear of being laughed at. Yet Rebecca had confided in him. He felt a need to reciprocate.

He sat down again. "I happened to run into Hugh Iverbrook in town a few months ago. He's a crusader against slavery, sits in the House of Lords, and he was telling me shocking stories about the conditions on the West Indian plantations. It reminded me of Teresa's adventure with the slave ship. Has Muriel told you about that?"

"No, though she did tell me about being abducted with your cousin. Oh, there was a slave trader involved in that, was there not?"

"There was." John recalled with great satisfaction having milled down the man responsible for that incident, but he doubted Rebecca would appreciate that particular reminiscence. "It was by way of revenge for her saving his slaves from drowning, thus putting him behind bars. She's a great gun, Teresa. You will like her."

"So you want to enter Parliament to join the campaign against slavery?"

"Yes." He grinned at her. "Only I haven't quite Iverbrook's singlemindedness. There are other ills to be rectified. The trouble is, and the reason I have never mentioned it to him before, his grace is a staunch Tory and I fancy myself on the Opposition benches."

It was the first time he had heard Rebecca laugh, and it delighted him. Only a few minutes since he had made her smile, also a first in their admittedly brief acquaintance. Having heard her story, he understood her usual solemnity, but it had troubled him.

Already her moment of mirth was past. "Will he not aid you, then?" she asked, with touching anxiety.

"I am first to prove my worth in foreign parts, before he will consider it. I am not sure whether he means me to be a clerk in Calcutta or a consul in Cameroon."

"Or a counsellor in Constantinople?"

"I dare not aspire so high! At least those are all warm areas of the globe." He feigned a shiver as the nurserymaid came in with a scuttle of coal to make up the fire. "On a day like this, even Cameroon sounds attractive. I believe I shall go in search of nuncheon, in the hope that Tom's cook will provide some hot soup. Will you come?" He stood up, leaned across the table, and touched her cheek with one fingertip. "This does not show any longer, you know."

Flushing slightly, she raised her chin and said with an air of resolution, "I *shall* go down. But I want first to make sure that Ned is not unhappy. Do go, and I shall follow in a few minutes." She folded the tiny pinafore neatly and went into the night nursery.

John waited for her. She was smiling when she rejoined him.

"He is half asleep, but he said he was sorry and gave me a kiss. What a dear boy he is, and Mary is a pet too, in general. They are the first children I have known since I was a child, and I am grown very fond of them."

"So am I. It's odd, I never took much note of my sister Pamela's offspring."

"Perhaps you *are* approaching your dotage, after all," she ventured, peeping at him nervously as if she was afraid he might object to her impertinence.

He laughed, and they went down together. The usual cold nuncheon buffet had indeed been supplemented with a steaming tureen of split pea soup.

"It's country fare," Muriel apologised, "but we are all family today and it is so good in cold weather."

Only her mother turned up her nose at the thick, savoury pottage. John seated Rebecca and helped her to a large bowlful, then buttered two golden-crusted rolls and set them on her side plate.

Lady Parr, having done without her companion for two days, was in a mood of thorough disgruntlement. Rebecca had scarcely begun to eat when her ladyship felt a draught and wanted her shawl.

"Pray exchange places with me, ma'am," offered John promptly. "It is so warm at this end of the table one might almost imagine oneself in Calcutta." He caught Rebecca's eye and saw her lips twitch as she repressed a giggle.

For the rest of the meal, Lady Parr contented herself with pointed comments about how fast some people's appetites recovered after an indisposition. John watched with some amusement as Rebecca manfully consumed every drop and every crumb, not wanting to offend him. He'd soon put some meat on her bones, he vowed to himself.

After nuncheon Tom went off to see his bailiff, and John accompanied the ladies to the drawing room, hoping to entice Rebecca into a game of backgammon to while away the time. In this he had no luck at all. First Cousin Adelaide's shawl must be fetched at last; then Cousin Adelaide's silks, horridly entangled after two days of neglect, must be sorted; then Cousin Adelaide, while she set an occasional stitch in her embroidery, must be read to from her newest book of sermons.

This last drove John from the room, wondering at Rebecca's cheerful patience.

His own patience was sorely tried as the foul weather continued over the next couple of days. He wished he was back in town, where a swift dash through the freezing rain to one of his clubs would provide congenial companions galore.

The only bearable part of the day was the mornings spent in the nursery with Rebecca. Otherwise, bored by Muriel's chatter and increasingly annoyed by Lady Parr's impositions on her companion, he was forced to seek out his brother. The political journals he usually read (with an eagerness that would have astonished his father) were not delivered. Not even the nearest neighbours ventured out to visit.

John's only consolation was the prospect of Teresa's arrival.

= 5 =

REBECCA WAS VERY much aware of John's boredom. It was difficult to be flattered at meeting him in the nursery every morning when she knew he had nothing better to do, but she found she enjoyed his company. Her lingering nervousness lessened as she saw his unfailing gentleness with the children, who adored him. He often made her laugh, and she was learning to respond to his banter.

As unflattering as his lack of any other occupation was his habit of wandering over to the window, gazing out at the freezing drizzle and muttering, "If this goes on much longer Teresa will have to go straight to Hull. Lord knows how long before I shall see her again!"

When, on the third day, the sun rose in a washed-out sky, Rebecca was glad for John's sake more than for her own. He had already gone riding by the time she went down.

Sir Andrew and Lady Graylin were expected the following afternoon. John returned early from his ride that day and hovered about the drawing room. At the sound of carriage wheels in the drive outside his face brightened. He rushed to the window, looked out for a moment, then strode out to the vestibule.

Muriel placidly folded her sewing and went after him.

"Help me up, girl," demanded Cousin Adelaide, to Rebecca's astonishment. Even Lady Parr, it seemed, was eager to see Teresa.

Curious to meet the woman who aroused so much enthusiasm, Rebecca followed, though it was none of her business to greet the visitors. She stood in the shadows by the staircase, watching.

A tall woman, in an excessively fashionable carriage dress of amethyst silk and a splendidly feathered matching bonnet, swept through the front door. Her face glowed with vitality and she laughed as she flung her arms round John in an exuberant greeting. He returned the hug with equal warmth.

"Mind my hat, John," she protested, her infectious laugh ringing out again.

A fair gentleman had entered behind her. Catching Rebecca's eye, he smiled slightly and shrugged his shoulders. Sir Andrew Graylin, she presumed. He was taller than Teresa, lean but tough-looking. He seemed resigned to his wife's delight at seeing her cousin.

Teresa withdrew from John's arms, her bonnet intact, and turned to embrace Muriel, though more temperately, while Sir Andrew and Lord John exchanged greetings. Tom arrived, to receive a hug that sadly upset his dignity.

Lady Parr, who had been standing near Rebecca watching this circus with considerable disapproval, moved forward now.

Teresa curtsied to her, then said with a wicked twinkle in her eyes, "Now I wonder, ma'am, did I do that right? You must know that Andrew is newly made a baronet, so I try to adjust my salutations accordingly."

Though Lady Parr looked a little offended, she said tolerantly, "I'm sure it is no longer my concern to teach you proper manners—but I know your funning ways. Allow me to felicitate you, Sir Andrew."

The others were adding their congratulations when a young black woman appeared on the doorstep, holding the hand of a little girl with a bright pink bow in her blonde hair. Rebecca guessed her to be about the same age as Ned.

She let go the servant's hand and ran forward, calling, "Papa, Mama!"

Teresa turned. "Chiquita, come and make your curtsy to Aunt Muriel and Lady Parr and your uncles."

Rebecca smiled at the child's grave and slightly wobbly curtsy, the tip of her tongue visible as she concentrated. Muriel kissed her, Lady Parr nodded approvingly, Tom pinched her cheek, and John picked her up and tossed her in the air, to her vast delight. He caught her, set her down, and engulfed her tiny hand in his.

"Come and meet Aunt Beckie," he said. "Teresa, Andrew, you are not acquainted with Miss Nuthall, I believe."

Rebecca had thought him unaware of her presence. Flustered, she stepped forward uncertainly, wondering whether to expect an embrace from the lively Lady Graylin.

However, Teresa merely greeted her with a friendly smile as Muriel explained that she was a relative. It was Lady Parr who made plain her subservient status.

"My companion," she said grandly.

John threw her a look of dislike. "Cousin Rebecca, this little shrimp is my niece, Esperanza, known to her mama as Chiquita and to her papa as Peri, with an 'i.' She is actually my first cousin once removed, but she does not care to be removed, do you, sweetheart?"

"No," agreed Miss Esperanza Graylin.

"All the same, pet," Teresa said, "it is time for you to be removed. You will like to see your cousin Ned again, will you not? Annie," she called to the servant. "Take Chiquita up to the nursery, if you please, and then come down to help me unpack."

Esperanza pouted.

"Pray let me take her up?" Rebecca suggested. "Will you go with me, Miss Esperanza?"

The child regarded her thoughtfully. "All right," she decided. "Can Uncle John come too?"

With one hand in Uncle John's and the other in Rebecca's, she skipped happily up the stairs.

Rebecca glanced back half way up the first flight. Teresa had her arm round her husband's waist, and his was about her shoulders. Her face was turned up to him, and at that moment he dropped a kiss on her nose. Rebecca looked quickly away, feeling like an intruder.

"Peri with an 'i'?" she said to John.

"P-e-r-i," he spelled out. "A *peri* is an Arabian fairy, I collect. Andrew spent some time in North Africa before he met Teresa."

"Not 'Rabian, Pershin," Esperanza corrected. "And *Chiquita* means a liccle girl."

"In Spanish. A family of linguists." John shrugged, then pulled a horrified face. "The devil—beg pardon, ladies—deuce take it, I had not thought, but doubtless I shall have to learn some outlandish tongue when I go abroad!"

"Me and Mama and Papa and Annie and Rowson's going to Russia."

"I wager you don't speak any Russian, shrimp."

"*Dobry dyen*," said Esperanza promptly.

"I can make up nonsense words, too."

"No, she's right," Rebecca put in. "It means good day."

John stared at her. "You speak Russian?"

She flushed. "Grandmère was Russian. My mother's mother. My grandfather was a diplomat, like Sir Andrew."

"Papa is a dip'mat," the child confirmed. "Where's Ned and Baby Mary? It's a lot of steps."

Her honorary uncle picked her up and set her on his shoulders. "You speak Russian?" he asked Rebecca again.

"Yes, or I did. Grandmère was an aristocrat and spoke French with my mother—the Russian aristocrats prefer French, I collect, or did in those days—but by the time I was born she wanted to speak the language of her childhood. As a matter of fact, I was brought up in a mixture of English, French and Russian."

"Famous! I expect Teresa and Andrew will be glad of your tutoring while they are here."

"Oh no, I could not presume to instruct them! Besides, I never learned to write it. Pray do not tell them."

"You are by far too retiring," said John severely. "Here

we are, shrimp. I expect your cousins are having their tea, with all sorts of good things to eat."

He and Rebecca stayed only long enough to be sure that Esperanza was comfortable with the other children and Nurse. However, when they reached the nursery door she jumped down from the table and ran after them with a milk moustache and a jam tart in her fist. She tugged at Rebecca's sleeve, fortunately with the other hand.

"Wait," she commanded stickily.

Rebecca crouched down to her level. "What is it, Miss Esperanza? You will be all right with Ned and Mary, you know. Your mama is just below-stairs."

"I know that! You can call me Chiquita, Aunt Beckie. I like you. Will you come and kiss me good-night?"

Properly flattered, Rebecca promised to come.

"The ultimate accolade," said John as the door closed at last behind them. "Must you return to your dragon now? I daresay I had best seek out Andrew and see if he can give me a few pointers on this diplomacy business."

He found the new baronet in the library with Tom. His brother stood up as he entered.

"Graylin has news for you, John," he said. "I'll take myself off and leave you to it."

With a slightly unsteady hand, John poured himself a glass of Madeira from the decanter on the side table. News brought by Andrew could only be from his grace or the Foreign Office. He was about to learn his fate.

"Consul in Cameroon?" he enquired with feigned nonchalance, taking a seat.

Andrew laughed. "Can you imagine how the duchess would react if you were sent to a deadly hellhole like that? Cheer up, it's not so bad. But I shall let you read it for yourself." He handed over two letters, one closed with the impressive seal of the Foreign Office.

John broke the seal and read the brief letter. He too laughed, though a trifle wryly. "St. Petersburg! Was it my mother, I wonder, who decided that I shall be safer with you to watch over me, or his grace who conceives that you might keep me out of trouble?"

"I am not in their graces' confidence, though you could ask Teresa whether her aunt had a say in the matter. It was my superior at the Foreign Office who told me where you are to be sent. Surely you do not imagine that because you are my wife's cousin I mean to be your nursemaid? Nor have I any interest in controlling your behaviour except insofar as my position at the embassy may demand it."

John flushed. "I beg your pardon. I must sound like a sulky child. Perhaps you know, for the letter does not say, what my work will be?"

"I will not pretend that I do not know, but I have been instructed not to give you your orders until we arrive in Russia." Andrew grinned at his indignation. "You are in no position now to demand the privileges of a relative!"

"I daresay I shall be set to transcribing reports," John grumbled. "I hope they will be secret, at least. I suppose I must read his grace's letter."

This missive was also short. As he had half-expected, it advised him to consider Sir Andrew his mentor, for the duke held a high opinion of his nephew-in-law. The irritating effect of a number of paternal homilies was softened by a draft for a thousand pounds drawn on a St. Petersburg bank.

John was nearly irritated enough to tear up that evidence of his father's continued affection. Fortunately he recalled in time the state of his purse, for though his income was generous and his gambling luck notorious, he had expensive tastes. He folded the note carefully and tucked it away in an inside pocket.

He glanced at the clock on the mantel. "No time to write a reply before changing for dinner," he said, his cheerful nature reasserting itself. He stood up and offered Andrew his hand. "I shall depend on you to tell me how to go on, you know, whether you like it or not."

The baronet shook his hand heartily. "Anything I can do, old chap, anything at all."

It was not until he was tying his neck-cloth half an hour later that John realized how neatly he had been manoeuvred into asking for advice. If that was an example of Andrew's diplomatic expertise, he was ready to learn from him.

Of course, though Andrew could not know it, that had been his intention all along.

Rebecca and Teresa were in the drawing-room when John went down. Teresa, superb in sapphire satin with her black hair gleaming in the candlelight, kissed him soundly on both cheeks.

"So you go with us. What splendid news! Andrew is still working on his cravat—you always put him on his mettle—but I could not wait to see you."

Rebecca was disturbed by their open affection for each other. They made a striking pair with a strong family resemblance, both tall and dark and brimming with energy. Sir Andrew seemed quieter, more reserved, very different from his wife, yet Muriel said it had been a love-match. Still, she could not help wondering if Andrew was as pleased as Teresa that John was going to St. Petersburg.

John turned to her. "Teresa told you? Of course she did, she is incapable of keeping such news to herself. No tropical wilderness for me!"

She smiled at his relief. "I hope you will like the Russian winter."

"Little pessimist! I shall hunt bears and wear their skins. Tom! Andrew has told you I am bound for Russia?"

The rest of the party came in and gathered round the fledgling diplomat, offering felicitations and a variety of conflicting advice. Rebecca retreated from the vociferous group. A little envious, she saw them, even Lady Parr, as a close-knit family. They were divided at times by opinions, taste, temperament, distance, but each member was always accepted as part of the whole. Despite her distant relationship she was a stranger, as much because she had not the habit of belonging as because she did not share their mutual past.

This feeling grew stronger when they went to dinner. The conversation turned to reminiscences. They talked of Teresa's voyage from Costa Rica to London under Andrew's aegis; of her meeting in Jamaica with Muriel and Lady Parr; of the Little Season in London, during which John had led Teresa from scrape to scrape; and of the Christmas house-party which had ended with Muriel engaged to Tom, and Andrew, to whom she had been betrothed, about to marry Teresa.

Rebecca listened, and ate the delicacies John piled on her plate. As had become his habit, he chose the best bits from the vast variety of dishes before them and pressed them upon her. This evening, however, he did so absently, scarcely looking at her, his gaze fixed on the vibrant loveliness of his cousin sitting opposite.

Teresa had attention to spare for everyone, but it was to her husband she turned for confirmation of a detail, to him she looked to share her laughter. Rebecca observed this, and her vague uneasiness was somewhat assuaged.

Muriel asked after Teresa's brother, now a Fellow at Oxford. Tom wanted more details of the Graylins' sojourn in China—he had read the report of Lord Amherst's embassy, but he knew Andrew had been sent to explore the hinterland more thoroughly than an official expedition could. Everyone had finished eating, but it took a strong hint from her mother to remind Muriel that it was time for the ladies to withdraw.

"Is Gayo going to Russia with us?" John asked Teresa as he held Lady Parr's chair. "How is the old rascal?"

"Swearing like a Chinaman," Andrew responded. "Fortunately his intonation is poor and even the Chinese did not understand him. The best that can be said is that it seems, thank heaven, to have driven the Spanish, French, and English profanity from his mind, to some extent. I am quite unable to persuade Teresa to get rid of him."

"Not that you have tried very hard. He's in our dressing room," Teresa added. "Go up and talk to him sometime,

John. He has a prodigious memory and will be glad to see you."

Rebecca was intrigued. Who was Gayo? She must have looked puzzled, for John said with a mischievous grin, "I'll go up now, and you must come with me, Cousin Rebecca. I cannot wait to make you known to Gayo."

Muriel smiled and nodded so Rebecca agreed, despite Lady Parr's frown. Doubtless she would be in for a scolding, but curiosity won.

On the way above-stairs, she thanked John for not committing her to teaching the Graylins Russian.

"You'll not escape so easy, my girl, for I rely on you to teach me everything you can force into this thick head of mine in the next few days."

"Languages are not your strong suit?" she asked gaily. Somehow teaching John was quite a different proposition.

He grimaced. "I understand French quite well, but I could never get my tongue around those peculiar sounds. As I remember it, Kolya's Russian sounded even more peculiar, so you will have your work cut out for you."

"Kolya?"

"Prince Nikolai Volkov. He came over here with the tsar—good sort of fellow. I daresay I shall meet him again in St. Petersburg, come to think of it. I don't suppose your grandmother taught you any good toasts?"

She laughed. "Only 'za zdorovye,' your health, which I suspect is rather too tame for your purposes."

"It will do for a start. First lesson tomorrow morning? Please, dear Cousin Rebecca. I can't promise to keep it secret from the others though, and they are bound to want to take advantage of your expertise." Not waiting for an answer, he opened the door to the Graylins' dressing room. "Now come and meet Gayo. He's the best linguist of the lot."

Rebecca was glad she had gone with him when Gayo turned out to be a parrot, a colourful green bird with flashes of red and blue on his wings when he spread them in his excitement at seeing them.

"Scummy son of a sea snake," he shrieked at John.

"That's affection speaking," John assured Rebecca, scratching the yellow nape of Gayo's neck. "He's most fluent in Spanish, of course, since he is from Costa Rica. His French isn't bad, either, though. Here, hold out your hand and let him investigate."

The bird had a wicked beak, but Rebecca refused to cry craven. She stood very still as he inched his way up her arm, though she could not help starting when he crooned "What a pity!" in her ear.

"That was not very polite, but he does seem to have slightly better manners with females," John observed. As they went back below-stairs, he told her the part the parrot had played in Teresa's adventures.

After the expected lecture on dereliction of duty, Lady Parr kept Rebecca busy the rest of the evening. It was not until she went up to her chamber that she had leisure to ponder the look she had seen exchanged between Muriel and Teresa when John had invited her to go with him to meet the Gayo.

It had been a glance of infinite significance: they thought John was attracted to her. They were quite wrong, of course. All he wanted was sympathetic audience with whom to talk about his fascinating cousin.

= 6 =

EVERYONE BUT LADY Parr put in an appearance at the breakfast table. Muriel was a little pale but announced bravely that she thought she was over her morning sickness.

"My dear!" Tom was shocked at her frankness.

Amused, Teresa patted his hand. "I fear I tend to have this effect on Muriel, though I have never known it operate so swiftly."

"We are all family here," said Muriel defiantly. "I am sure everyone knows that I am . . . "

"Muriel!"

Tom's thunderous expression made Rebecca feel ill with apprehension. However, everyone else was laughing at him.

" . . . Breeding." John obligingly finished his sister-in-law's sentence. "Don't be gothic, Tom. Of course we know."

His face sheepish, Tom muttered, "I am glad you are feeling better, my dear."

"Poor Annie is in a bad way for the same reason." Teresa saw no reason to let the indecorous subject drop. "She and Rowson were married as soon as we arrived back in England, you know. Rowson insisted on a 'proper Church wedding'—he refused to trust any of the parsons we met abroad. I have tried to persuade Annie that she ought not to travel, at least until she is feeling better. Aunt Stafford would take her in, and she could join us later."

"I'm sure she would be welcome to stay here," Muriel offered.

"She is determined to go with us, and I cannot blame her, for Andrew needs Rowson. I shall not insist on separating them, but I fear she will have a difficult time caring for Chiquita. At least neither of them suffers from sea—*mal de mer.*"

Rebecca saw her catch Sir Andrew's eye and substitute the more acceptable French phrase for the unpleasantly graphic "seasickness." The gentleman did have some measure of control over his outspoken wife, then. Annie, she remembered, was the black maid who had brought Chiquita into the house, and Rowson must be Sir Andrew's servant. If she was as ill as Muriel had been, the maid would indeed have a hard time looking after the little girl, who seemed to be as lively as her mother.

Muriel was speaking. "I meant to ask you anyway, Teresa, but since you have brought up the subject—will you not consider leaving Esperanza with us while you are abroad? Edward and Mary would be thrilled."

"No," said Teresa flatly. "I beg your pardon, I do not mean to offend. I am sure she would be happy here, but I do not care to be parted from her."

Tom intervened. "It cannot be thought suitable for a child that age to be dragged about the continent."

"Remember, Cousin, that she was born in China and has spent most of her young life abroad. She's a sturdy child, no wilting flower."

"I believe we should consider Muriel's kind offer, Teresa," said Sir Andrew. "It might be better for Peri to be with children her own age, and Annie would only have you to take care of."

"No."

"At least we should discuss the possibility."

"There is nothing to discuss. My mind is made up, Andrew."

"We shall discuss it later." Though quiet his voice was determined, with a hint of annoyance.

Teresa nodded. Rebecca searched for a sign in her face

that she feared her husband's anger. She saw only an equal determination. Did Teresa fear nothing, or had she nothing to fear? Rebecca glanced at John to see how he reacted to this threat to his idol.

He was looking thoughtful, but not in the least concerned. Perhaps he considered it a husband's right to beat his wife—or perhaps he anticipated no such outcome. Rebecca longed to believe that it was possible for a man to express his wrath in words, not blows.

When John spoke, his words were so irrelevant to her thoughts that it was a moment before she took them in.

"Cousin Rebecca is going to teach me Russian."

All eyes turned to her. Muriel seemed to be surprised, Tom sceptical, Teresa and Sir Andrew interested. Rebecca flushed and looked down, biting her lip.

"You speak Russian?" Teresa sounded pleased.

"A little. I used to, when I was a child."

"I hope you will be willing to include Andrew and me in John's lessons?"

"I never learned to read, nor write it. And I daresay what I learned from Grandmère must be nursery language, of little use to you."

Andrew gestured dismissively. "Vocabulary we can find elsewhere. It's the pronunciation we are having trouble with."

"Terrible trouble," Teresa confirmed, laughing. "Do say you will help. It will not be so great an imposition, for we leave in three days."

Rebecca looked around. John was still unwontedly contemplative, the Graylins alert, expectant. In three days they would all be gone, taking with them the colour and vivacity they had brought into her life. She would return to the placid existence in the Danville household for a day or two, then back to London with Cousin Adelaide. Back to the uneventful hours which had been blissful after her uncle's house and now seemed—dull?

She must make the best of those three days.

"I'll do it."

"Splendid." Andrew grinned at her.

"Will you mind if Annie and Rowson join us?" Teresa asked hesitantly. "I know it is a lot to ask."

"Don't forget Esperanza," John put in.

"In for a penny, in for a pound," said Rebecca with an air of reckless bravado.

"Then the sooner we begin the better." John smiled, and nodded encouragingly. She had a feeling he had expected nothing less of her. "But you must not give up your walks. I'll go with you and you shall coach me on the way."

"We'll join you," Andrew proposed.

John looked less than pleased. "But you already have an unfair advantage, having begun your studies earlier," he grumbled.

"It may be the only time available," Rebecca pointed out. "My first duty is to Cousin Adelaide. I shall have to ask her if she can spare me in the afternoons."

"It is intolerable the way she ties you to her side!"

Tom frowned at his brother's outburst. Muriel said quickly, "I shall talk to Mama. I daresay I can think of something to keep her occupied for a day or two."

When the four of them set out across the fields some time later, Rebecca was glad of the Graylins' presence. Though not directed at her, John's anger had made her wary of him. She stayed close to Teresa's side.

The pressure of their expectations suddenly seemed overwhelming. "I don't know where to start," she confessed.

"Tell us a story," Andrew proposed. "A faery tale perhaps? Something to give us the feel of the language."

So Rebecca told them one of the tales of the witch, Yaga Baba, and her hut that scuttled about on four chicken's legs. The richly rolling syllables sounded out of place in the Lincolnshire countryside, but her pupils listened intently.

"Again, with a translation, if you don't mind?" requested Andrew.

She complied, stopping now and then to let them repeat

words and phrases after her. Teresa and Andrew were quick to pick up the intonation. John, though he had a good memory for the meaning of words, persisted in sounding thoroughly English.

"I warned you, remember?" he said laughing to Rebecca as she tried patiently to explain the difference between two similar letters. "I have no ear for it. But pray do not give up on me altogether. It will be useful to understand even if I cannot make myself understood."

"Yes, that may do very well," said Andrew thoughtfully, but despite Teresa's teasing he refused to explain.

When they returned to the house, they found that Muriel had taken her mother to Spalding on a shopping expedition. Nuncheon became a lesson in the Russian names of various foods, and then the class adjourned to the library. Annie and Rowson joined them there.

At first Rebecca found the maid's black face distracting. She was soon won over by the girl's willingness to learn, and found her an apt pupil. Her husband, Sir Andrew's servant and long-time travelling companion, was a short, wiry man whose weatherbeaten face made him appear older than his years. Showing a rough and ready grasp of essentials, he ignored the claims of grammar and syntax and was soon able to request hot water, demand a meal, or ask the way to the nearest inn.

Rebecca discovered she enjoyed the rôle of teacher, especially when Esperanza came down for a half hour's instruction. The little girl's enthusiastic interest in Yaga Baba and her wandering *izba* delighted her.

"I can hear better if I sit in your lap," Esperanza suggested hopefully.

As she lifted the child, Rebecca surprised a look of satisfaction on John's face. She could not imagine why he should be so pleased that Esperanza liked her.

John had chafed all evening at Lady Parr's demands on her companion. When her ladyship returned early from a round of visits next day, claiming a headache and insisting that Rebecca abandon the lessons to attend her, he reached a decision.

"Teresa, I'd like word with you," he said as the others straggled out of the library.

"Of course. What is it?" His cousin resumed her seat and looked at him expectantly.

He ran his fingers through his hair. "I don't know quite how to put it. You are worried about whether Annie will be able to look after Esperanza, are you not?"

"A little. It is no great matter."

"You must have noticed how fond she is of Rebecca already. Ned and Mary adored her too. And she is a good teacher, isn't she?"

"Excellent." Teresa smiled at him affectionately. "I fancy I can guess what you mean to propose, but I wish you will tell me anyway."

"Take her with you! Rescue her from that abominable woman. She can continue our lessons and I daresay she will not mind helping with Esperanza. Besides, she will be a companion for you, too."

"Annie has always provided all the female companionship I need on our travels."

"But Annie is only a servant, after all. Rebecca is a lady, refined and sensitive."

"And spiritless. I do not mean to disparage her, but she has not one half of Annie's courage and capability."

"You wrong her!" John thought of Rebecca's life with her uncle and her bold escape. That story was not his to tell, but he could remind Teresa of the river rescue. "I told you how she saved that urchin from drowning when she might have climbed out by herself. Admittedly, her disposition is retiring. That does not indicate a lack of bravery."

Teresa frowned. "Perhaps you are right, though she gives an impression of timidity, and you cannot deny that she is far from lively."

Her searching look brought a slight flush to John's

cheeks. "If she is really so timid, she will refuse to go, but she deserves a chance at something better than a life of slavery with Muriel's mother," he protested.

"I am loath to condemn anyone to that fate!" Teresa's eyes danced. "It was bad enough being her protégée. Oh, very well, John, I will speak to Andrew about it. I expect he will be delighted to keep his Russian instructress, if she agrees to go and if Lady Parr can be persuaded to grant her permission."

"Bless you!" John caught her hands and kissed her cheek. "I'll not allow that her ladyship has any say in the matter, though, if Rebecca chooses to come with us."

"I doubt she will make so adventurous a choice," she warned.

He shrugged. "If she prefers her present life, at least I will have done what I can to rescue her from it."

He was aware that his suggestion had surprised and puzzled his cousin. He found it difficult to explain to himself why he was so concerned over Rebecca's fate. It must be that having saved her life he felt a certain responsibility for her, he decided, trying to ignore his apprehension at the thought that she might refuse.

Later that afternoon, Teresa reported to him that Andrew was very much in favour of the plan.

"You had best broach it to Rebecca at once," she continued. "She will have preparations to make if she is going with us, and we cannot delay the voyage to wait for her."

"I think you had best ask her."

"Why? It is your notion, after all."

"But it is your daughter she will be looking after, and you and Andrew will be her pupils. Besides, I don't want her to get it into her head that I . . . well, the sort of notions that you females get into your heads."

"You think that the slightest expression of interest will start any female setting her cap at you? Of all the vain, self-satisfied, conceited . . . !"

"Of course you are different," said John hurriedly. "All the same, I wish you will ask Rebecca."

Unable to deny that considerable numbers of predatory females had indeed thrown the handkerchief in the direction of her eminently eligible cousin, Teresa agreed.

The opportunity arose after dinner. Tom and Andrew had gone off to play billiards. Lady Parr was temporarily occupied in criticising her daughter's performance on the harp. Rebecca was wondering tiredly whether she dared slip away to her chamber when Teresa took a seat on the sofa beside her.

John lounged nearby with an unconvincing air of listening to the music. He appeared to Rebecca to be trying to lurk inconspicuously, no easy task for a gentleman of his size in an elegant drawing-room. Teresa's words distracted her.

"I have a great favour to ask of you."

"A favour? Of course, anything I can do to help."

"Wait until you have heard me out. I want you to come with us to Russia."

"To Russia!" She was so astonished she could not think of anything more sensible to say.

"We are loath to lose your help with our language studies, but quite apart from that, I have noticed how fond Chiquita is of you. You must have heard that we are worried that Annie will not be able to care for her properly. It would be such a relief if you would agree to help look after her."

"She is a darling, and I have thought that I should like to take care of children, but . . . to Russia!"

John abandoned his pose of inattention. "Do say you will go. Indeed, I hardly know how we shall manage without you. I need a great deal more coaching, you must admit, or I shall be quite useless when I arrive. And surely you cannot prefer your present life to such an adventure. You may never have such a chance again." His voice was low, to avoid being overheard by Lady Parr, but his eager impatience with Rebecca's uncertainty was obvious.

It frightened her. To be sure, Teresa would be there, but Sir Andrew would be her employer, with authority over her.

And Lord John, how would he treat her once he was no longer her pupil? The rôle in which she knew him best—indulgent uncle—would be left behind, and she could not guess what sort of man he might turn out to be.

"You must come!"

His imperious demand was too much for her composure. Half blinded by tears, she fled.

Lying on her bed in the darkness of her chamber, curled in a knot of misery, she felt a fool. Teresa must think her behaviour extraordinary, an inexplicable response to a generous offer. No doubt the offer would be withdrawn, for no one would want to employ a governess of such excessive sensibility. John, too, must be disgusted with her. Though he knew her past, it was not to be expected that so self-confident a gentleman should understand her fears.

There was a soft knock at the door. Before she could answer Teresa came in, carrying a branch of candles which she set on the dressing table. Rebecca scrambled to sit up, blotting her eyes with the back of her hands.

"I'm sorry," she choked out.

Looking unwontedly grave, Teresa sat on the edge of the bed and patted her shoulder.

"John did not mean to upset you. He is greatly distressed. I bear his most sincere apologies."

"Oh no, it was not his fault. Indeed I am sorry to be such a peagoose."

"He told me that he should have known better than to press you, after you honoured him with your confidence."

There was a questioning note in her voice. Rebecca was tempted to try to explain her panic, the terror that overwhelmed her at the sound of an imperious male voice. But though they had somehow slipped into the spurious intimacy of first name terms, she did not know Teresa well enough to trust her with her shameful story. Lady Graylin, lively and intrepid, would think her a ridiculous coward.

"He must not blame himself," she repeated helplessly.

"I wish he had not interrupted before I had time to

explain properly. Of course we do not expect you to give up your present position for nothing. A governess and tutor combined deserves higher remuneration than a lady's companion, that goes without saying."

"That is not why I hesitated," Rebecca protested, then she realized that Teresa was teasing her in an effort to rally her spirits. She managed to smile. "I promise you I am not so mercenary. But I need time to think."

"Time is what we do not have, my dear. We must leave the day after tomorrow, with you or without. Perhaps talking to John will help you make up your mind. Will you see him?"

"Oh dear, I must look a shocking fright!" She slipped off the bed and peered into the mirror on her dressing table. Her eyes were red-rimmed, her face blotchy, and her hair escaping wildly from its coiled braids.

Teresa poured some water from the ewer into the basin. Rebecca splashed her face then poked a few hairpins into the disarray above.

"That will do very well," said Teresa firmly. "He is far too concerned to notice your appearance. I do hope he can allay your apprehension, for the more I think about it, the more I see that we shall find it difficult to manage without you."

John was waiting on the landing, leaning against the balustrade with his back to her. Dressed in black, in accordance with the dictates of the long-discredited George Brummell, his tall, broad-shouldered form was an impressive silhouette against the lights in the hall below.

Rebecca went to stand beside him.

Without looking at her, he said quietly, "Forgive me."

"There is nothing to forgive." She laid her hand on his arm, feeling the restless energy pent in the taut muscles. "I must learn to overcome my stupid sensitivity."

"You have nothing to fear from me." He turned, his dark eyes serious. "Never. Not ever, I promise you. I cannot deny that I have my faults, but brutality to women is not one of them. Will you come?"

His gentleness, his wry smile, were irresistible.

"I will come," she said.

His natural exuberance won through. "You can come out of hiding, Teresa," he whooped. "She'll go with us!"

Lady Parr's reaction to the news was quite the reverse. After a long tirade on ingratitude, she prophesied dire consequences. Rebecca listened patiently to her reproaches, but John stormed off in search of his brother.

"Tom," he cried, bursting into the billiard room, "you must do something about Rebecca's fortune."

"Devil take it, you've ruined my shot." Tom straightened with an indignant glare. "Just when I was about to get my revenge over Graylin."

"Rebecca's fortune?" asked Andrew, regarding the table thoughtfully and chalking his cue. "Do I gather that Miss Nuthall is not going to accompany us to Russia?" He bent over the green baize and took careful aim.

"Yes, she is, but there's no knowing how long you will need her, and it is intolerable that she should be dependent on such as Lady Parr."

"Just what am I supposed to do about this mythical fortune?" enquired Tom sourly, watching Andrew score a cannon.

"I gather her uncle receives the income until she is twenty-five, unless she marries. That seems scarcely just when she no longer resides with him. There must be some way to ensure that the money goes to her."

"I suppose I might have my lawyer look into it. There! A hazard! All even again. But don't mention it to Rebecca for there's no knowing what may come of it."

"Thanks, old fellow," said John with a sigh of satisfaction.

=== 7 ===

THE BUSTLING PORT of Kingston upon Hull merged with the grey overcast as the brig *Daisy O* sailed out into the Humber estuary. Standing at the rail, with John at her side, Rebecca pulled her cloak close about her. The sense of shared adventure was as frightening as it was exhilarating.

She shivered.

"You are cold?" John asked. "Both wind and waves will pick up as we near the North Sea, I collect. We had best go below to join those blasé world travellers."

"Is it not amusing to see Esperanza make herself at home on board?" Rebecca was glad of his steadying arm as the deck rolled beneath her. "She kindly told me I might take the bunk since she prefers to sleep in a hammock."

"You will not mind sharing with her?" He helped her down the companionway, ducking to avoid the low beam on which he had earlier hit his head.

"No, how could I object after Teresa told us how she shared a cabin with Muriel, Cousin Adelaide, their abigail and Annie all the way across the Atlantic! And Sir Andrew shared with her brother and the parrot."

John laughed. "I was properly put in my place for grumbling at the size of my accommodation. Only think, I have a space almost as big as a horse's stall all to myself. At least Gayo is lodged in the saloon this time."

The *Daisy O* was laden with cotton and woollen goods from the mills of Lancashire and Yorkshire, and machinery besides, but she had been designed to carry passengers too.

The four tiny cabins and cramped saloon were adequate, if not as luxurious as Teresa jokingly claimed.

Rebecca was too busy to notice the crowded conditions. First thing each morning she dressed Esperanza, brushed her hair and tied it with her favourite pink ribbon. After she dressed herself and they broke their fast, Rebecca took the little girl up on deck for fresh air and exercise, usually accompanied by John. Most of the rest of the day was occupied in Russian studies.

Sir Andrew had decided that Rebecca and John must learn the Russian alphabet. Their first morning out of port, he sat them down at the table in the saloon with a list of letters and their English equivalents. Rebecca stared at it in dismay.

"Cheer up," said John, "I daresay it is not as bad is it looks. Even I managed to learn the Greek alphabet without too much trouble."

"This is derived from the Greek," Andrew told them. "If you want something really difficult, try learning to read Chinese."

Gayo added what was probably a pungent oath in Chinese.

Andrew and Teresa took charge of Esperanza, leaving John and Rebecca to struggle with the *t*'s that looked like *m*'s and *r*'s that looked like *p*'s and a sort of a *w* with a tail that was pronounced "shch."

Each day, as soon as Annie recovered from her morning sickness and was able to care for Esperanza, Rebecca resumed the rôle of teacher. The time flew by, and soon the *Daisy O* was threading her way past the Danish islands. The weather was fine, and they all spent as much time as possible on deck, practising their Russian conversation as they watched the scenery glide by.

John had quickly mastered the alphabet, but his tongue still tied itself in knots when he tried to speak the language. Teresa laughed at his pronunciation, saying Gayo's was vastly better, and though John joked about it Rebecca could see that he was mortified. Andrew, however, was not at all disturbed.

"The important thing is that he should understand," he assured Rebecca.

So she walked the deck with him, speaking in Russian while he responded in English. She told him about her childhood, memories revived by the use of the language she had learned at her grandmother's knee. Whenever she paused he was quick to prompt with a question, and she wondered wistfully whether he was at all interested in understanding her as well as her speech.

One sunny morning they stood by the rail, gazing at the distant line of the Polish coast. A brisk westerly bellied the sails of the *Daisy O* and she cut through the waves with a regular, gentle rocking motion. Behind them in a sheltered nook, Esperanza sat dressing and undressing the rag doll Annie had made for her, crooning to it in a mixture of English, Russian, Spanish and some African language.

Every now and then, Rebecca glanced back to make sure her charge was safely occupied. She happened to be looking when a sudden gust of wind seized the doll's best dress and whirled it away.

Esperanza cried out in dismay, jumped up and ran after the scrap of bright blue cloth, the naked doll clutched to her chest. Rebecca called to her, but her voice was lost in a sudden spate of orders from the duty officer and the rush of sailors to the rigging.

A stronger gust struck and the ship heeled. Rebecca reached for the rail behind her, keeping her balance with difficulty.

Esperanza was sent sprawling. John leaped towards her but the ship heeled further and she slipped towards the rail, wailing in fright. The doll flew over the side and vanished in the wind-tossed spray.

Diving across the deck, John slithered the last few feet and caught the child by the ankle. Her little hands were already clutching air above the water. Rebecca watched in breathless horror as they continued to slide, then John fetched up against the rail, too big to pass between the bars.

Sails lowered, the ship began to right itself. John rolled onto his back with Esperanza clutched to his chest as she had held the doll a moment since.

Rebecca pulled herself towards them along the rail against the now vigorous rolling of the *Daisy O*. A pair of sailors came running, their bare feet confident despite the motion. One took Rebecca's arm and steadied her.

"Cap'n says ye'd best go below, miss. There do be a squall ablowin' up. Seth'll bring t'babby. That were a neatish piece o' work, m'lord!"

The other was picking up the sobbing Esperanza as John struggled to his feet.

"Dolly!" she wept. "Dolly's drownded."

John took her from the sailor. His face was scraped, he was breathing hard, and he limped a little as they made their way below, but he was grinning.

"You see," he said simply, "we sportsmen are not altogether useless."

While Teresa fussed over Esperanza and Annie promised to make a new doll, Rebecca told them what had happened as she cleansed John's wound. His gaze was on Teresa's face, and he flushed when she came to throw her arms around him, kiss his good cheek and thank him fervently for saving her daughter. He watched her as she went into her cabin to fetch a salve from her medicine chest, even as he shook hands with Andrew and accepted his expressions of gratitude.

Rebecca was sad for him, and almost angry with him. The long days of enforced intimacy at sea had shown her beyond a shadow of doubt that Teresa adored her husband. Their frequent disputes quickly blew over, leaving their love strengthened. Though she was fond of her cousin she often mocked him, openly comparing his profligate life with Andrew's successful career. Rebecca longed to shake John and tell him to forget her.

"Here is the ointment." Teresa came back with a small glass vial. "Will you put it on, Rebecca? You only need the tiniest bit. Perhaps you should join the Navy, John, since

61

you are becoming expert at saving people from drowning."

"I only rescue females, and only the pretty ones." He reached for Rebecca's hand and kissed it. "Thank you, gentle nurse. And thank you, Rowson."

He took the offered glass of wine from Andrew's servant, whose services he was sharing for the voyage since his own valet had refused to travel. Rebecca was glad of the distraction. She turned away, hoping that no one had noticed her blush. It was most disconcerting to be suddenly reminded of the indecent condition John had seen her in after pulling her out of the river.

Her confusion had not escaped Teresa's observant eye. Rebecca was in her cabin that evening, preparing for dinner while Annie gave Esperanza her supper in the saloon, when Teresa knocked and came in.

"I could not help seeing that John's words distressed you," she said, sitting down on the bunk with the graceful movement natural to her. "Gentlemen can be thoughtless, but forgive me, I could not see any harm in it. It was something of a compliment, rather, if a mild one. But I will not allow him to discompose you."

"Oh no, you must not blame him." Rebecca concentrated on brushing her hair fiercely, then began to braid it. "I . . . I was simply embarrassed by a memory."

"Do you care to talk about it? Shared, it may lose its sting."

Though Teresa's forceful personality was at times somewhat overwhelming, Rebecca had come to admire her forthright honesty. She knew the concern in her voice was genuine. Half against her will, she found herself describing how John had stripped her clothes off her that cold day by the river.

"Oh dear, I quite see why you are thrown into confusion at the memory," Teresa frowned. "Has John been teasing you about it, or making advances? That would not be like him, for he is a gentleman if he is nothing else. Besides, you and he seem to be on easy terms."

"No, he has never mentioned it. And he is not likely to make advances to me, for he is heels over head in love with you. He has been wearing the willow for you these many years."

Teresa laughed. "John wearing the willow for me? If it seems so it is because he has used me as an excuse for escaping matchmaking mamas. He is born to be a crusty old bachelor like our Uncle Cecil."

"Do you think so? He admires you greatly."

"Admiration is not love, and seldom leads to thoughts of marriage. No, take it from me, my dear, the duke will find him some sinecure where he can leave the work to his underlings and he will go merrily and uselessly on his way, just like Uncle Cecil."

Rebecca turned to face Teresa. "I wish you will not tease him," she said bravely. "He is very much aware that his life has been frivolously wasted, that his accomplishments are not such as serious people think important. Have you not noticed how often his joking is against himself?"

Teresa looked at her with dawning respect. "You may be right. Certainly I cannot accuse him of not applying himself to the study of Russian, though his efforts meet with little success."

"He is not unsuccessful. His comprehension is excellent. Not everyone can be lucky enough to have a gift for speaking foreign languages. I believe he is determined to do well in whatever position awaits him in St. Petersburg."

"And you believe he will rise to the challenge."

"Has he ever been challenged before? Sir Andrew is a younger son with his way to make in the world. Lord Danville is heir to a dukedom, expected to take his place as landowner and member of the House of Lords. What did anyone ever expect of John?"

Though she smiled at this impassioned speech, Teresa was thoughtful. "He was given an ample income and left to win his spurs on the town. No one can deny his preeminence in that regard. He is a splendid shot, a superb rider, top sawyer, lucky gamester, popular with the gentlemen, and pursued by females of high and low degree."

"You see, he has excelled where he has made an effort.

Is there any reason to suppose he will do less well at anything else that takes his interest?"

"You have convinced me. I daresay he will be ambassador in no time. Let me help you pin up your hair."

"Thank you." Rebecca did not protest at the return to a joking tone, nor did she contradict the assumption that John's chosen field of endeavour was to be the Corps Diplomatique. If he had not disclosed his desire to go into Parliament, it was not for her to reveal it.

She realized that in confiding his hopes to her he had shown his trust as fully as she had when she told him of her uncle's violence.

Not another word of disparagement passed Teresa's lips, and Rebecca noticed that John grew less self-conscious about his poor pronunciation. When the others conversed in Russian, for Teresa and Andrew's grasp of the language was already excellent, he joined in, sometimes in stumbling Russian and sometimes in English. Nonetheless, when the *Daisy O* sailed into the Gulf of Finland and St. Petersburg was just a day or two away, his usual cheerfulness faded and he often fell silent.

The day before they were due to land, Rebecca found him on deck, leaning on the rail and gazing moodily at an island that lay ahead. She went to stand beside him.

Though she longed to ask him what was troubling him, she said only, "There are more ships visible now than we have seen throughout the voyage."

"Yes, because we are approaching the harbour, and because it freezes all winter so the merchants are making up for lost time now that spring is on the way. There are Russian naval vessels about, too. That island is the naval base of Kronshtadt. It guards the approaches to St. Petersburg."

"It will be wonderful to walk on solid land again."

"I suppose so. I wish Andrew were not so devilish secretive about what I shall be doing at the embassy! If they expect me to be able to speak the lingo, they are in for a disappointment," he said gloomily.

"Andrew does keep saying you will not need to."

"How am I to succeed at any job without it? And if I am a failure, his grace will not help me to a seat in Parliament."

"There must be a way to enter Parliament without your father's help. I am certain you can do it if you put your mind to it."

He smiled wryly and patted her hand. "You are the only creature in the world with any faith in me. Do you really think I can do it? I daresay I shall be as useless at that as at all else, but I have been talking to Annie about her experiences as a slave and I am determined to join the fight. Look, that ship is sailing towards us. That is the flag of the Imperial Navy, if I am not mistaken."

Even as he spoke, the Russian ship took up a parallel course and hailed the *Daisy O*. An answering shout rang across the water. Sailors on both vessels scampered to lower sails and their wakes died as they slowed. A pinnace was lowered from the Russian ship's side.

The captain of the *Daisy O* appeared on deck, a thick sheaf of papers under his arm. Sir Andrew joined him, leafing through more papers, as a Russian in an elaborate uniform climbed up the rope ladder lowered for him. Salutes were exchanged and the three retired to the bridge. Rebecca and John watched the official go through both stacks of papers with studious care. He produced a stamp from his satchel and stamped several, then took out some more documents and added them to the piles. Once more salutes were exchanged, and the Russian departed, somehow preserving his dignity despite the swaying rope ladder.

Andrew joined them, shaking his head ruefully.

"The most bureaucratic country in the world." He showed them five or six different seals and signatures. "Nothing can be done without permission from at least three ministries and, in our case, the Russian embassy in London. Not to mention letters of introduction from our Foreign Office to the Russian ministers, the Imperial Court, and Lord Cathcart, our ambassador. It's amazing they ever get anything done."

"How did you get papers for me?" Rebecca asked. "I only joined you at the very last moment."

"I'm afraid you are classified as a servant. Since most Russian servants are serfs, and thus a form of property, they are simply added to their masters' papers. John was more difficult, but it is wonderful how a determined duke can cut through red tape even of the Russian variety."

John snorted. "He must have been very eager to place me under your eye."

"It's true you will be reporting chiefly to me. And I think this is the moment to explain what you will be doing, before we are surrounded by listening ears and prying eyes. Pray excuse us, Rebecca."

The two gentlemen strolled off to a part of the deck out of earshot of both Rebecca and the crew. She could see the tension in John's broad shoulders as he bowed his head to listen to the slight figure beside him. She turned away, a prey to her own forebodings.

With a nationful of prospective Russian teachers in the offing and Annie no longer plagued by nausea, she saw her usefulness to the Graylins at an end. Though she did not for a moment suppose that they would cast her off, her future was uncertain.

She leaned miserably against the rail, wondering if she should offer to go back to England on the next ship, whether Cousin Adelaide had already found a new companion. Or perhaps she should look for a position as a governess in a Russian family, where she could teach both English and French. At least then she might see John occasionally—and the Graylins of course.

"Rebecca!" John was returning to her, a spring in his step, grinning. "Splendid news! I wish I could tell you but Andrew says no one is to know, not even Teresa."

He seized her in a bear hug and swung her around till she gasped for breath.

= 8 =

JOHN WAS PROVIDED with lodgings in a house belonging to the British Embassy, which was shared by most of the unmarried embassy staff. As son of a duke rejoicing in the official, if vague, position of attaché, he had three spacious rooms and he was allotted a personal valet.

Like all the servants, except the English butler, the man was an English-speaking Russian, assigned by the Russian Foreign Ministry and doubtless reporting thereto. John realized what Andrew had meant about prying eyes.

His first evening in St. Petersburg, he dined in the common room. Most of his fellow-diplomats were present, in honour of his arrival, along with a few guests from other embassies and one or two Russians. A long table ran down the room. Silver gleamed on the spotless white cloth and crystal sparkled in the candlelight. Slightly disappointed, John felt he might as well be attending a convivial bachelor dinner in London.

The military attaché, Colonel Sir Humphrey Wharton, performed the introductions, then they all gathered round a side table. On it were a number of bottles, and a couple of dozen dishes, most of which John did not recognize.

"*Zakuski*," said the slim young man standing next to him, the Honourable Sebastian Crane. "Hors d'oeuvres. Pickled fish, pickled mushrooms, pickled cabbage, pickled bees' knees for all I know. That revolting-looking mess is the best caviar, which is never exported. Then of course there's cheese, radishes, sausage and so on if you don't feel adventurous. Allow me to pour you a glass of vodka, my lord."

John accepted a plate filled with various tidbits that someone else pressed on him, and cautiously tried the salted sturgeon. It was delicious. He took the glass Mr. Crane handed him and sipped.

"They drink this by choice?" he choked, his throat on fire.

Mr. Crane and a couple of bystanders laughed.

"Yes, but not like that." Mr. Crane raised his own glass in a toast, then tossed the entire contents back. "If you do it right, it misses the epiglottis and goes down quite smoothly. You don't even have to taste it. Try again." He topped up John's glass.

After two or three painful attempts, John caught the knack. A glowing warmth spread outward from his belly.

"Not bad," he admitted.

The second secretary arrived and they sat down to dinner. A tolerable Hungarian wine was served with the meal. Thirsty after the salty *zakuski*, John indulged freely, nor did he refuse a snifter of the excellent cognac that followed.

"The Russkis brought it back from Paris by the hogshead," someone explained when he commented on its superiority.

"Much went also to England, *nyet?*" said a Russian seated opposite, grinning.

A Frenchman some way down the table scowled.

At peace with the world, John leaned towards him and said genially, in atrociously pronounced French, "There is nothing to compare with French wines, monser. *Reeang dew toot.*"

That, he thought with great satisfaction, should establish his reputation as an appalling linguist.

After dinner, the Honorable Sebastian invited John to join a group of the younger diplomats at a popular tavern. The friendly Russian, a somewhat dandified gentleman named Count Boris Ivanovich Solovyov, went with them.

As they left the house, a sleepy *drozhky*-driver offered his services. Crane waved him away.

"Let's walk," he suggested. "Clear our heads before we start again."

Chatting and laughing, they strolled through the dark streets of St. Petersburg. On the way from the harbour to the embassy, John had noted the wide thoroughfares, lined with the magnificent classical palaces of the nobility. Now they plunged into a maze of lanes and alleys behind the mansions. An occasional rush torch showed tenements crowded round squalid courtyards where dirty snow still lay in piles, hidden from even the noonday sun. There were wooden huts, too, leaning drunkenly askew. Now and then John heard raucous laughter or the sound of steady cursing.

They crossed a bridge over a canal and came to another wide street, though less splendid than those they had left behind. On the opposite side a door stood open. From it issued a hubbub of voices and the strains of a lively tune played on unfamiliar instruments.

"Balalaikas play tonight," said the Russian as they went up the steps and entered a crowded room hazy with tobacco smoke. "Is fine welcome for new visitor. Allow me to offer you champagne, milord."

He turned away, waving his ebony cane to summon a waiter, and Sebastian Crane murmured in John's ear, "Watch out. Spy."

John nodded his comprehension. His heart beat faster and an involuntary smile curved his lips. His mission was off to a good start.

The count, Boris Ivanovich he insisted on being called, challenged him to a game of picquet. They sat at a small table at the side of the room. The waiter brought fresh cards, and two bottles of champagne.

"Yeshcho nagrablennoye voini," Boris Ivanovich remarked, indicating the bottles.

More spoils of war. John looked at him blankly, feigning incomprehension.

"You do not speak our language? Odd, for diplomat, is it not?" He eased the cork out of the first bottle and poured.

"*Da*," said John, breaking open a pack of cards and shuffling. "*Nyet*. To tell the truth, I'm not really much of a diplomat." He confided the story of the botched duel and his subsequent exile.

"This duel, it was a joke? You English are truly strange nation. In Russia we take our honour seriously."

They began to play. The count was a fairly skillful player and John concentrated hard until he had fathomed the other's style. In a few minutes he knew he was better. He set out to win modestly—he had no desire to become known as a lucky gambler but, though Andrew had said the embassy would cover his losses to some extent, neither did he choose to be thought a dupe.

He sipped sparingly at his champagne.

"You prefer *krasnoye vino*?" asked his opponent. "Red wine? Or brandy?"

"Thank you, no. The champagne is excellent. However, though he has his mistaken notions, the duke taught me in early youth that drink and cards don't mix and I have found the precept serves me well."

"Another interesting oddity. Few Russians are able to drink with moderation." The count gestured towards a large table nearby where a dozen or more hussars were toasting each other noisily.

John glanced at them occasionally as he played. Several of them had girls on their knees or leaning against their shoulders. Once more he might almost have imagined himself back in London at the Royal Saloon, except that now and then, after a particularly spirited toast, the soldiers tossed their glasses over their shoulders to smash on the floor.

He caught snatches of their conversation and gathered that it was a farewell party. Five of the young officers were leaving next day for a garrison in the south. It was the sort of information he was listening for, but not being seated with them he heard no details. He needed an introduction to military circles.

"Do you know Prince Volkov?" he asked the count.

"Minister Mikhail Denisovich?" The man was startled. "I have seen him only, never introduced. Is very important person. Why you ask?"

"Must be his son." John laughed at the idea of the dashing young blade he had known rising to ministerial status. "He was in London in 1814 as aide-de-camp to your emperor. Kolya, his name was."

"*Knyaz Nikolai Mikhailovich. Da,* he is in Imperial Guards, I believe. I am not acquainted, but perhaps Vladimir Dmitrievich can help you." He called to one of the officers at the next table.

The hussar extricated himself from the embrace of his doxy and stumbled over to join them. His face was red, his waxed moustache drooping, and his scarlet, silver-laced uniform jacket unbuttoned.

"Boris Ivanovich!" he cried, and embraced the count, kissing him heartily on both cheeks.

The count fended him off and brushed fastidiously at his elegant coat. Switching to flawless French, he performed the introductions.

"Captain Prince Vladimir Dmitrievich Vasilyevski, Lord John Danville."

Before he could dodge, John in his turn was subjected to a hug and kisses from the drunken soldier.

"My dear English friend, you must call me Volodya," he insisted in atrocious French.

John was glad to agree, since he was sure he would never be able to get his tongue around the fellow's Christian name and patronymic, let alone his surname. In equally bad French he explained that he wanted to contact Prince Nikolai Volkov.

"Nikolai Mikhailovich? Of course, I take you tomorrow. Vodka!" he shouted to a passing waiter. "You drink with me, very sad day, little brother he go away." He burst into tears.

A younger hussar left his companions, who were now

singing a maudlin song about birch trees on the steppes, and came to weep on Volodya's shoulder. To John's relief, Sebastian Crane appeared at that moment to suggest that it was time to leave. Count Boris Ivanovich paid the thirty-five rubles he owed and they stepped shivering into the cold night.

"Devilish sentimental race," observed Mr. Crane.

The following morning John woke late. He requested a bath, and his servant, Fedka, offered a choice of English or Russian. John was curious to experience the Russian version, but a glance at the clock dissuaded him. As it was, he did not reach the embassy until after noon.

On the way to Andrew's office he passed Sir Humphrey in the corridor and heard him mutter, "Noble ne'er-do-well!" as he ostentatiously consulted his pocket watch.

Andrew was more welcoming. He met John in his outer office, where sat an English and a Russian clerk, and drew him into the inner sanctum, closing the door behind him. Despite this precaution, he put a finger to his lips as he waved John to a chair. He sat down behind a vast, empty desk on which he promptly put his heels.

"Well?"

John described his evening in detail, omitting only his own ideas and Crane's warning. He finished with the military attaché's aside a few minutes since. Andrew was laughing at this when the English clerk put his head round the door.

"I sent Fedorenko for the samovar, sir."

"Thank you, Harvey. Now, John, we've ten minutes before the fellow returns. You have made an excellent start. You've established that you don't speak or understand Russian, and your execrable French will lend weight to that, while allowing you to communicate with those who don't speak English. Confiding the story of the duel was a masterstroke."

"I thought it might help," said John modestly.

"It will be all over the city in a day or two and no one

will be surprised that you spend your time carousing instead of working. Nor will they wonder at your deigning to report to me occasionally, since I am lucky enough to be married to your cousin. And it sounds as if Colonel Wharton is already convinced that you only obtained the position through your father's influence."

"Which is true, of course. The only problem is that Volodya was so drunk we made no arrangements to meet and I can't for the life of me recall what his name is. Captain Prince something. Without him I've no entrée into military circles."

"I wouldn't worry about that. These Russians have hard heads and he will probably turn up. Even if he doesn't, it's early days yet and you will meet other soldiers. You might even call on your friend without him. I can find out where he lives, and princes are not the unapproachable beings here that they are at home."

"They seem to be two a penny!" John was saying as the door opened and Fedorenko carried in a tray with glasses in silver holders and a plate of *zakuski*. He was followed by a servant bearing a tall metal contraption, rumbling and hissing with steam escaping from the top."

"*Spacibo, Makar Ilych,*" said Andrew. "Yes, there are a lot of princes. They are not necessarily connected with the Imperial family, since the tsar's children are grand dukes and duchesses—*vyeliki knyaz*; actually that translates as grand prince, but no matter. Often, I collect, the princes of the ordinary sort are neither influential nor rich. In the early days of Muscovy there were many petty princes, and since every one of their offspring took the title, they have proliferated beyond measure."

John accepted the glass of tea offered him by Fedorenko and the Russians withdrew.

"Thanks for the lecture," he said softly. "Do I have to drink this stuff?"

"Certainly. As a 'diplomat' you must learn to live with the national idiosyncrasies of your hosts, and drinking tea at all hours is essential to Russian civilisation, as to English. I will not force you to put jam in it, as they often do, but we must not let Makar Ilych suppose that you do not care for it after he went to the trouble of fetching it."

"No, I can see that that would not be wise." John sipped the clear amber liquid. "Not bad, when it's not ruined with milk and sugar as English ladies prefer it. By the way, how are Rebecca and Teresa?"

"Teresa took an instant dislike to the curtains in the drawing room, or so she claims. I suspect it is an excuse for exploring the shops of St. Petersburg, which is how she and Rebecca are spending the day. Teresa hopes you will find time in the midst of your dissipations to visit her. At least you cannot escape the ambassador's ball next week, so she will see you there."

There was a knock on the door and Harvey again appeared.

"Excuse me, sir, there's a Russian asking for Lord John." He consulted a card. "*Kapitan Knyaz Vladimir Dmitrievich Vasilyevski*, my lord. He is waiting in the vestibule."

Glad though he was that the hussar had tracked him down, John could not help resenting the clerk's smooth Russian pronunciation. As he went below-stairs, he reminded himself that his lack of talent in that direction was a positive asset to his job of collecting military intelligence.

Volodya greeted John like a long-lost friend, with a repeat of the previous night's embrace. John suspected that this was a custom he would not easily adjust to. He submitted without a perceptible shudder, and slapped the short, chubby young man on the shoulder in return. They exchanged 'bong joor's.

The captain had a *drozhky* waiting outside the embassy gates, driven by a serf in a long peasant coat and felt boots. Making laboured conversation in French, they drove through streets a-bustle with carriages and pedestrians. John was again impressed by the extravagant mansions, their white marble pillars standing out against walls of pale blue or yellow or green stucco.

The *drozhky* stopped before one of the largest.

"*Vot dvoryets Volkovykh,*" the captain announced. "*Ici palais de Volkov.*" He explained that Prince Nikolai Mikhailovich spent much of his time at his father's house though he also had quarters in the tsar's Winter Palace and in a nearby barracks. If he was not at home, the genial hussar was willing to take John all over the city in search of him.

A liveried porter ushered the gentlemen into a high-ceilinged entrance hall whence a magnificent double stair of marble swept up to the upper regions of the house. He gave their visiting cards to a footman, one of three waiting in the hall, who hurried above-stairs with them. Moments later Kolya ran down, beaming a delighted welcome.

"John, my dear fellow!" he cried in slightly accented English, seizing both his hands. Having spent several months in England, he knew better than to kiss him. "What the devil are you doing in St. Petersburg?"

John grinned at his friend. Tall, thin and lively, Kolya looked the same as ever. Though his hair was light brown and his eyes hazel, the shape of the latter gave his long face an oriental slant that supported his claim to a Tartar princess somewhere in his family tree. He was dressed in the uniform of the tsar's own *Preobrazhensky* regiment of the Imperial Guards, dark green with red sleeves and facings.

"It's good to see you again, Kolya. I'll tell you all about it later. I believe you know Volodya, who was kind enough to bring me to you."

"*Knyaz Vladimir Dmitrievich, nyet?*" Kolya and the captain shook hands, apparently not being on hugging terms.

John did his best to look blank during the ensuing brief conversation in Russian. Kolya thanked the hussar and offered refreshments, which were refused. Volodya did not want to interrupt the reunion of old friends which ought to be carried on in English, milord's French being as bad as his own. He was on duty tonight, but perhaps Nikolai Mikhailovich would be good enough to convey to milord his invitation to join a party of friends the following evening.

Kolya translated, while John nodded and smiled.

"*Enchantay*," he accepted, and the captain took his leave.

"Come up to my rooms," Kolya suggested, starting up the stairs. "Stepka, some refreshments at once! Now tell me, John, how do you come to be in Russia?"

"I'm in disgrace," John confessed, and told again the story of the duel, this time with various embellishments that he knew would amuse his friend. "I have already told the tale to one of your countrymen, who was flabbergasted that Englishmen could joke about an affair of honour."

Kolya laughed. "English are indeed curious nation. Here, this is my sitting room." Turning to the icon hanging on the wall with a lamp burning before it, he crossed himself, then shrugged. "Old childhood habit. Tell me, how is your friend Mr. Fitzsimmons?"

They were talking of mutual acquaintances when three servants brought refreshments. A number of bottles and dishes were set out on the table in the window, then one of them dismissed the others, bowed, and spoke to Kolya in a low voice.

"Stepka says that my father has heard of your arrival and hopes you will dine with us today. I have told him how kind Duke of Stafford was to me in London and he wishes to meet his son. It will not be amusing evening I had planned for us, I fear," Kolya said.

"I shall be honoured to meet the prince," John said with more politeness than truth.

"Do not fear, most of my family speaks English, to some degree at least. We had for many years English governess, as I think I have told you once." He informed the servant that milord would stay to dinner and the man left. "Let me pour you some wine, or will you try our *pivo*? It is nearest thing to your ale. I must go for one hour or two to palace this afternoon. Will you come with me? It is not so exotic as Carlton House of your prince, or Brighton Pavilion that

76

they call 'Little Kremlin,' but I think you will enjoy to see it."

Kolya drove a *troika* to the Winter Palace. John exacted a promise to teach him the art of driving three horses abreast, the outer two of which were harnessed so that their necks curved away from the centre. It looked much more difficult than even a four-in-hand.

Before going about his business, Kolya seconded a subaltern to show John the splendours of the tsar's principal residence. Though he occupied a couple of hours agreeably enough admiring the superb classical architecture and magnificent furnishings and artworks, he was glad of his friend's return.

On their return to the Volkov mansion, John was introduced to what seemed like hordes of brothers and sisters and aunts and cousins and hangers-on. The prince and princess greeted him graciously, but he was not unhappy to find that there were more important guests who occupied their attention. The younger members of the family were as lively as Kolya. Unabashed by the presence of their elders, they made John feel at home, involving him in their games and music. He thoroughly enjoyed the evening.

While he was waiting for a convenient moment to take his leave of his host, he overheard a fragment of conversation. It was in French, the preferred language of the aristocracy. One of the distinguished guests said something about the possible future emancipation of the serfs. The minister responded with a vigorous exposition on why the Russian peasant would never be capable of using his freedom to his or anyone else's advantage.

John was reminded of his grace's obstinate opposition to reform of Parliament. Having made his farewells, he mentioned this, laughing, to Kolya.

"Is no joke," said his friend fiercely, escorting him out into the hall. "Condition of serfs is disgrace. When I inherit,"—he crossed himself as if to ward off that day despite his disagreement with his father—"I free every one on our estates."

"Does the Minister know this?"

"*Da*. We have often disputes. I am in trouble with tsar for my views, too, but still my father protects me, or I will—would—be in exile like you, to Moscow at least. Tsar Aleksandr Pavlovich was once progressive; now he listens only to Arakcheyev. Bah!"

On the way home in the Volkov carriage, John was thoughtful. He was surprised to find a serious side to his companion of many a lark. He had been tempted to tell Kolya of his own ambitions. However, besides a certain unwillingness to expose himself to raillery, it suited his purpose better to be considered an unthinking scapegrace. Little as he relished deceiving Kolya, particularly after his family's enthusiastic welcome, his duty to his country must come first.

He found a game of faro in progress in the staff residence. Nothing loath he joined in, drowning his misgivings in vodka. It was a positive pleasure to be surrounded by Englishmen.

John had every intention of calling on his cousin and Rebecca. In fact, he rose early one morning with that intention, only to find them out. He stayed half an hour to play with Esperanza and talk to Annie. Otherwise, his time was fully occupied by the outings and entertainments proposed by his new acquaintances. Before he realized it, the evening of the ambassador's ball arrived.

In London he had generally avoided such tame events, unless coerced by his mother into escorting her. Now he found himself looking forward to it, particularly when he learned that Kolya was to attend.

As a member of His Excellency's staff, however superfluous, he was kept busy for some time looking after the earliest arrivals. Even the censorious Colonel Wharton had nothing to complain of in his behaviour. Lord John Danville was, after all, a gentleman of the highest *ton*, and bred up to such occasions. Outwardly nothing was visible of his rising sense of anticipation except, perhaps, a tendency to glance rather often at the entrance to the ballroom, where Lord Cathcart was greeting his guests.

He saw Andrew move towards the door and gracefully extricated himself from his present companions.

Two ladies were curtsying to the ambassador as he approached. Teresa, as always, was strikingly lovely. John's gaze slid over her appreciatively and came to rest on the girl beside her. He drew in a long breath at the magical transformation.

A vision in white and silver, her dark gold hair released from its braids and coiling in shining ringlets to her slender shoulders, Rebecca smiled at him. Their eyes met. No longer a frightened waif, she was timid still, but expectant, hopeful. She was beautiful.

= 9 =

"You would not believe, John, the trouble I had persuading Rebecca to come tonight," said Teresa, laughing. "She would have it that it was not her place as a governess to be dancing the night away. I managed to persuade her not to leave me to face a ballroom full of strangers without her support."

Rebecca blushed. She had not only allowed herself to be persuaded to attend the ball, she had accepted as a gift the delightful confection of white satin and silver net she was wearing. Her hair, freed from its severe plaits, was dressed in careless-seeming ringlets.

"Of course you came," John murmured.

Shyly she raised her eyes to his face. He was smiling at her in manifest approval. She smiled back, glad she had given in.

"Will madam deign grant me the first waltz?" He performed an elaborately fanciful bow, to her, not to Teresa as she had expected. "Andrew, there will be a waltz, will there not?"

"Oh yes, I believe so. The starchier Russians still disapprove but the foreign colony would not turn out for less, I collect. You'll save a waltz for me, won't you, darling?"

"Of course," agreed Teresa promptly. "And I expect John to do his duty by standing up with me too. You will not find any English country dances here of course, John, though there may be a quadrille and a cotillion. I made enquiries so as to be prepared. The popular dances are mazurkas, which are Polish, and what they call *anglaises* and *écossaises*, neither of which I believe would be recognized by the English or the Scottish. Rebecca and I have been practising all week."

"As have I not, so I must be excused from sporting a toe with any but you and Rebecca, which suits me well enough."

They moved on into the ballroom. Andrew went about his duties but John stayed with them, chatting about their impressions of St. Petersburg. Teresa voiced her approval of the shops on the Nevski Prospekt, admitting ruefully that they had seen little else.

The orchestra began to play, and several couples took to the floor.

"John, you must introduce me to your *feya*." A tall, thin Russian had materialized at John's elbow.

"Faery," Rebecca interpreted, involuntarily relapsing into her rôle of tutor before she realized the stranger was referring to her. She felt her cheeks grow hot with embarrassment.

"Allow me to present Prince Nikolai Mikhailovich Volkov, a.d.c. to his Imperial Majesty. Dash it, Kolya, I don't even know your present rank."

"*Polkovnik*. That is colonel, *mesdames*." The prince kissed Rebecca's hand, to her confusion, and bowed gallantly to Teresa.

"My cousin, Lady Graylin," John completed the introductions with Teresa first in formal order of precedence. "And this is Miss Rebecca Nuthall, who is cousin to my sister-in-law. Beware of Kolya, Rebecca. He is used to sweeping the ladies off their feet."

"You understand *feya*, Miss Nuthall. You speak Russian?"

"My grandmother was Russian," Rebecca confessed shyly. She liked the look of his merry face and the twinkle in his slanted eyes.

Asking about her grandmother, he quickly put her at her ease. He wrote his name down on her dance card for an *écossaise*, then proposed introducing her to his family.

"They will welcome any relative of Lord John," he assured her.

"I am only a very distant relation, and a connexion by marriage besides." Rebecca wanted to tell him that she was a governess and hired companion, but she was afraid he would think her presumptuous for coming to the ball. She looked to Teresa for advice, but she was deep in conversation with the first secretary and his wife, who had visited them soon after their arrival. John was busy charming a large elderly Russian dowager as he found her a seat.

Prince Nikolai laughingly insisted that a Russian grandmother amply compensated for any distance in her connexion to John. She allowed him to lead her around the side of the room, though she cast a nervous backward glance at Teresa, who nodded encouragement.

Of course he was a friend of John's, and surely nothing could happen to her in a ballroom, but she hoped he would not be excessively angry when he discovered her station in life.

The Volkovs greeted her with open friendliness. The princess enquired into her family tree and managed to discover a remote relationship. One of Kolya's younger brothers requested a mazurka. Rebecca stood chatting with two sisters who, when they found that she knew nothing of London fashions, favoured her with their own opinions of the latest St. Petersburg modes.

The first dance ended, and John came looking for her. He brought with him a young man he introduced as the Honourable Sebastian Crane. Mr. Crane seemed to be an obliging gentleman. Besides putting down his name on Rebecca's card, he begged both Kolya's sisters to stand up with him, and even approached the elderly princess. She rapped his knuckles coquettishly with her fan and sighed.

"Ah, *monsieur*, but I danced till dawn in my time."

Mr. Crane was listening politely to her reminiscences when John bore Rebecca off.

"I never realized before," he said, "that one of the chief duties of a minor diplomat is to keep the ambassador's guests happy. Come, the music is beginning."

Rebecca had practised the waltz with Teresa. She had thought it would be alarming to be held so close by a man, and it had been an act of bravado to accept John's invitation. Yet when he took her in his arms she felt safe, protected, though suddenly there was something wrong with her breathing.

He swung her onto the floor. She concentrated on her steps at first, till her breathing settled, then ventured to look up. He was smiling down at her and she smiled back, suddenly exhilarated.

"How pretty you are tonight! I'm sorry I have not had time to visit you since we arrived. Are you enjoying life in St. Petersburg?"

"Oh yes. I thought there would be nothing for me to do, but I have been very busy. Now that we are settled, Annie is much occupied with her duties as abigail, so I have been taking care of Esperanza."

"Surely Teresa does not confine you to the nursery?"

"Hardly. Am I not here tonight? She has been a deal too good to me. Indeed, I feel more like a younger sister than a governess, or even a companion. I ought not to accept so much, but it is excessively difficult to refuse her."

"Don't I know it! My cousin is irresistible, in more ways than one. I hope you do not regret being persuaded to come tonight?"

"I have never been to a ball before, and I was afraid such a crowd of strangers would be overwhelming. At first it was, with the bright lights and the jewels sparkling, and everyone talking at once. But you are here . . . and your friend is very kind and charming. I am prodigious glad I came."

"You have never been to a ball before? What a shocking confession! I could not have guessed it from your dancing; you are light as a feather. I trust you mean to attend many more? I shall do my best to be present at every one so that you are not overwhelmed."

The ready colour mounted to Rebecca's cheeks. "I ought not. But if Teresa invites me, I shall!"

The music came to an end with a swirl. John stopped a waiter and presented Rebecca with a glass of champagne. She sipped it, and sneezed as the bubbles rose to her nose.

"Oh dear, is that another first?" John asked, amused. "It will probably give you hiccups too. I'd best find you some lemonade."

"No, I shall drink it very slowly and learn to like it. Will you take me back to Teresa now? I am sure you ought to be about your duty, taking care of the ambassador's guests."

"You are one of them, my dear. I shall therefore now make polite conversation. Have you seen the Winter Palace yet, Miss Nuthall?"

"I have not had the opportunity, my lord. I have several times visited the Nevski Prospekt, however. It is a splendid thoroughfare, is it not, and the several bridges greatly enhance its attractiveness."

"The chief attraction is the shops, I understand," John teased. "I should like to drive you and Teresa about the city one day. Kolya has been teaching me to drive a *troika*."

"Is that how you have been spending your time? Oh, I beg your pardon, it is none of my business."

He seemed to be about to speak, then a shadow crossed his face and he shook his head, almost angrily, she thought.

"Like you, I keep busy," he said lightly. "In fact, you are right, I ought to be doing my duty. Now where has Teresa disappeared to?"

Prince Nikolai overheard these last words.

"If you are seeking Lady Graylin in capacity as chaperone," he said, "allow me to relieve you of necessity, my friend. Miss Nuthall is promised to me for next dance, I believe. *Mademoiselle?*" He bowed and held out his arm.

The lively figures of the *écossaise* made Rebecca hot and a little tired. She was glad to sit out the dance after it with the prince, who amused and shocked her with tales of the Imperial Court in the reign of Tsar Pavel Petrovich.

Among other instances of insanity, he told her, the tsar had been obsessed with uniforms, down to such details as the cut of a collar and the number of buttons.

"Is that why almost all the Russian gentlemen are wearing uniforms?" she asked.

"No, it was Pyotr Veliki—Peter the Great—who did that, as means of controlling nobility. Not only military, but every rank of our civil service has its own. You see my revered papa over there beside my mother? That is uniform of highest rank, and stars he is wearing are especial honours."

Prince Nikolai sounded proud of his father's elaborate coat with its flashing diamonds and vast quantity of gold braid. Rebecca murmured admiringly, but privately thought the plain elegance of the English gentlemen's black and white much to be preferred. John in particular looked splendid in his evening dress.

Her next dance was with Sebastian Crane. At first the figures of the quadrille gave them no leisure for conversation, until it was their turn to stand and watch the other couples in their set.

"Your cousin's up to every rig and row," said Mr. Crane admiring.

"My cousin?"

"Danville." He brushed aside her attempt to explain that John was not really her cousin. "Comes in to the embassy at noon, stays half an hour, an hour at most, then off he goes to play with the natives. Wish I knew how he gets away with it, even if his father is a duke."

"He's not really a diplomat," she offered hesitantly.

"I'll say he's not! Cathcart keeps our noses pretty much to the grindstone, though I will say this for the old boy, he puts on a good show. What do you think of the decorations?" He waved his hand in a comprehensive gesture.

Amid the general glitter, noise and movement, Rebecca had not even noticed the decorations. She was too concerned about what she had heard of John to take any interest in them now, but a certain anxiety in the young man's tone warned her that she must make some comment.

From the centre of the ceiling hung what looked like a

flying worm made of green silk. Rearing over it was a strange four-legged brown creature somewhat resembling a bear, with a suit of armour balanced on its back. Rebecca glanced around the room. The walls were hung with banners, a red cross on a white ground. It dawned on her that it was the twenty-third of April, St. George's Day, and doubtless the ball was in honour of the patron saint of England.

Before she could think of something complimentary to say, he went on, "I was in charge of it, you know. Had the deuce of a time making that armour stick together, and I'm afraid the horse isn't quite right."

"I think it's a very clever idea, and the dragon is splendid," Rebecca reassured him.

He beamed in gratitude as they reentered the pattern of the dance.

Her effort was repaid. Mr. Crane not only put his name down for an *écossaise*, he subsequently brought several gentleman of various nationalities to be introduced to her. Since John and Teresa were also determined to provide her with partners, she was soon engaged for every dance.

Faces and names merged in her mind. When supper was announced at one o'clock in the morning, she was relieved to see John's scrawl on her card, not another stranger's. Then she remembered what Mr. Crane had told her, and worry began to gnaw at her again.

John came to fetch her. "What's wrong, Rebecca?" he asked. "Has some young puppy been annoying you?"

"No, everyone has been very kind." She wanted to ask him about his position, about the way he spent his time, but he had very firmly turned the subject last time it arose. Perhaps he regretting ever having confided his doubts and ambitions. He seemed to have distanced himself from her and returned to a life little different from that he had led in London.

"You must not let anything spoil your first ball. Save your troubles for the morrow, or rather later today. Another glass of champagne will help."

He seated her at a small table and brought her a selection of delicacies from the buffet, then set himself to cheer her up. She found him irresistible. Admittedly she did not try very hard to resist. He soon had her laughing at his diplomatic efforts to prevent the wife of the French ambassador from coming face to face with the wife of the Russian Foreign Minister.

"It seems madame once made some comment about Russian fashions which was taken as a personal affront. It's a wonder their husbands did not call each other out."

"One of my partners—I cannot remember his name, but he was Russian—would talk of nothing but duels and insults and avenging his honour."

"They seem to be quick to take affront. I step carefully, I assure you. I have had enough of duels."

"He boasted of having fought a dozen, but perhaps it was nothing but talk. Russians seem to love display." She confided her distaste for the gaudy uniforms.

"None of them can hold a candle to our own Prince Regent's taste in dress," he assured her. "George IV, I mean. Of course, Prinny is one of a kind, and he does not attempt to force the rest of us into his mould."

"It all seems so . . . wasteful, so frivolous."

He looked at her, his dark eyes serious. "Frivolity is no bad thing, you know, in moderation. Perhaps I have had too much in my life, but you have had too little. Enjoy yourself, Rebecca, while you have the chance."

She frowned. There was a tantalising hint of a hidden meaning behind his words. Before she could begin to puzzle it out, her next partner came up and addressed John in Russian, begging his pardon for interrupting their tête-à-tête.

John looked blank. Rebecca knew he was perfectly capable of understanding the simple words. Why was he pretending not to?

The Russian apologized in French and repeated his explanation of his interruption. John stumbled through a response in the same language, not only his pronunciation but his grammar atrocious.

As Rebecca went off on her partner's arm, she glanced back and saw John's self-satisfied expression. She remembered how pleased Andrew had been at his inability to speak Russian. She had all the clues, she thought, but there was no time to put them together before she was whirled into the dance.

= 10 =

JOHN WAS NOT the only member of the embassy staff to put in a late appearance on the day after the ball. In fact, being more accustomed to going to bed at dawn, he arrived before Andrew and was waiting in his office, with his heels on the desk, when his superior turned up.

"Fedorenko has the day off," said Andrew, closing the door. "We can talk."

"How is it that your desk is still as empty as the day we arrived?" John enquired, yielding his place.

"The kind of papers I deal with are mostly kept in a locked safe. Besides, a great part of my usefulness to the Diplomatic Corps is my ability to remember details without writing them down."

"I can see that would come in handy in our business. I may have something of a talent that way myself, for I can always recall which cards have been played, and by whom. I've not yet heard anything worth remembering, though."

"You will. You have other worthwhile talents, too. Cathcart was impressed with the way you handled that impossible Frenchwoman."

John was pleased, but he grumbled, "That's all very well, but I nearly came to grief last night. I was with Rebecca when someone addressed me in Russian. She knew very well that I ought to be able to understand."

"Did she comment?"

"No, she just looked surprised and puzzled, and I don't suppose anyone noticed, or guessed why."

"Perhaps you had best avoid her company."

"No! That I will not. And I cannot avoid Teresa, who is equally likely to give me away."

"She is not! Teresa is equal to anything."

"So is Rebecca. But that is beside the point. There seems to be a general impression that they are both cousins of mine, so I cannot avoid either without causing talk. I think I should explain the situation to Rebecca." John did not mention his unhappiness that she should think him sunk once more into a life of dissipation.

Andrew frowned. "I cannot like it. The slightest hint that you are not the scapegrace you appear to be, and your usefulness will be at an end."

"Your opinion of Rebecca seems to be as low as your opinion of me. She will never betray me deliberately, and she is more likely to do so inadvertently if she does not know the truth. The same applies to Teresa, of course."

"Very well." Having made up his mind, Andrew was decisive. "I shall tell Teresa, and you may tell Rebecca. You must not think that I do not value Rebecca. She has many excellent qualities, or I should not trust my daughter to her, but she has not Teresa's force of character."

"If you knew what her life has been like, you would understand and appreciate her courage," said John softly, and took his leave.

He went straight to the small house the Graylins had hired. A Russian servant admitted him and showed him into the drawing room, which was crowded with visitors of both sexes. John remembered how quickly Teresa had gathered about her a circle of friends after she arrived in London knowing no one. The years had only added to her poise and charm, without detracting one whit from her vivid loveliness. Now gentlemen and ladies alike clustered about her, laughing and talking in at least three languages.

Rebecca's corner of the room was quieter. She sat with her back to the window, a sunbeam playing with the golden lights in her hair. Her face brightened when she saw John.

He smiled at her as he crossed the room, but the smile faded when he recognized her companions. Kolya, the womanizer—well, John could hardly take exception to that, and at least he had brought one of his sisters. The fourth member of the group, however, was Count Boris Ivanovich Solovyov, dandy and spy.

How the devil had the wretched man wormed his way into an acquaintance with Rebecca?

By the time he had bowed to the ladies and spoken to Kolya, John had recovered his poise. He greeted the count with easy courtesy, then turned back to Rebecca.

"I see you are engaged at present, Cousin, but I want to remind you that you promised to drive with me one of these days. May I call for you tomorrow afternoon?"

"Oh dear, Princess Volkova has invited us to drink tea tomorrow. Perhaps the next day?"

He remembered that Volodya had asked him to attend a military review that day, before a night of carousing. The hussar was a useful contact and he did not want to offend him. After some discussion, it was fixed that the earliest afternoon that both he and Rebecca were free was a week hence.

In no good humour, he exchanged a few words with Teresa then went up to the nursery to see Esperanza.

"Dusha moya!" Gayo greeted him. The parrot's vocabulary was grown much more decorous since he had been living in the nursery.

If being addressed as "darling" by a bird was not enough to raise John's spirits, the little girl's delight at seeing him cheered him and he spent some time playing with her.

Annie was apparently occupied elsewhere, since a Russian maid was in charge. John knew that a Russian coachman had been hired to drive the ladies about. He wondered if all these servants, too, were in the pay of the Foreign Ministry. He must warn Rebecca to be careful of what she said even in the safest-seeming places.

Rebecca had already come to the same conclusion. She

longed to ask Teresa's opinion of the curious incident at the ball, but if her suspicions were correct it was best to mention it to no one. Overheard by the wrong person, the information might endanger John.

On the other hand, if she was wrong it looked very much as if he was so disgruntled by his position that he had abandoned any effort to succeed and had returned to his former dissolute life. The possibility disturbed her.

She was too busy to worry about him overmuch. She took seriously her duties as governess, and had made a game of teaching Esperanza her ABCs and the Russian alphabet together. The child was a joy to be with, lively and loving and as intelligent as her parents.

However, most of Rebecca's time was spent with Teresa. Enlisted at first as a companion to her employer, she imperceptibly slipped into being her protégée. She tried to protest.

"Indeed I cannot accept any more clothes. You know a hundred people here now, and do not need me to go into company with you."

"Fustian!" said Teresa briskly. "If I did not give my dresses to you I should have no excuse to buy new ones, and I do love shopping for pretty things. It is most fortunate that we are much of a height and that you are not too young to wear bright colours as I do. Besides, I am practising my skills as chaperone, so that when Chiquita makes her come out I shall know how to do it properly."

So Rebecca went to afternoon teas and balls and musicales and the theatre. Prince Nikolai and John were often in attendance at the same parties, and both sought her out. However, she had no opportunity to speak privately with John, and she noticed that he generally left early, in search, she presumed, of less respectable entertainment.

The day came when he was to take her driving. Spring had at last invaded St. Petersburg. The air was balmy, trees were greening, and fur coats and hats, if not yet laid away in camphor, were at least not in evidence.

John brought a bunch of violets, as if he had guessed she would wear her new lilac pelisse. She pinned the sweet-scented flowers to her bodice and happily allowed him to hand her up into the carriage he had hired.

The groom jumped up to his perch behind. As they drove off, John explained the finer points of driving a *troika* as opposed to a pair or four-in-hand. Rebecca was not very interested, but she enjoyed listening to his voice as he demonstrated his newly acquired expertise. Dextrously he wove his way through the bustling traffic on the Nevski Prospekt, dashed across the bridges, past the colonnades of the Kazan Cathedral, to the great square in front of the Winter Palace.

John grinned at Rebecca's gasp of amazement.

"Spectacular, ain't it?"

She had thought herself inured to the splendour of the mansions of the nobility, but the tsar's Winter Palace dwarfed all the others. It seemed to stretch forever across the far side of the square, an endless vista of blue-green stucco, white pillars, rows of windows, with statues decorating the roof balustrade.

"I have never seen anything like it," she said lamely.

"Over a thousand rooms, or thereabouts. I wish I could show you the inside too. Perhaps Kolya can smuggle you in."

"Do you think so? I shall ask him."

He frowned. "I did not know you were well enough acquainted to make such a request. I warned you that he is a rake, did I not?"

"He has never been anything but perfectly proper to me, I promise you. I like him." Rebecca tactfully changed the subject. "What is that building over there?"

"With the golden spire? That is the Admiralty. And the golden dome is the Cathedral of St. Isaac. It is still under construction, I collect. These Russians have a liking for gold, from the braid on their uniforms to the roofs of their buildings. The cathedral in the Peter-Paul Fortress is gold-roofed too. Would you care to see it? It is on an island in the Neva River, facing the palace; we might walk along the embankment since the weather is so clement."

It was the opportunity Rebecca had been awaiting. She eagerly agreed.

He drove closer to the river, then left the *troika* in the groom's care. There were several people strolling along the granite embankment, alone, in couples or small groups. John and Rebecca walked a short way, then stopped to gaze at the turbulent stream, racing down to the Gulf of Finland with chunks of ice and the melted snows of a Russian winter.

Rebecca shivered, reminded of the Lincolnshire river, little more than a brook compared to this mighty torrent, from which John had pulled her. She was sure he must remember too, but he was by far too gentlemanly to mention the incident.

"Are you cold?" he asked. "This sunshine is deceptive."

"No." The monosyllable hid a sudden rush of affection for him. He was not merely gentlemanly, he was kind. He was everything a man should be except, perhaps, responsible. Rebecca longed to ask about his work for the embassy, but she could not think how. After all, it was none of her business. "Is that the fortress," she asked, pointing across the Neva at another gold-spired building.

"Yes, that is it. You must have heard the noon gun? It is fired from there. The place is used as a gaol for prisoners of state."

"Prisoners of state?"

"Traitors, spies, those whose views differ from the tsar's."

"I do not like it." She shivered again. "No, I am not cold, truly, but that place is sinister—it makes me shudder. Pray let us walk farther."

"Of course, you fanciful creature." He took her kid-gloved hand and tucked it under his arm, warming it against his side as they went on. "There is something I want to tell you, Rebecca."

She looked up at him eagerly, "Oh yes, what is it?"

He hesitated, as if searching for words, and flushed slightly. "Perhaps you have wondered why I spend my time . . . why I live as if I had never left London?"

"You do not owe me any explanation. Because you confided in me once, you must not think I should ever presume to expect . . . "

"I *want* to explain. I do not want you to think ill of me. You see, I am collecting information for Andrew. Only Lord Cathcart knows that I am not the dissolute wastrel I appear to be."

"I guessed," she said softly, casting a frightened glance at the prison on its island, so close, so threatening. "When you pretended not to understand."

"That was Andrew's notion, of course. Famous, is it not? They talk quite freely in Russian in my presence. My own idea seems to be working quite well, too."

She smiled at the deprecating tone that could not hide his pride. "What is that?"

"I told several of the fellows that . . . dash it, I ought not to tell you."

"Pray go on, John. You cannot leave me in suspense."

"Well then, I made it plain that I will not gamble when I am . . . uh, that is, when I have been drinking. So if I refuse to play cards they assume that I am inebriated, and they do not mind their tongues as they would if I were sober. Which I am, of course," he added hastily. "Or nearly, at least."

"You will be careful, will you not?" she begged, half shocked and half amused. "I know that when gentlemen have been drinking, they do not always act or speak as they mean to when sober."

"I am not so easily befuddled, but I am careful, and you must be too. Never say a word about this, even to Teresa, though she knows. There are ears everywhere in this suspicious country." He paused while an innocent-looking couple passed them. "By the way, how did you come to be acquainted with Count Solovyov?"

"I was introduced to him at the embassy ball." She

wrinkled her nose. "I do not much care for him, but one cannot cut everyone one does not care for. At least, I think one should be able to but Teresa says it would not be *comme il faut* to refuse when he asks for a dance. Fortunately he is more interested in Teresa than in me."

"Good. She will know how to handle him."

"Why, John? Is he dangerous? But I have seen you talking with him several times, and even playing cards."

"It is as difficult for a gentleman as for a lady to cut an unwanted acquaintance without unpleasant consequences. More so, in fact."

"I daresay he would challenge you to a duel? Yes, of course he would. The Russians are so horridly bloodthirsty. Pray talk to him whenever he chooses!"

Not until she was back home, changing for dinner, did Rebecca realize that John had not answered her question about Solovyov. Not in words, anyway. His very unwillingness to do so made her resolve to be especially cautious when Count Boris Ivanovich was about.

She remembered the grim bulk of the Peter-Paul fortress and shuddered again. Its golden spire, shimmering in the sunshine, had pierced the sky like a brandished sword.

$=11=$

WALTZING WITH PRINCE Nikolai made Rebecca feel daring. It was odd, she mused as he spun her round the floor, how different it was from the safe, protected feeling she knew in John's arms. Oh dear, that was a shockingly intimate way of putting it! Her face growing warm, she amended her thoughts hastily—when she danced with John.

"Penny for your thoughts, Miss Nuthall," offered the prince teasingly. "Is fine English idiom, *nyet*?"

"Indeed, sir, you have an excellent command of English."

"*Nu*, enough of this 'sir'! My *imya-otchestvo* is Nikolai Mikhailovich."

"Alas, I cannot return the compliment. People would stare if you called me Rebecca."

"No, in English there is nothing between formality of surname and familiarity of Christian name. What was your father's name?"

"Ian," she said dubiously. "It is a Scottish name."

"Ah, those Scots, what fighters! I remember at Waterloo—magnificent. But Ian is not very different from our Ivan." At that moment the dance ended. The prince's bow to his partner was a model of formal elegance. "Permit me to procure refreshment for you, Rebecca Ivanovna."

"How pleased Grandmère would be to hear me named in Russian style!" Rebecca curtsied, laughing with delight. "Thank you, Nikolai Mikhailovich."

As he escorted her into the supper room, the prince repeated his offer of a penny for her thoughts. She had had time to think of an answer by now, and she told him how impressive she had found the Winter Palace.

He looked at her shrewdly, as if he guessed she was prevaricating, but forebore to press her. "It is superb, is it not?" he responded. "Tsar Nikolai decreed that all buildings in St. Petersburg except churches must be *odin sazhen*—six or seven feet—lower."

Despite her words to John, she was not quite bold enough to ask Nikolai Mikhailovich outright if he could show her the interior. "John says the rooms are splendid, too, and beautifully decorated," she ventured to hint.

He laughed, reading her mind. "I am sorry, but I cannot introduce you into Winter Palace. However, I will ask my mother to do so. To Princess Volkova, all things are possible. Are other sights in St. Petersburg that I can show you. You have surely strolled in Summer Garden, but I can take you inside summer palace of Tsar Peter. Perhaps you have seen Senate Square?"

"No, I do not believe so."

"Then I take you. Now, may I offer lemonade or champagne, Rebecca Ivanovna?"

"Lemonade, if you please, Nikolai Mikhailovich."

As the prince turned away to call a waiter, John spoke softly in Rebecca's ear, startling her.

"Nikolai Mikhailovich? I do not like to hear you so intimate with a rake." His voice was severe and he was frowning.

Rebecca was annoyed. "Even if I called him Kolya, it is not your business to reprimand me."

"I beg your pardon, Miss Nuthall," he said stiffly. "I presumed upon our slight relationship to offer a word of advice, not of reprimand. Pray excuse me."

He strode away. She saw him speak briefly to their hostess and depart from the ball, leaving her miserable.

It was several days before she saw him again, and the occasion was not propitious. She was standing with the prince in Senate Square, admiring the huge bronze statue of Peter the Great on a rearing horse, trampling a serpent beneath its hooves. Nikolai Mikhailovich had told her how Tsar Peter's obsession with building a city on the swamp by the Neva had led to the deaths of thousands of serfs brought in to construct it.

With a passion altogether Russian, he was explaining his views on the emancipation of the serfs when John drove up and hailed them. He was scowling, and Rebecca felt a tremor of fear.

"Excuse us a moment, Kolya," he said with icy politeness. "I want a word with Miss Nuthall." He drew her aside.

She went willingly, realising that her fear was not for herself but that he and the prince might come to blows. She did not understand why John should be so antagonistic towards his friend.

"What is it, John?" she asked, smiling at him hopefully.

He made a visible effort to relax. "I have just received an invitation to the tsar's midsummer fête at Peterhof. Teresa tells me you are going. Will you allow me to escort you, Rebecca?"

"Oh drat!" Her face fell. "Prince Nikolai asked me on the way here, and I had no good reason to refuse. Oh John, I had much rather go with you."

"Perhaps we can make up a party," he said with attempted lightness. "Do you mind if I join you now?"

She was quick with a warm assurance that that would be delightful. They went to look at Prince Lobanov-Rostovsky's new palace with its fierce stone lions standing guard, but conversation was stilted and even Kolya seemed subdued.

Rebecca hated to feel she had come between good friends. John had shown signs of being overprotective before, such as his efforts to shield her from Cousin Adelaide's sharp tongue. Having rescued her from the river's greedy grasp, he seemed to feel some sort of responsibility for her, but to quarrel with Kolya because of her was nonsensical. The prince was all that was gentlemanly towards her; if his manner was sometimes more impetuous or sentimental than an Englishman would consider proper, he was, after all, not English.

She regretted the breach, but whatever his differences with the prince John seemed to have forgiven her. He spent that evening quietly at home with the Graylins and gave every appearance of enjoying himself.

Evenings at home were few and far between. The days and weeks passed swiftly, the nights grew shorter, and in no time Rebecca woke to the morning of the tsar's fête.

Though John had said no more about it, she hoped that he would go with them. When they boarded the boat without him, she scanned the low, marshy banks of the Gulf of Finland as if she expected to see him riding there. When they reached Peterhof, the gilded statues posed about the cascade and channel leading down to the gulf from the palace reminded her of his comment on the Russian love of gold decoration. Though the hundreds of fountains sparkled more brightly in the sun than the jewels of the throngs of Russian gentry, she scarcely saw them. She was searching the crowds for his face.

He did not come. Kolya was amusing, the yellow-and-white palace was charming, the grounds were delightfully laid out in woods and groves and grottos. Rebecca smiled and admired and chatted but her mind was elsewhere.

The day was endless. Near midnight the sun set at last, but there was no true night at midsummer and the thousands of lanterns hanging from the trees and bushes glowed dimly useless in the dusk. The Russians, accustomed to their White Nights, pursued amusement with unabated vigor. Rebecca wilted.

"I shall take you home now," the prince suggested. "It is not proper to leave before His Majesty has retired, but if I care not for his policies why should I care for his protocol?"

Andrew decided that he and Teresa ought to observe the rules and stay. Teresa was in two minds as to whether to entrust Rebecca to Prince Nikolai, but she was pale with fatigue and quite willing to go. The prince borrowed a calèche and driver from a fellow-officer and soon they were on their way back to the city.

Rebecca slept most of the way, rousing only briefly when the rising sun shone on her face. It was still the small hours of the morning when they reached the Graylins' house. The prince knocked on the door, then handed her down from the carriage as it opened.

Behind the drowsy Russian servant, John appeared in the hallway.

"So you are back at last!"

"Fête continues. Rebecca Ivanovna was *burnt to the socket* so I brought her home," the prince explained, obviously pleased with his English idiom.

"I expected to see you there, John."

"The stupidest accident! I shall tell you tomorrow when you are rested."

Rebecca obeyed the implied suggestion and retired wearily to her chamber. If the gentlemen meant to fight there was nothing she could do about it. What incomprehensible creatures men were!

Below-stairs the incomprehensible creatures eyed each other warily.

"I should like to know why you take such a prodigious interest in my little cousin," John demanded.

Kolya shrugged. "At first, simply because she is pretty; then, because she is your cousin; and now because I like her. She has a simple soul. She is natural, not hiding troubled depths like our capricious Russian women."

"Much you know about her. Besides, she is not my cousin, merely a distant connexion. My cousin Teresa employs her as governess."

"So she told me."

"*She* told you? Devil take it, what a well-plucked 'un she has turned out to be!"

"If it were not for that, I might even have married her and settled down," said Kolya seriously. "However, I am not in position to anger my father by marrying English governess. Ah John, I believe my soul is English! I prefer your women, your language, your constitution."

Always rendered acutely uncomfortable by the Russian propensity for discussing their souls at the slightest provocation, John went to pour them each a glass of brandy. So Kolya had considered marrying Rebecca—for her, a splendid catch indeed. Then why was he so glad that Kolya had rejected the notion?

It must be because, despite Rebecca's Russian grandmother, she was thoroughly English and he could not imagine her living happily anywhere but in England.

Satisfied with this explanation, John handed Kolya his brandy. He was a good fellow after all.

"You, too, are very interested in welfare of Rebecca Ivanovna," said the prince enquiringly.

"I do not want to see her hurt. She is my cousin, after all," John reminded him.

Kolya's knowing look was lost on John, who was unaware of contradicting himself. "Of course. I mean no hurt, but perhaps you fear she will fall in love with me?"

"Nothing of the sort! It is just that you may raise her expectations."

"And she will set her cap at rich Russian prince?"

"Rebecca has by far too much delicacy of mind to do anything so vulgar. I wonder that you like her if you think her capable of it."

Kolya laughed. "I roast you, my friend. Let us be serious. I wish to invite Rebecca Ivanovna to visit my father's *dacha*. It is pleasant in summer to take picnic and seek mushrooms in woods. Was my intention to ask Sir Andrew and Lady Graylin, but perhaps you think better I invite large party?"

"Much better. I shall be delighted to go. You know, Kolya, you speak devilish good English, but you always forget 'the' and 'a'."

"Is on purpose, of course," said the prince, grinning. "Must do something to distinguish self from proper English gentleman."

Laughing, the friends walked home arm in arm through the bright June morning.

When John returned to the Graylins' house after a few hours of sleep, Teresa and Andrew had returned but were still abed. He found Rebecca in the nursery with Esperanza.

"Hello, hello, *dushenka*," Gayo screeched.

"On the whole I preferred his scurrility to his endearments," said John disapprovingly. Rebecca laughed.

Esperanza's greeting was as rapturous as the parrot's.

"Uncle John, listen to my ABC," the little girl insisted when he put her down after a hug of Russian proportions.

He listened gravely as she recited the alphabet.

"That was so good, shrimp, that you deserve a reward. I shall take your teacher away for a while so that you can play."

Esperanza pouted. "It's more fun if Aunt Beckie stays, and you too."

"We'll be back in a few minutes. I promised Aunt Beckie to exculpate myself this morning."

"Expate?"

"Make my excuses."

"Were you naughty?"

"Very!"

"Oh. Don't be angry with him, Aunt Beckie."

"I shan't make him stand in the corner, pet." Rebecca led the way down to the drawing room and took her favourite seat by the window. "Well, my lord?"

John stood leaning on the back of a chair, looking down at her enquiring face. Kolya was right, she was a devilish pretty girl. "I did mean to go with you, to be sure, but after all, you scarcely needed me when you had Kolya to escort you. Did you enjoy the fête?"

"Yes, excessively, and Peterhof is a charming place. But I could not help wondering why you were not there."

"It was these wretched, deceptive White Nights." He began to pace. "One forgets the time. I did not reach home until six or seven yesterday morning, and then Fedka, my valet, misunderstood me and failed to wake me. There was no way to avoid blotting my copybook, either by not attending the fête or by arriving after the tsar, which I had been assured was near a capital crime."

"Prince Nikolai told me you are not allowed to leave before him, either."

"Precisely. I decided that no one would miss so insignificant a person as myself, whereas by some unlucky chance I might be noted arriving late. I've no desire to draw attention to myself, so I did not go. I'm sorry if my absence spoiled your pleasure." He did not feel sorry in the least.

"Oh no, Nikolai Mikhailovich is an amusing companion."

That was not what John wanted to hear. "I was surprised to see you return home alone with him."

"There was a coachman. It was perfectly proper, and Teresa said I might. Is it not odd, John, that I was not at all afraid? To think that eating breakfast alone with Cousin Tom used to make me shake in my shoes! I believe it is your doing. I feel safe with you, so I am more confident with other gentlemen who have never offered me harm."

He sat down and took her hand. "I am glad of it. But beware of overconfidence. There are so-called gentlemen who do not deserve your trust."

"Count Solovyov, for one?"

"Yes. I believe you can rely upon Kolya, but most of these Russians are paradoxical folk. You think you know what they are about, and then you are confounded." He stood up again and moved about restlessly, feeling her gaze following him.

"You have made many friends among them, though?"

"Friends—call them acquaintances rather. I spend so much time with Russians that I scarcely see my compatriots at the embassy. Besides, they despise or envy me because I seem to do nothing useful. I do not know how it is, but though I live much as I used in London, I find it tedious. Only the work I am doing is worthwhile."

"Hush!" she said in alarm.

He nodded abstractedly. "I must suppose it is because my companions are so different in temperament from what I am accustomed to. Nor can I like their code of honour, though I cannot claim that all Englishmen subscribe to my own, let alone obey it. The Russians will not lie to a gentleman, true, but they think nothing of lying to a female or a serf. And then, they will not bear the slightest insult, yet they seem to me to go out of their way to insult others in an effort to prove their bravery. They seek out opportunities for duels, while any decent Englishman does his best to avoid them."

"To be sure." Rebecca's amusement was ill hidden.

"Oh, I know what you are thinking," he said ruefully. "I'm a fine one to talk, am I not? But that was not meant to be a serious affair, after all."

"I know, John. I am teasing. That does not mean I am not interested in what you are saying."

"I need to tell someone. You see, it has made me question my own code. Why should it be a matter of honour to pay one's gambling debts and not one's tailor? Why is it acceptable to cheat a husband but not at cards?" He hesitated. "I should not be saying such things to you. I never keep my tailor waiting overlong, I assure you."

"I do not pretend to understand what gentlemen think honourable. Why is it permissible to beat a wife but not a servant?" She was pale and trembling.

Again he sat down beside her and took her hand. "I am a villain to trouble you so, Beckie. I hoped you had put that behind you."

"It is not so easily forgotten."

"There are few marriages like your uncle's, I wager. Look at Andrew and Teresa. Muriel is perfectly happy with Tom, and my parents go on quite comfortably together. But enough of that. Try to put it all out of your mind. Kolya is planning an excursion into the countryside and I have already accepted. He means to invite you and the Graylins, among others. Do say that you will go."

"I expect so. Both Teresa and Andrew grow tired of the city."

"And you?"

"I do miss the countryside, even though I have discovered that I thoroughly enjoy parties and balls and the theatre. It would be nice to spend part of the year in the city and part in the country."

"That is what I have always done, and it suits me very well." He stood up. "It will be interesting to see how the Russians amuse themselves in the fields and woods. I had best let you go back to Esperanza now. I promised her not to keep you long."

"She does enjoy your visits," Rebecca said as they went out into the hall. "She told me you are her favouritest uncle, and her favouritest gentleman except Papa."

"I am very fond of her, and of young Ned, too. I daresay Mary will improve with age. You know," he added in surprise as he took his hat and gloves from the servant, "I have enjoyed my evenings here with you and Esperanza and Andrew and Teresa above anything else I have done in St. Petersburg!"

Pondering this extraordinary fact, he took his leave.

$=12=$

Jaded he might feel, but John continued to frequent the company of the young Russian officers. His patience was beginning to bear fruit. Nearly every day he had some tidbit to report to Andrew, and a pattern was emerging.

While news of troop movements and garrisons were useful, Andrew was eager to gain an insight into the plans of the military command headed, of course, by the tsar. He urged John to see more of Prince Nikolai.

"I hate to spy on a friend," John said gloomily. After their midnight discussion, he was once again on intimate terms with Kolya.

"You have yet to report a single word he has said. I must assume he is singularly close-mouthed about matters of state, whatever his opinion of the government. If it helps, I shall release you from any obligation to repeat anything he may let drop. I hope you feel no such qualms about those to whom he has introduced you."

John spent that very evening at a gaming house with Kolya and a few other members of the tsar's staff. As was his habit, not wanting to draw attention to his presence he avoided either winning or losing large sums.

The White Nights were past, but dawn still came early. The sun was already rising when one of the company proposed adjourning to a popular brothel.

It was not the first time a convivial evening had ended with such a suggestion. John had always declined; even in London a certain fastidiousness had kept him from the many houses of ill-fame after a disillusioning visit of exploration at an early age. Nor had he set up a mistress in St. Petersburg, feeling that the language barrier would prevent the friendly relationship he preferred.

In fact, he had not lain with a woman since that lying jade Minette had deceived him with Rawley, thus precipitating the duel responsible for his presence here.

Kolya, sharing his preference for a more stable liaison, had a ballet dancer under his protection.

"I'm off to see Dunyashka," he said. "Come with me, John? Her little sister is visiting. Is obliging girl." He sketched a shape with expressive hands.

John went. The dancer's sister, Katyenka, turned out to be a pretty blonde with merry eyes and red, pouting lips. Her figure lived up to Kolya's gestures, and she was more than willing to *oblige*. John drank a glass or two of wine with her, kissed her, gave her a few rubles and departed. It was the yellow hair that put him off, he decided. It reminded him of Minette. Dark hair was really much more attractive, the kind that had gold lights in sunshine. And besides, Katyenka was too buxom for his taste.

As he sauntered home through the pale light of the early morning, he remembered that tonight he had given himself a holiday. Instead of working he would spend a delightful evening with Rebecca and the Graylins.

He was looking forward to Kolya's expedition, too. He had already visited the Volkov's country house. Once he had stayed overnight after an unsuccessful bear-hunt and again after bagging several brace of snipe in a satisfying display of superior English marksmanship. It was a pleasant place. Rebecca would enjoy strolling through the birchwoods.

Half of July passed before a convenient day for Prince Nikolai's expedition arrived. St. Petersburg was full of dust and mosquitoes, the canals were growing odorous, and most of the wealthier Russians moved out of town to *dachas* in the villages of Tsarskoye Selo or Peterhof.

Prince Volkov's favourite summer home lay in the opposite direction, some twenty miles north of the city on the Karelia Peninsula, between the gulf and Lake Ladoga. Towards this, one sunny morning, drove a convoy of a dozen carriages: *troikas*, *kibitkas*, *drozhkis* and *brichkas* and one large, clumsy *tarantass*.

"I did not know you had invited so many!" Rebecca exclaimed as Prince Nikolai's *troika* took the lead.

"Once I involve my mother, it was inevitable," he sighed. "Still, they are all friends of mine, except for count. Mama has inexplicable fondness for Boris Ivanovich."

Rebecca had not noticed Count Solovyov among the others. She did not like him, and John had as good as told her he was dangerous, but surely he could not do anything to imperil John today. She resolved to put him out of her mind.

Crossing the Neva, they soon left the marshland behind and entered a region of sand dunes and forests. A refreshing breeze sprang up. Rebecca wished she dared remove her bonnet to enjoy it to the full.

"The air smells of pine," she said. "It is delightfully cool here."

"It is always pleasant here between lake and sea. Peter the Great had one of his many country residences here, at Blizhniye Dubki. In fact, it was near here that he rushed into sea in November to save people from sinking boat, which caused his final illness. Peter mirrored Russian soul sometimes heroic, sometimes brutal, sometimes sentimental. How sane you English seem in comparison. Even your mad King George merely talked to trees."

Princess Volkova had gone ahead the previous day, with her daughters and an extraordinary number of serfs. The party arrived to find a sumptuous picnic spread on rustic wooden tables in the shade of a grove of oaks. As Kolya handed Rebecca down from the *troika*, she thought she saw her hostess frown at them. It puzzled her, for the princess had always been friendly. Surely she did not suppose that her son intended anything more than a mild flirtation with the English governess?

She quickly forgot the moment as the two young princesses swept her off to join a merry group at one of the tables.

After nuncheon, the livelier members of the party took rush baskets and wandered into the woods to search for mushrooms. The cool green hush beneath the birches was shattered by gay voices. All the Russians knew just what they were looking for. There was much good-natured teasing as they instructed Rebecca, John and the Graylins, before spreading out in small groups among the silvery trunks.

Kolya and his younger sister stayed with Rebecca and John. Rebecca was distracted by the play of light and shadow as the sun shone through the leafy branches, and it was John who found the first mushroom.

They laughed at his air of triumph as he placed it with the utmost care in Rebecca's basket.

"Take care of it for me, and I shall have it for dinner," he said, grinning. "All the same, Princess, I'd wager you saw it first and it was only your politeness to a guest that allowed me the prize."

She giggled, and proved the truth of his guess by filling her own basket with astonishing rapidity.

Kolya had arranged for carriages to meet them at the far side of the wood, to drive down to the seashore when the afternoon had grown cooler. As host he was obliged to be there first, so they did not linger in the wood. They waited a few minutes by the sandy track before the others began emerging from the shade of the trees.

One of the last to arrive was Count Solovyov, escorting a young lady with whom he exchanged amorous glances. However, their dalliance must have been more a matter of words than of deeds, for he carried two respectably filled baskets.

He handed them to his coachman. The serf fumbled, spilling the mushrooms on the sand. Instantly Solovyov lashed out with his cane, slashing the man across the shoulders as he dropped to his knees to scrabble after the mushrooms. A kick caught him in the ribs and he went sprawling with a croak of pain.

Rebecca turned away blindly, sick with shock. John was beside her; she hid her face against his waistcoat and his arms closed about her, strong, comforting, protective.

"Enough, Count!" That was the prince's contemptuous voice. "Let the man pick them up. You are distressing the ladies."

But the princess addressed some lighthearted, inconsequential remark to the count's companion, and there had been no pause in the chatter of the others.

Rebecca raised her eyes to meet John's.

"They do not care," she whispered.

"I care." His arms tightened as he bent his head towards her.

"Rebecca Ivanovna!"

John released her at once, only keeping one hand beneath her elbow to support her.

Kolya's slanting hazel eyes were full of concern. "I am sorry you should witness this when you are my guest, though, alas, such things will happen as long as Russia has serfs. Are you all right? Shall I drive you home?"

"N-no, I shall be all right. I do not want to disrupt your party, and I should like to see the sea."

"You may count on me to take care of my cousin," said John gently.

Kolya nodded and went to see to the rest of his guests. Only the Graylins and the Russian gentleman who had gone with them were not yet arrived. They ambled out of the wood a few minutes later, with empty baskets, and the procession set off for the beach.

Rebecca was more shaken than she was willing to admit. The odd thing was that it was not the image of the beaten serf that kept recurring in her mind, it was the feeling of John's arms holding her close.

John too was shaken. He had to admit to himself that if

Kolya had not spoken at that moment he would have kissed Rebecca, right there in front of everyone. A brotherly kiss, of course, just to reassure her that she was safe. It was gratifying that she had turned to him in her distress. That was why his heart had swelled with joy until he thought he would suffocate—he was simply glad to be of service for once.

Andrew was the only other person in the world who viewed him as a competent, useful human being. And Andrew kept him very busy for the next couple of weeks. He saw Rebecca only fleetingly, in a crowd, and the remembered impact of her slender body and trembling lips faded.

It was sultry afternoon at the beginning of August when Andrew suggested that they leave his office in the embassy and walk by the Fontanka Canal.

"I have nothing to do for an hour or two," he said as he opened the door into the outer office, "and it may be a little cooler there. This place is like an oven."

John followed, bursting with curiosity. They crossed the embassy courtyard, waving away a persistent *drozhky* driver, and were strolling along the Fontanka before Andrew spoke a word about anything other than the weather.

"But on the whole I prefer the English climate," he concluded, and grinned at John's impatience. "For one thing, it bores foreigners beyond bearing and they soon cease to listen."

"Not only foreigners! Cut line, Andrew. You never brought me here to babble about your love of April showers."

"True. I believe we can talk safely here, though to make a habit of it would arouse suspicion. There are not too many others walking here at midday. First, I want to tell you what a splendid job you have done and to convey the ambassador's congratulations and thanks."

John flushed. "I forgot Cathcart knew what I was doing too."

"He means to send the duke a most favourable report of

your ability. I confess to having doubted that you would be helpful. Forgive me."

Suppressing an urge to embrace him Russian-style, John shook his hand with English formality.

"You know, I'm devilish glad you married Teresa," he said irrelevantly. "Well, now that you have emptied the butter-boat, let's hear what you really have to say."

"Your reports all point to a serious build-up of troops in the south, on the Turkish border and in the Caucasus. Yet as far as we can tell, none of the high command is down there. Cathcart thinks Alexander's attention is divided between dissipation, mysticism and the fear of internal revolt. He doubts there is room left for foreign adventures, nor stomach for it after the long fight with Napoleon. Yet if there is a chance of an attack on Turkey or Persia, we need to know. I am going south to find out."

"Let me go! You have a wife and child to think of."

"I thank you, John, and I expected nothing less of you. But this mission requires fluent Russian. I must do it myself. Ah, there are Teresa and Rebecca. I asked them to meet us here. Will you give Rebecca your arm and follow while I explain the situation to Teresa?"

To the couple strolling behind, it soon became obvious that though no voices were raised the Graylins were in the middle of a serious altercation. John gave Rebecca a brief explanation of what was afoot and then, exchanging glances of complicity, they moved closer to eavesdrop.

"You *shall not* leave me behind!" hissed Teresa. "Nothing could be better calculated to raise suspicion."

"It will be given out that I go only to Moscow, to visit our consul there. No one will miss me when I slip away."

"*I* shall. How do you mean to explain why you are not taking your wife to see the glories of the old capital?"

"You have a point," Andrew admitted unwillingly. "But once I leave Moscow I shall be travelling fast and light."

"Are you saying that I am incapable of travelling fast and light? You know better."

"Indeed I do, my dear. You must see though that it is out of the question to take Peri, even if Annie were not growing larger daily."

"She is big, isn't she?" Teresa was momentarily diverted. "I wonder if she will have twins? No, I see that we cannot take Chiquita, but after all it is not like leaving her in a distant country. I shall have no qualms whatever about entrusting her to Rebecca, and John will be here to take care of them."

Rebecca flushed with pleasure at the compliment, but John thought she looked a little anxious. He smiled at her reassuringly. He was pleased himself that Teresa at last considered him dependable enough to be left in charge.

"As you will," Andrew was saying resignedly. "It will take a week or two to obtain the necessary papers for travel to Moscow, so . . . "

John slowed his steps, drawing Rebecca back out of earshot. They paused, as if admiring a mansion on the opposite embankment of the grey-green, sluggish Fontanka.

"It's my belief," he said, laughing, "that Andrew has got exactly what he wanted. He knows very well how to handle my cousin."

"He wanted Teresa to go with him?"

"I'd lay a monkey on it. If he had simply proposed such a scheme, she would have insisted on taking Esperanza. As it is, she feels she has won half the battle so she is generously prepared to give in on the other half. Of course, it all depends on whether you are willing to accept responsibility for Esperanza and the household."

That thought seemed to have dawned on the Graylins, for at that moment they turned back.

"Rebecca!" Teresa held out both her hands. Beneath the azure ostrich plumes bobbing on her extravagant bonnet, her lively face was half mischievous, half pleading. "I have such a big favour to ask of you. John must have explained the situation. I want to go with Andrew. Will you look after Chiquita for me?"

Rebecca took her hands. To John's surprise, the anxiety had vanished from her eyes and she looked proud and self-confident. How she had changed since the day he met her!

"I am honoured that you trust me," she said. "Of course I will do it. How long do you expect to be gone?"

They walked slowly back along the canal, clarifying details that could not be freely discussed where they might be overheard. Just before they reached the bridge where Teresa's carriage was waiting, John recognized the slightly mincing walk of a gentleman coming towards them.

"Solovyov!" he warned.

Rebecca clutched his arm, but she said in a determinedly bright voice, "Do you go to the ballet tonight, Cousin?"

When the count reached them they were discussing the relative merits of opera and ballet. He bowed, smiling, but his eyes were cold.

"Good day, *mesdames, messieurs*," he greeted them. "Is family party? I may join? To stroll by Fontanka is *priyatno*—pleasant—in hot weather, is it not?"

"Very pleasant, but I fear we cannot ask you to join us," said Teresa with a convincing assumption of regret. "Sir Andrew escaped only briefly from his duties and is about to return to the embassy, while Miss Nuthall and I have shopping to do. Good day, Count." She shepherded Rebecca towards their carriage.

Andrew consulted his watch, tut-tutted, nodded to Solovyov, and went to hand the ladies into their *brichka*. The count frowned as he looked after them.

"I'm off to find a beefsteak," said John. "Care to join me, Count?"

"Ah, you Englishmen, always you must eat *bifsteks*. Come, I show you best in St. Petersburg."

Swallowing a sigh, John went with him.

$==13==$

IT WAS THE end of August before Andrew managed to gather together the requisite permits, internal passports, authorisation for post-horses and letters to the military governor of Moscow, all signed and sealed by the officials of several departments in three ministries.

Teresa had been chafing at the bit for a fortnight. The very day after Andrew came home and spread the papers triumphantly on the table before her, they were off. Rebecca stood on the front steps with Esperanza, John, and the weeping Annie, waving as Rowson drove the creaking *tarantass* down the street. Teresa blew a kiss as they turned the corner, and they were gone.

Rebecca had a hollow feeling inside. She had been sure she could cope, but faced with the reality her assurance wavered as she suddenly thought of a dozen things that could go wrong.

Esperanza gave her no time to brood. Her agitation at the departure of her parents showed itself in a flurry of boisterous excitement. Pulling away from Rebecca's hand, she danced down the steps and began to climb the ornate iron railing separating the house from the street.

"Look at me, Uncle John. I can go right to the top!"

"Be careful, Esperanza, you will hurt yourself." Rebecca hurried after her.

"Don't call me that, I'm Chiquita. I can jump from here."

"No you can't," said John. "Even I could not jump from there. Come down, shrimp."

"Call me Chiquita!" she insisted, and launched herself at Rebecca shouting, "Catch me, Aunt Beckie!"

Taken by surprise Rebecca managed to break her fall, but she sprawled on the ground and a wail went up. Heart in mouth, Rebecca stooped over her—scraped hands and knees and a rip in her pretty new dress.

She picked her up, hugged her, and carried her sobbing into the house.

"Silly cuckoo,"she said lovingly. "You should have listened to Uncle John. Let's wash your hurts and put a plaster on. I expect Annie can mend your dress."

"To be sure, Miss Beckie." Annie dried the child's eyes on her apron. "I'll fetch some warm water from the kitchen, and the ointment from my lady's medicine chest." She bustled out, leaving Rebecca to coax a smile from Esperanza.

Rebecca was glad when she returned. She was glad also when John decided to spend the rest of the day with them. He kept Chiquita amused during the painful business of washing her grazes, then carried her up to the nursery, and read to her.

"What a pity," Gayo commiserated.

After nuncheon John drove them to the Summer Garden. They met Kolya walking there with his married sister. Rebecca did not know her well as she lived in Moscow, but she had two small children with her and Chiquita quickly made friends with them. Princess Zoya was as sociable as her younger sisters. Rebecca soon felt at ease with her and thoroughly enjoyed the afternoon. On parting they made plans for the children to play together another day.

John stayed to nursery tea before going off to an evening engagement. He had left the embassy's bachelor quarters and taken a room in a house nearby, far enough for propriety, near enough to be of use. Rebecca was relieved to have him within reach, but after a successful first day in charge she was once more confident of her ability to manage.

In the absence of her chaperone, she found her social life

considerably curtailed. She did not mind; it was good to have time again for reading and Annie proved an excellent companion. Intelligent and practical, the African girl was full of stories about her travels with the Graylins. Esperanza adored her, and soon settled down.

Rebecca often spent the evenings with Annie, reading and sewing. Together they perused the latest sensation on the St. Petersburg literary scene, a fairytale in verse called *Ruslan and Ludmila*. Annie was particularly interested in it because the author, Aleksandr Pushkin, was the great-grandson of an African prince who had somehow become godson to Peter the Great.

When Rebecca mentioned this to John, he claimed acquaintance with the poet.

"He's a minor official in the Foreign Office, but I doubt he spent even as much time there as I do in the embassy. A dissipated libertine," he added with a grin, "and I speak as one who knows."

"His poetry is charming. I suppose it would not be proper for you to invite him here. Annie would so love to see him."

"Impossible. He was transferred from St. Petersburg to the south before the poem was published. A sort of internal exile. It seems to be quite common here. The tsar even exiles people to Moscow, or to their country estates."

"Why was Pushkin exiled?"

"His excesses are legend, and he is something of a radical, too, I collect."

"You have a great deal in common, then," Rebecca suggested teasingly.

"No, we have not!" John was revolted. "I never wrote a line of verse in my life! Now, are you ready to go? I hope your cloak is warm enough and Chiquita is well-wrapped. It is decidedly chilly outside."

They spent a splendid afternoon in the Summer Garden, trying to catch the leaves as they drifted down from the trees, and running through the rustling russet heaps of those already fallen.

"I have not had so much fun in a long time!" Rebecca exclaimed as John lifted Chiquita up to the carriage seat beside her.

"I fear you have been very dull since Teresa left," said John, leaning across to pick a yellow birch leaf from her hair. He presented it to her, frowning in thought. "There are so few entertainments to which it is proper for me to escort you alone."

"I do not mean to complain. I like the peace and quiet, and besides Princess Zoya has been prodigious kind in inviting me to go with her to parties now and then."

"She is gone back to Moscow though." He gave his three horses the office to start.

"Will she see Mama and Papa?" Chiquita demanded, a trifle tearfully. "Will Misha and Natasha see my Mama and Papa?"

Rebecca devoted her attention to soothing her, but she noticed that John remained thoughtful as he drove them home.

Chiquita ran above-stairs to tell Annie how many leaves she had caught. John helped Rebecca take off her cloak and followed her into the drawing room.

"I have an idea," he announced, warming his hands at the Russian stove built into one corner of the room.

"Heavens, is that all? I quite thought you were trying to hatch an egg."

"Like a broody hen, was I? Well, I have hatched out a famous notion. You will like it excessively, I wager."

"Do you mean to tell me what it is?"

He considered. "No, it shall be a surprise. Only be ready, and warmly dressed—your cloak would be best, I daresay; the hood will conceal your face—tomorrow at eight."

"John, tell me what I am preparing for!"

"No, only don't dress too fine. You'll enjoy it, I'll go bail. I was there last week."

Not another word could she pry from him, even when she was in the hired *troika* being driven to the unknown destination. She had dressed with a feeling of excited anticipation, ignoring Annie's words of warning.

"I misdoubt his lordship'll lead you into mischief, Miss Beckie. A mort of trouble he caused my Miss Teresa."

Rebecca tossed caution to the winds. Had John not rescued her from the briars more than once? He would not land her in a scrape, she was sure. She leaned back against the carriage seat, admiring the still beauty of moonlight on the waters of the Neva—and John's skill with the reins.

The first clue she had was the distant, haunting strains of Gypsy music. As the wild fiddling grew louder, she saw by the light of flickering rush torches a circle of caravans with swarms of people milling about them. Colourful uniforms mingled with Romanies' bright-hued garb in a kaleidoscope of animation.

"Exotic, ain't it?" John pulled up at the end of a row of carriages. "The Gypsies in England are a poor lot compared to these. There is more room for nomads in Russia. This tribe camps here for the winter, but in the summer they have the freedom of the steppes." He gave the reins to the groom, thrust his whip into the capacious pocket of his overcoat, and helped Rebecca down.

"Can I have my fortune told?"

"Of course. I thought that would amuse you so I have a purseful of silver for crossing palms. Let us go and watch the dancing first, though."

As he escorted her towards the bonfire at the centre of the camp, careful to protect her from the crush, she kept her hood close about her face. Though a number of the Russian officers had females on their arms, she suspected that they were not of the first respectability.

Not for the world would she have been so poor-spirited as to spoil John's treat in the interests of propriety. Clinging to his arm, she smiled up at him.

The violin's tune ended with a flourish as they reached the clearing by the fire. A handsome girl in flamboyant scarlet and yellow, gold-sashed, completed her final gyration with a low curtsy, her dark head held proudly. A cheer went up and coins showered at her feet. Two small boys scrambled to collect this largesse while the girl herself moved with lithe dignity into the shadows. Rebecca saw the glint of silver braid and guessed that a hussar waited for her.

Tambourine and czymbalom joined the fiddle for the next dance. A couple ran out into the clearing. Rebecca watched entranced as they swayed and swirled and leapt with impossible agility and astonishing stamina. She was breathless by the time the man caught his partner in a final dramatic pose.

"Like it?" John's grin told her he knew the answer. She realized he had been watching her face more than the dancers. "They make the waltz look positively staid, do they not?"

"It was . . . it was . . . I cannot find the words. Will they dance again?"

A couple of Guards officers were arguing with the musicians, who had laid down their instruments.

"Later, I expect. Come, let us find the Gypsy queen and have your fortune told."

They were directed to a large caravan set somewhat apart from the rest. A torch flared above the open door. John went up the steps and exchanged words in his mangled French with someone inside, then beckoned to Rebecca.

An old woman, her hair covered by a white kerchief, sat at a table before a black curtain embroidered in gold thread with strange symbols. A similar cloth covered the table, on which rested a crystal globe, a pack of cards, and an oil lamp. The dark eyes that appraised Rebecca from head to toe were unexpectedly keen, and the voice that bade her be seated was commanding.

She obeyed, and John gave the Gypsy a few coins.

"Now you will leave, milord," the woman said in heavily accented English.

Startled, he shook his head. "No. I don't know how you

guessed who I am, but I will not leave the lady."

She scrutinized him, her gaze piercing, then nodded. "You do well to take care of her. You may stay. Now, *barynya*," she switched to Russian, "give me your hand."

Her fingers were knotted with rheumatism but her clasp was firm. Rebecca was disappointed when the fortune she told was the usual rigmarole about a tall, dark, handsome stranger, great peril, a long voyage, and true love waiting at the end. John was the stranger of course, and the fact that she was a foreigner made the long journey an obvious deduction. Sooner or later most people met with some sort of danger, and as for true love . . .

She stole a glance at John. He was flipping through the Tarot deck, apparently unheeding, though she could not be sure if he was just pretending not to understand Russian. She suppressed a sigh.

. . . As for true love, John was not the marrying sort and she must put such farfetched notions out of her mind. She thanked the fortune-teller and declined an offer to seek further revelations in the crystal.

"Milord!" said the Gypsy sharply, "the cards are now attuned to you. I will read them."

Rebecca nearly giggled when John dropped the pack as if they burned him.

"No, thanks! I don't go in for such taradiddles, begging your pardon, ma'am. Are you finished, Rebecca? Let's be off, then."

The torchlight outside seemed bright after the mysterious dimness in the caravan. The violin was playing again, soaring above a rhythmic clapping from the crowd.

"Let's go and see what they are doing now," John suggested eagerly, his hand on Rebecca's arm to steady her on the rickety steps.

As she stepped to the ground, the dancing-girl in red and yellow dashed across in front of them. A short, wiry Gypsy chased after her, slashing at her with a willow switch. Rebecca cried out as the girl stumbled and fell. The man was upon her, his arm swinging in vicious blows about her bare shoulders. She crouched there, protecting her head with her arms, no sound escaping her lips.

With a muttered oath John strode towards them. He pulled his whip from his pocket and raised it to strike, then he glanced back at Rebecca and seemed to falter. The Gypsy looked up. In one agile bound he was facing John in a fighter's crouch.

A knife glinted in each hand.

The two men circled warily. John was a head taller than his opponent, who was within easy reach of his whip, but the whip was no protection against the deadly danger of a thrown knife. Afraid of distracting him, Rebecca did not dare stir even when the girl brushed past her and fled up the steps.

She heard urgent voices in the caravan behind her. She was about to go up and beg the old woman to intervene when a tall, well-known figure strolled into view and stood arms akimbo regarding the combatants.

"Kolya!" Rebecca gasped.

The fortune-teller spoke sharply from the top of the steps. Only one word was comprehensible—"Volkov." The Gypsy flashed a sullen glance at his queen. For a moment it was touch and go, then he shrugged. The knives disappeared and he faded into the shadows between the caravans.

Rebecca ran to John, reaching the safe circle of his arm just as Prince Nikolai clapped him on the shoulder with a laugh.

"Well, John, we both know uses of having influential father, *nyet*? Who is your fair charmer?"

"No one you know." John sounded on edge. Glad that the light was behind her, Rebecca bowed her head and pulled the hood tighter. "I must take her home now. My thanks, Kolya. I shall see you tomorrow."

"Think nothing of it, old fellow," said the prince genially. "*Do svidanya.*"

"Until tomorrow."

John drove in silence for some way. Clouds hid the moon and the poor quarters they traversed were ill-lit. Her mind whirling with the events and emotions of the past few hours, Rebecca was glad of the time to compose herself.

"I'm sorry your evening was spoiled. I ought not to have taken you there."

John's voice was still strained, and Rebecca found that her nerves were not yet settled.

"It was not spoiled. I would not have missed the dancers for the world. But I was so frightened for you."

"I don't mind admitting I was in a bit of a quake myself," he said wryly.

"How fortunate that Prince Nikolai was there!"

"Yes, and how fortunate that he did not recognize you." Though John suspected that Kolya had guessed the name of his companion, he knew his friend would never betray her. On the other hand, it was just as well if Rebecca did not repose too much trust in the Russian.

He took her home, paid off the carriage, and after assuring himself that she was recovering from the shock, he went for a walk. He needed to think.

The streets were still, though high above a wind scattered ragged clouds across the sky, now hiding now revealing the moon. The glassy waters of the Fontanka reflected the white circle briefly, then plunged into darkness, then gleamed again. John leaned against the balustrade. Ideas and images raced through his mind, some clear and some obscure.

He should not have taken Rebecca to the Gypsy camp. It was no place for a respectable female, though he had not suspected how dangerous it could be. It had been a delight to see her face as she watched the dancers, yet he had had to steer her away from the dancing bear, remembering how its trainer had whipped and prodded it into performing on his last visit. She was oversensitive to violence. Not that he enjoyed seeing animals mistreated; he had never frequented cock fights or bull-baiting at home, but he had not actively disapproved. He had never really considered such matters until he met her.

He liked to think he would have gone to the rescue of the Gypsy girl even if Rebecca had not been there.

It was growing chilly standing still. He wandered on, passing a noisy tavern without the least desire to go in. Looking back, his life seemed one long vista of taverns and gaming houses and rowdy companions.

He could not blame his dissatisfaction on the Russians. Even in London, he realized, he had been searching for something more. One by one his friends had moved on. Some had ended in the sponging house, or fled to the Continent, but others had married, taken their seats in the House of Lords, retired to the country to tend their acres, or otherwise converted to a life of sober discretion. New faces had always replaced them, and a few of the old lingered still. Bev, for instance, showed no sign of repentance and could always be counted on for a lark. Of course, that was about all one could count on him for.

And that, thought John in dismay, was exactly what his grace had said of Bev. Oh lord, was he in danger of turning into the sedate, serious person his father wanted him to be?

Alarmed, he went into the next tavern he passed and ordered a bumper of brandy. It was a shabby place, patronized by labourers and minor clerks, who fell silent when he entered and stared to see a gentleman among them. None spoke French, let alone English.

John drank his brandy and went home to bed, thoroughly blue-deviled. Even his room depressed him though it was a pleasant place, spacious and well-heated. He was not used to living alone, with only a servant. In London most of his friends had hired bachelor apartments, whether they could afford them or not, but despite his profligate habits, he had always stayed in his parents' house.

To his astonishment and horror, he was forced to admit that he missed his family.

=14=

IT WAS PAST noon when John was awakened by the arrival of Kolya.

"Get up, lazyhead. We shall miss first race."

"Lazybones. Sleepyhead. Race?" John rubbed his eyes. He had had a restless night with disturbing dreams.

"Today is day of horse-races at Tsarskoye Selo. You remember, I am to ride in fourth race. So get up your sleepy bones and come."

John quickly recovered his spirits in the lively atmosphere of the race track. It was largely a military event, with officers riding rather than the trained jockeys he was used to. Many of his acquaintances were there, several of them taking part, and the tsar had honoured the occasion with his presence. The betting was enthusiastic for the honour of the various regiments was at stake.

With no axe to grind, John laid his wagers on the horses and riders that looked best to him. He won a considerable amount on the first three races, and put his winnings on Kolya in the fourth. The prince led the field from the start and came in two lengths ahead of his nearest rival. Again John bet everything on the next race, and again he was lucky.

"Not lucky, astute," said Kolya, grinning, and bore him off to celebrate.

It was a riotous celebration. They started with champagne and the inevitable *zakuski* in the quarters of one of Kolya's fellow-officers at the nearby military camp. When two more members of the Preobrazhenski regiment won their races, the party spread to the officers' mess, and then throughout the camp, growing noisier as it expanded.

Kolya invited John and several others to dine at a restaurant in St. Petersburg. The sun was setting as the boisterous group drove into the city. There was much uproarious laughter when they found that the prince, in anticipation of his victory, had already reserved a room and ordered a banquet. Turtle soup, asparagus, veal, game and sturgeon were washed down by oceans of wine, and more oceans of vodka followed for the toasts. The floor was littered with smashed glasses by the time there was a general move to adjourn to a gambling hell.

John found himself walking across a bridge with Kolya at his side, some way behind the others. He was pleasantly tipsy, and when Kolya started singing the ballad of *Styenka Razin* he joined in with *Annie Laurie*. After a couple of discordant verses, they somehow ended on the same note.

"Splendid," said Kolya. The word appealed to him and he repeated, "Splendid, splendid, splendid. England is a splendid country."

"*Annie Laurie*'s Scottish," John objected.

"No, no, my dear fellow, Annie is an African. But what I mean to say is that it is all thanks to England that I won the race today. Was it today?"

"Think so. Don't quite follow you, though. In Russia, not England, wasn't it?"

"It was in England that I learned to judge horses and to ride like an Englishman."

"Yes, England has the bes' horses and riders in Europe. In the world. In the universe. You speak ex . . . ex . . . splendid English when you're topheavy, Kolya."

"It is my English soul speaking. England has not only the best horses but the best gentlemen." He put his arm round John's shoulders and said solemnly, "I model myself on the English gentleman. You are my model, John."

"No!" Shocked, John stopped and stared at his friend. "Not me. Bad model. Very very very bad model. Best choose someone else, old fellow. Choose Andrew or Tom or even his grace. Dozens of 'em to choose from." He waved his arms and nearly overbalanced.

"Come and have some brandy," Kolya suggested pacifically, pulling on his sleeve, and they caught up with the others as they entered the gaming house.

That night John forgot his rule about mixing drinking and gambling. His luck was in, and the pile of rouleaux and vowels grew before him whether he played faro or boston or whist. In an effort to change their luck, his companions dragged him off to another hell, but he went on winning. They moved again. Somewhere along the way he lost sight of Kolya and found himself singing *Annie Laurie* again, in a demented counterpoint to a chorus of melancholy Russian soldiers. There was a girl on his knee, and another leaning on his shoulder.

When he woke the next morning, he was in a small white-washed room. Just enough sunlight fought its way through the grimy windowpanes to set hammers pounding in his head, and there was a foul taste in his mouth.

He ventured to move slightly, and a straw mattress rustled beneath him. The sheets were none too clean.

A rickety table and two chairs stood against the far wall, on which hung an icon. The only other furniture in the room was a chest, made of cheap deal but lovingly carved by inexpert hands. The door of the room was ajar and his greatcoat hung from a nail behind it.

John had no idea how he had got there.

He sat up with a groan and swung his legs off the bed. At that moment a plump, cheerful-looking girl with an untidy yellow pigtail thumped the door open and set down a hissing samovar on the table. She turned to regard him.

"*Vy prospalsa, dusha moya?*"

Had he slept it off? John pretended not to understand, alert though his head was pounding. Why had she called him "darling?" He groaned again. He remembered nothing but the implications were obvious.

"*Chai?*" she offered, pouring a glass of tea.

He took it gratefully, refusing the lump of coarse beet sugar that went with it. The hot liquid revived him somewhat, though when he stood up he felt a bit shaky. Taking his top coat from the nail he hunted through the inside pocket.

There was a gold three-rouble chernovetz, two Imperials, worth ten roubles apiece, and a handful of silver. In one of the other pockets he found a twenty-five rouble note. He had a vague memory of winning large sums last night. Had he gambled it all away again, or had he been robbed?

He looked at the girl. Her expression was enquiring, not in the least guilty. He put the Imperials and the note on the table, patted her cheek, and departed.

The narrow staircase stank of cabbage soup. By the time John reached the courtyard he was feeling decidedly nauseated. Fortunately a *drozhky* driver was just setting out to look for passengers. His suspicion vanished when John tossed him a silver rouble and he drove him home.

At least, John had intended to go home. The *drozhky* pulled up in front of the Graylins' house, and he realized he must have given the wrong address. It was too complicated to explain, so he gave the man another rouble, and stumbled up the steps to knock on the front door. Rebecca would give him something to ease the pain in his head and the queasiness in his stomach.

The Russian servant who opened the door started back in dismay before recognizing him.

"Milord! *Shto vy* . . . "

"Who is it, Vanya?" Rebecca stepped into the hall. "John! Heavens above, what have you been doing? You look as if you have been dragged backwards through a bush, at the very least. Come in and sit down."

Suddenly aware that he had slept in his clothes, lost his hat, and neither combed his hair nor shaved, John hung back.

"I'd better not." Unwisely he shook his head. He winced.

Rebecca seized his hand and tugged him after her into the drawing-room.

"Sit down," she insisted. "What is the matter?"

"Kolya won a horse-race yesterday," he explained sheepishly. "We were celebrating last night."

Her expression changed from concern to indulgence. "Ah, then I can guess what ails you. Wait here a moment."

She went out, to return a few minutes later with a glass of aromatic tea. He sniffed it suspiciously.

"It is one of Teresa's herbs. Annie has learned all about them and she says this is what you need. Drink it up and you will soon feel more the thing."

He obeyed, feeling like a small boy who had hurt himself being naughty. She was treating him just as she had treated Esperanza when she fell from the railing.

The tea helped, but the departing discomfort left room for his anger and disgust with his own behaviour. He did not want Rebecca's amused tolerance; he wanted her to see him as strong, capable, worthy of her respect. He thought he had had that respect, but now he had lost it. It would have to be earned again.

His dejected musing was interrupted by the servant.

"It is *Knyaz* Nikolai Mikhailovich Volkov, *barynya*. Are you at home?"

John made a quick gesture of denial, but Rebecca smiled and nodded.

"Yes, show him in, Vanya. Perhaps he too is in need of some herbal tea."

Kolya was immaculate in a fresh uniform, smoothly shaven, at worst a trifle paler than usual. He kissed Rebecca's hand, then tossed a package of papers and a clinking leather pouch on the small table beside John.

"I came to return these to you." He shook his head in mock reproach, grinning, as he took in his friend's condition. "You had devil's own luck last night—begging your pardon, Rebecca Ivanovna."

John picked up the papers. "Then I did win! I was not

sure whether I had dreamed it or been robbed."

"In that case, it is good thing that I kept them for you. You have won fortune, my dear fellow. Among those papers you will find vowel for Count Kirsanin's *dacha* at Peterhof. As I remember, his bath-house is exceptional. I suggest we go and inspect your property—Russian bath will make you new man."

"Yes, do go," Rebecca urged. "I daresay fresh air and exercise will help."

John grimaced, but had to agree that powerful remedies were called for. He heaved himself to his feet, apologised to Rebecca for having visited her in such a state, and made his way carefully towards the door.

"I bring him back to you tomorrow right as trivet," Kolya promised Rebecca. "Was grand celebration."

Rebecca had been a little shocked to see John in such a disreputable condition. At the same time, she could only be glad that he was sufficiently at ease with her to turn to her for comfort. It was odd that the gallant gentleman who had supported her and given her confidence in herself should ever be in need of her aid. She wished she had been able to do more for him.

She went above-stairs to the nursery, where she had a difficult time explaining to Esperanza why Uncle John had not gone up to play with her.

"Prince Nikolai came to take him to Peterhof," she said. "He was in a hurry and one must not keep a prince waiting. They will return tomorrow and I expect Uncle John will come to see you then."

"*Cochon*," observed Gayo reproachfully.

Esperanza giggled. "That means pig in French. He's not s'posed to say that."

At last they settled to lessons. It was peaceful in the sunny room. The parrot was muttering to himself over a dish of sunflower seeds. Annie sat by the window sewing and Esperanza was drawing a flower with coloured chalks to illustrate the letter *F*. Rebecca had a book open on the table before her, but she was still thinking of John when a hurried step was heard mounting the stair.

Had he come back? It did not sound like his tread, yet nor was it the stolid gait of the Russian servants.

Annie dropped her sewing and struggled to lift her heavy body out of the chair. "That's . . . " she began, when Rowson burst through the door.

"Miss Beckie! Annie! You're all safe then? Where's his lordship?" As he spoke, Rowson enfolded his wife in his arms and planted a hearty kiss on her brown cheek. Dressed in a Russian peasant smock, sheepskin jacket, and felt boots, he looked travel-worn, weary and agitated.

"Rowson! Where's my Mama and Papa?" Esperanza abandoned her chalks and flung herself at him. He caught her with one arm and gave her a quick hug, the other arm still about Annie's swollen waist.

"That's what I've to talk to Miss Beckie about, missy." He sent a glance of appeal to Rebecca.

"Go down to the kitchen, Chiquita, and tell Cook I said you can have a *sladki pirozhok.*"

Esperanza pouted. "I don't want cake, I want my Mama and Papa."

Rowson dropped to his knees and put his hands on her shoulders. "Be good, missy. Sir Andrew and my lady bain't with me right now, but they's jist fine, I promise."

She looked at him seriously, then turned to Rebecca. "An apple tart?" she bargained.

"Yes, scamp, you can have an apple tart. Off with you, now." Rebecca clenched her fists in her lap, hoping her apprehension was hidden from the child.

Rowson closed the door behind Esperanza. "Ifn you don't mind Miss Beckie, I'll sit down. It's a long way I've come, and fast."

"Of course, Rowson." She was amazed at how calm her voice sounded. "Now tell us what has brought you back alone."

"Annie, love, come sit aside me." He helped her to the

table, seated her and dropped onto the chair next to her. She clung to his hand. "I think we be safe here, but I'll talk soft and careful-like. You know what Sir Andrew was up to, don't you, miss?"

Rebecca nodded. "Yes, roughly. They are all right, are they not? You promised Chiquita."

"Aye, miss, they was all right when I left, and safe and sound by now I don't doubt. But there's no denying the Russians guessed what's up and was after us. Sir Andrew decided 'twas best to head for the Turkish border. Not far away from it, we wasn't. Only summun had to warn his lordship, being as how he's in the same business. No one takes note on a servant, so I bin riding day and night for more days than I c'n count."

"Lord John has gone to Peterhof with Prince Nikolai. I have no idea how to reach him." Rebecca stood up and wandered restlessly to the window. "What should I do? If you have brought us the news already, I daresay it has reached the Russians here. No one knows where John is now, but he will be arrested as soon as he comes back to St. Petersburg. Oh lord, what shall I do?"

She leaned her forehead against the window pane, cold despite the sunshine. He would ride back down that street, cheerful, restored to his usual exuberant health, and they would be waiting for him. There must be some way to warn him!

A group of four uniformed horsemen was cantering towards the house. The chill of the glass ran throughout her body.

"Rowson, come here. Look."

He hurried to her side. "That's the Pavlovski regiment, as garrisons the Peter-Paul fortress," he confirmed grimly. "Looks like we're in for a mite o' trouble."

The thunderous knocking at the front door could be heard even from their position on the third floor. It stopped suddenly, to be succeeded by pounding feet on the stair. Rebecca felt the blood drain from her face as she turned to face the intruders.

The door swung open and crashed against the wall. A short, thin officer strutted into the room. Rebecca recognized by his insignia that he was a lieutenant, and though she had been uncertain of the uniform, his snub nose confirmed that he was of the Pavlovski regiment. The massive trooper who loomed in the doorway behind the lieutenant was also snub-nosed. She remembered with half-hysterical irrelevance how Kolya had told her of the founding of the regiment by mad, snub-nosed Tsar Pavel Petrovich.

"*Vashi dokumenty!*" the officer snapped.

Rowson stepped forward. "We are servants, your excellency. We have no papers."

"Your names." He checked their names against a list, pointed to Annie and Rowson, then hitched his thumb over his shoulder. "You and you—out."

Rowson hesitated, glancing back at Rebecca.

"Go on," she insisted. "You must take care of Annie. I daresay he only wants to ask me some questions."

Despite her brave words, she felt very alone when the two had gone, Annie in tears. Behind her back, she gripped the windowsill as if it could save her from being swept away.

"Revekka Ivanovna Nootall." The lieutenant rolled the *r* with more than usual Russian gusto, and leaned on every syllable. "You are not servant."

"I am a governess," she replied with all the composure she could muster.

"You entered Russia as governess, on passport of Sir Andrew Graylin. Then you go into highest society, to balls, theatre, everywhere. Is curious, *nyet*?"

"Lady Graylin was kind enough to take me to parties." To her chagrin her voice was shaking. "But I am a governess."

"What you know of Graylin's business in south?"

"Nothing. I was told they were to visit Moscow."

"Where is Lord John Danville?"

"I do not know. He does not report his movements to me."

"But you know he is spy! And Graylin also!" His stabbing forefinger threatened with an almost physical shock. "Perhaps you too are spy?"

"No! They are not spies. I am not."

"Tell me why Graylins went to south."

"To see Moscow."

"Where is Lord John Danville?"

"I do not know. Indeed I do not!"

"I think you know. I think you will tell my colonel when he asks." He gestured to the trooper.

The soldier marched forward and gripped Rebecca's upper arm. She stumbled after him down the stairs. The world seemed to swim about her head, but she saw the pale, frightened faces of the Russian servants and heard Esperanza crying in the kitchen. Of Annie and Rowson there was no sign.

In the street, they shackled her wrists and tossed her up on a horse before one of the other troopers. Grinning, he pulled her roughly against his chest, his arm round her waist. He smelled of cabbage and sweat, and despite the warmth of his body she could not stop shivering. The streets passed in a dream, until they crossed the Neva and she saw before her the sinister gate and gold cathedral spire of the Peter-Paul fortress.

They rode through the square stone gateway, beneath the sneering double eagle. She was lifted down from the horse and hustled into the nearest building. Her escort paused before a door and knocked. A gruff voice bid them enter.

As they obeyed, a familiar figure slipped past them and out of the room. Rebecca caught only a glimpse of his face, but it was enough.

It was Count Boris Ivanovich Solovyov. And he wore an expression of malicious satisfaction.

The next few hours were a nightmare of repetition. "Why did the Graylins go to the south? Where is Lord John Danville?" She stood before the hard-faced colonel, obstinately insisting that she did not know. They did not touch her, just let her stand there, the shackles biting into her wrists. At last she crumpled to the floor, barely conscious.

They carried her out. Her ankles were fastened together with iron rings and a length of chain. Supported by a trooper on either side, she was taken along gloomy passages, down steps worn in the centre by the feet of countless prisoners, until they stopped before a black hole in the wall.

A dank, noisome miasma rose to her nostrils. The soldiers let go of her, then a hand between her shoulderblades propelled her forward to sprawl on slimy stone.

Behind her, the door clanged shut.

== 15 ==

JOHN WHISTLED AS he cantered back towards St. Petersburg, Kolya keeping pace at his side. The cold wind off the Gulf of Finland was invigorating. He was full of energy, ready to slay dragons if any should present themselves.

"It is great pity you will not be here next summer to enjoy the *dacha*," Kolya observed.

"Yes, it's a pretty place. I'll bring Rebecca and Esperanza out to see it one day soon, but I shall have to sell it."

"Count Kirsanin will be anxious to buy it back, at good price. You are wealthy man, John."

"Free of his grace's apron strings at last!" He laughed, touching the package of papers in his greatcoat pocket. Russians were as punctilious as Englishmen about paying their gambling debts; he had no fear of being cheated.

The road entered a birchwood. The graceful trees were leafless now, but the white trunks grew so close together it was still impossible to see very far into their midst. Not until they were nearly level with it did John notice the ramshackle *tarantass*, drawn some way off the road, and the hobbled nag beside it.

At that moment a man ran towards them, shouting.

"My lord! My lord!"

So unexpected was the sight of him that it was a moment before John recognized Rowson in his peasant garb. He drew rein at once.

"What the devil are you doing here?"

Rowson glanced at the prince, who tactfully moved out of earshot.

"Sir Andrew sent me back to warn your lordship. The Russkis tumbled to his lay and him and her ladyship lit out for the border. He reckoned they'd be after you for sure, and right he was. Oh my lord, I don't know how to tell you."

"What is it man? Out with it."

"I got Annie and Miss Esperanza away safe enough, my lord, but they've taken Mistress Beckie to the fortress."

An icy hand clutched at John's heart and the blood drained from his face. "Beckie! Oh God, no!"

His anguished cry brought Kolya to his side. *"Shto s toboy?* What is wrong, John? Can I help?"

His long face with its slanted eyes was full of concern. The fact that he was on the other side seemed irrelevant. He was a friend—and his father was a powerful man.

"Rebecca has been arrested. Surely Prince Volkov can arrange her release? Will you ask him?"

"Arrested? *Bozhe moy*, do not tell me she is in Peter-Paul fortress."

"Rowson thinks so. I have heard stories . . . "

"Better not to think of them. John, I will do what I can for you, but it is useless to approach my father. Already he has warned me not to entangle self with English governess."

"You do not think he had her arrested because of you?"

Kolya shook his head. *"Nyet.* It is because of your profession, I do not doubt. Perhaps as bait to lure you."

"You know what I have been doing?"

"Am not blind, my friend. If not you, then another. Is best each country knows what others plan, then no nasty surprises. We are allies, after all. Now let us move off road and think what is best to do."

John dismounted and followed him into the wood. He felt utterly helpless. Here was no dragon to be faced with sword and spear, but a multi-headed hydra of bureaucracy with an army to back it. If he rode up to the fortress and demanded admittance they would grant his wish. He would find himself in a cell, less able than ever to help Beckie.

"If I gave myself up, would they release her?"

Kolya tied his horse to a tree before responding. "Possibly. Perhaps not. You must not do this until we have tried all else. I know you love Rebecca Ivanovna but . . . "

John stared at him, not hearing the rest of his sentence. Of course, he loved her. How could he not have realized it? That explained everything, made everything simple. Whatever was necessary to ensure her safety he would do, even to facing a firing squad at dawn.

He was calm now, ready to make plans, ready to listen to Kolya, who knew his way about in this benighted country. When a shriek of "Uncle John! Uncle John!" preceded the eruption from the *tarantass* of a small figure bundled in a fur robe, he managed to grin at her as he caught her and tossed her in the air.

"Are you having a splended adventure, Chiquita?"

"Oh yes, 'cept Annie cries a lot. I want Aunt Beckie."

Annie's tired face appeared between the panels of the *tarantass* cover. Her tight-curled black hair was hidden by a peasant shawl but inevitably she was conspicuous. John loved Rebecca and feared for her, yet he also had responsibilities to the little girl and the faithful servants.

"I'll tell you what," he said to Esperanza, "You and Annie and Rowson shall go and stay in my new house and Auntie Beckie shall join you there as soon as she can. You will like it. There is a stream in the garden with a little bridge over it."

"You come too."

"I'd like to, but I have work to do in St. Petersburg. Now hush a minute, there's a good girl, while I give Rowson directions. The sooner you are off the better."

"Good idea," Kolya approved.

John explained to Rowson how to find the *dacha* and offered him some money.

"Sir Andrew give me plenty for the present, my lord."

"You may need more. In fact, you had best take all I have on me. I shall try to be in touch shortly, but if things go wrong you will have to get them home as best you can. I know Sir Andrew has the utmost faith in you, and I do too. Here." He gave the man the purse full of his winnings, amounting to several hundred roubles. "Now off with you. There's not much traffic on this road at this season, but the fewer see you the better."

While Rowson hitched up the nag, John carred Esperanza to the wagon and set her down with a kiss.

"Take care of her, Annie."

The maid looked at him with trembling lips.

"And you'll look after Miss Beckie, my lord?"

"You may be sure I shall," he said grimly and stood back as the *tarantass* lurched into motion.

He and Kolya mounted and followed the clumsy vehicle till it reached the road safely. They watched for a moment as it rattled away, then turned their horses' heads in the opposite direction.

"The first thing you must do," said Kolya, "is to speak to your ambassador. Rebecca Ivanovna is a British citizen, after all, and has committed no crime."

"No doubt they will expect that and be waiting for me."

"Aha, I have a wonderful notion. I get you hussar's uniform, not officer, just trooper. You are large enough and no one looks at face of soldier in uniform."

"I have no moustache. All hussars wear a moustache, do they not?"

"I know many people in theatre, will find false moustache." Kolya appeared to be enjoying himself.

"Suppose it were to fall off? I shall be out on the streets, not strutting on a stage. I should prefer to dress as a peasant, like Rowson."

"My dear John, no one will believe you are serf! Your bearing is of nobleman of many generations. Is not exactly arrogance—no, is unconscious pride. Hussar, even common soldier, walks with swagger. Lord John Danville, son of Duke of Stafford, cannot walk like peasant."

John was about to protest this aspersion on his acting ability. If it would help Rebecca, he would become the most obsequious serf ever seen. But Kolya held up his hand.

"Wait. I have it. Is nothing in world more arrogant than palace footman, yet no one notices man inside livery. Powdered wig will hide dark hair. You shall become footman of Tsar Alexander!"

"That's a devilish good notion. Besides, it's more likely for a footman to be sent on an errand to Lord Cathcart. You can get me a livery?"

"Certainly."

"But all this will take time. I shall have to hide in the meantime."

"You shall stay with Dunyasha."

"Your ballet dancer? Yes, that would do. I could pretend to be her cousin, perhaps, and as a favour to her you have found me employment at the palace."

"I daresay I can trust a man in love not to touch my *chère amie*?" Kolya's grin changed to a frown. "Is pity you do not speak Russian, though Dunyasha knows some French."

"I'm delighted to hear you have not found out all my secrets. I understand Russian very well and can make shift to speak a little, though badly. However, as a high-and-mighty palace footman, I shall insist on using French. No one will wonder at it if it is bad French."

"What fine conspirators we are! Now let us turn our minds to reaching Dunyasha without having you arrested on way."

This was accomplished without incident. That very evening Kolya brought the livery, a magnificent outfit adorned with lace and ribbons in which John felt like a regular popinjay. Kolya and Dunyasha went into fits of laughter when he put on the curled and powdered wig, and the dancer continued to giggle quietly whenever she looked at him. Kolya soon sobered.

"Is little problem," he said. "Tsar's footman brings message to ambassador's residence, but he is not likely to see ambassador in person."

"I have thought of that. Lord Cathcart must be told to expect me. It would look odd if you asked for an interview with him but you know Sebastian Crane and can visit him without arousing too much comment. He does not know what I was up to, but he's a good-hearted fellow and I daresay he would help. Or does everyone know by now that they are after me?"

"No, has been kept quiet. When ambassador hears news, will claim diplomatic immunity for you. If you are already in cell, will be more difficult. I shall see Mr. Crane tonight, then. I know his usual haunts."

"I need some money, Kolya. I gave Rowson all I had."

"My purse is yours, my friend."

To his own surprise, John flung his arms around the prince and kissed him on both cheeks.

"Hell and damnation, I've been here too long," he muttered, flushing to the roots of his wig. "You're a good friend, Kolya, but I shan't need your money if you can redeem some of these vowels for me." He handed over the package of papers. "Don't let Count Kirsanin have his villa back, though, until we are ready to move Rowson out."

Laughing, Kolya took the package. "They will think I have won them from you! I see you tomorrow. Take care of milord, Dunyashenka, *dusha moya*." He kissed the girl and departed.

John spent an uneasy night planning and replanning what he would say to Lord Cathcart, and trying not to think of the stories he had heard of the Peter-Paul fortress. He did his best to remember Rebecca as she had been at her first ball, but the memory that recurred was her white face when he had rescued her from the river.

He paced up and down his narrow chamber. If the bastards had hurt her, he would create an international incident as soon as he reached home. He would persuade his grace to speak to Prinny, Prinny would raise the matter with the tsar, and heads would roll. The Russians would learn that an Englishwoman was not to be mistreated with impunity. Vengeful thoughts raced through his mind and he did not sleep till dawn.

He met the ambassador the next afternoon. Lord Cathcart was not encouraging.

"Of course I shall do what I can, Danville, but the courses of action open to me are very limited. In fact, before I can do anything else I shall have to obtain confirmation of Miss Nuthall's arrest from the Foreign Ministry, and then lodge a formal protest with them. You know how enamoured of paperwork they are in this country. It will go from ministry to ministry and I cannot hold out hope for a speedy resolution."

"But in the meantime Rebecca is in a dungeon that has driven strong men to madness! There must be something we can do!"

"Crane tells me Prince Nikolai Volkov is acting for you?"

"Yes, but his father cannot be approached in this."

"A pity. Yet Prince Nikolai is a popular man. He has contacts everywhere, and an excessive reliance on seals and signatures can work both ways. Nor are Russian officials incorruptible. I can let you have some money, though naturally I cannot afford any public connexion with anything you may choose to do."

"Thank you, Lord Cathcart, I am well beforehand with the world. And you have given me food for thought."

"If Crane can be of any assistance to you without compromising the embassy, you may tell him he has my permission." The ambassador hesitated, then went on, "You know, you are accredited to the embassy and I can get *you* out of the country without great difficulty. Ah, no, I see that it is out of the question." He stood up and shook John's hand. "She's a nice child, Danville. I wish you well."

That was poor consolation, John thought bitterly as he straightened his wig in the hall mirror before venturing back into the streets. Here he was dressed as a clown while Rebecca . . . but that did not bear thinking about.

Instead, he concentrated on Lord Cathcart's cautious suggestions. If Kolya could obtain papers authorizing Rebecca's release, then they must spirit her out of the country before the fraud was discovered. Esperanza and Annie and Rowson would have to go with them. Crane might be useful as liaison with Rowson in Peterhof, which was unlikely to get him into trouble.

It would be best to leave by ship, for the nearest border was hundreds of miles away. Yet shipping was already sparse at this season, the traders afraid of being trapped in the Baltic ice. The chance of finding one who was willing to aid the escape of the fugitives seemed meagre. John wondered if it would be possible to hide in his dacha all winter.

Kolya was waiting to hear how the interview with Lord Cathcart had gone. He shook his head.

"As I expected, he can do little. But do not despair, his idea is excellent. Only, I think, will not be order for release, which is more likely to be questioned. We will have papers saying Rebecca Ivanovna is to be transferred to different prison, so will be no questions when she does not return. Perhaps we shall hint also that tsar is interested in bold Englishwoman who is spy. That will explain my presence. You shall be soldier of my Preobrazhenski regiment. We are Foot Guards, so you will not need moustache. You will drive *brichka* to carry away prisoner. Ah, is grand plan. I see it all."

"Do you think it will be safe to spend the winter at the *dacha*?"

"No, absolutely no. Count Kirsanin urgently wants to buy back *dacha*. His mother is very angry. Is no problem. If we bring Rebecca Ivanovna safe from fortress, I have ship waiting."

"How can you do that?"

"Is Finnish ship now loading cargo at quay just down Neva from fortress, will take you to Helsinki. Is best I can do. Finland is part of Russian empire, but Finns hate Russian government. They will help you. Besides, Captain Jotuni owes me favour."

"A Finnish sea-captain owes you a favour!"

"I am obliging fellow, John. Are many, many people owe me favours like Captain Jotuni, who is smuggler of sables. Is lucky for us, *nyet*?"

"I am not about to argue with that. I just hope the right people in the right ministries are among those indebted to you."

"Those who are not," said Kolya with a gesture that seemed to include half the officialdom of the Russian Empire, "are eager to do favour for son of my father, or at worst can be bought. Is fortunate you are rich man. I go now, is much to be done. You must stay hidden here. Best not to risk going out without need."

"I wish there was something I could do!"

Nothing in John's life had ever been so difficult as the period of waiting that ensued. He was alone much of the time, since Dunyasha was rehearsing for a new ballet and Kolya could only spare the time for brief reports of his progress. He found it hard to eat, until Dunyasha scolded him, telling him he must be strong to rescue his sweetheart. She had thrown herself heart and soul into the plot. International politics meant nothing to her, but she knew a romantic drama of thwarted love when she saw one.

Kolya's motives seemed to be a combination of deep, sincere friendship and love of excitement. He approached the task of collecting the necessary documents with a gusto that John had to admire. He brushed aside with a laugh a question as to what the consequences would be when his part in the rescue became known, as it inevitably must.

"Is not important. One must take risk for fair lady in distress, *nyet*?"

On the third day, Kolya reported that he had all the necessary documents save one. That one would have to be forged but he had found a man to do it, at a price. For a thousand roubles, it could be done in two days. For two thousand, by tomorrow afternoon.

John handed over two thousand roubles, enough to

purchase twenty serfs. If providing funds was the only thing he could do to hasten Rebecca's release, by an hour or by a minute, he would gladly give up every penny he owned in the world.

"Then tomorrow is the day?" he asked eagerly.

"Tomorrow evening," Kolya confirmed. "Tonight, Mr. Crane fetches servants and child and takes them to ship. I consent to Count Kirsanin's pleas and sell the *dacha* for gold. Tomorrow you are ready to go at six, dressed up in pretty green and red uniform."

"Six? It's dark long before that these days!"

"We wait till Captain of Guard has drunk some vodka to console self for night duty. I have arranged for suitable officer to be at post this week."

"You are amazing, Kolya. If you ever visit England again . . . "

"I come to stay with Lord and Lady John Danville. Is understood. Now let us look again at map of fortress."

Once more they went over the details of their plan. John had rehearsed the stride, the salute, the correct stance for "attention" and "at ease," until he felt sure he could pass as a trooper in his sleep. Fortunately it was most unlikely that a common soldier would be called upon to speak in the presence of an officer. Dunyasha promised to polish his buttons and boots till they shone.

They all avoided mentioning the possibility that something could go wrong.

The next evening John was ready well before Kolya sauntered in, promptly at six.

"Let's go!"

"Patience, my friend." Kolya went to Dunyasha's cupboard, took out a bottle of cognac and filled two glasses. "Spot of—Dutch courage, you say?—will not hurt. Drink."

John was dubious. "I don't need it. Besides, I've not touched a drop of spirits since your infamous celebration."

"Drink. I must tell you something you will not like to hear."

"Something has gone wrong!" He shivered, cold with dread.

"No, no, nothing is wrong. Is warning that I did not want to give before."

Puzzled, John took the glass and gulped the brandy. It left him warmed but clear-headed.

"Tell me."

"Dungeons are most unpleasant. Is possible Rebecca Ivanovna will not be able to walk."

John fought down the fury that threatened to overcome his commonsense. To play his part, he needed to be calm. "It will be my delight to carry her," he said softly.

"Ah, but you must not carry in arms like lover. Over shoulder is best, I think. Discomfort is small price to pay for freedom."

He nodded his understanding. "Let's go."

With Kolya riding ahead, John drove the *brichka* through the busy, lamp-lit streets of St. Petersburg and crossed the Neva by the Dvortsovy Bridge. He did not spare a glance for the splendid palaces he would never see again, the golden domes and spires gleaming in the moonlight, the myriad stars reflected in the river's glacial waters. At last they halted before the massive stone gateway of the Peter-Paul fortress.

Kolya gave the password and they trotted beneath the arch.

$==16==$

REBECCA BLINKED AT the lantern light, raising her head from the straw pallet on the stone floor. In the week she had spent here, she had grown used to seeing no one from dusk till dawn. Any change was threatening.

It was the friendly guard, the one who had slipped her an extra bit of bread with the thin cabbage soup of her daily meal. He had congratulated her solemnly two days ago when they took off her shackles and moved her to this cell above ground. At least it was dry, and though she could not see out of the high window there was daylight for a few hours each day.

There was a rumour, he had whispered to her, that the English ambassador was enquiring after her.

That had given her a measure of hope. She had ventured to ask whether he had heard of an English milord who had been arrested. He had not. If John was free, he would never abandon her. She clung to that certainty.

"Come, *barynya*," said the guard, his friendly snub-nosed face worried. "They are taking you away."

"Who? Where to?" She struggled to her knees and he lent his hand to help her to her feet.

He glanced behind him and muttered in her ear, "They say Aleksandr Pavlovich himself wishes to see you."

"The Tsar? But why?"

"Who knows?" He shrugged. Incomprehensible whims were to be expected of a being so god-like. "At least, it is one of his officers who has come for you. We must hurry."

Stumbling along the passage behind him, Rebecca tried to dismiss the fact that Prince Nikolai was one of the tsar's officers. He was only one of many. If she let herself believe that it was he, the disappointment of finding someone else awaiting her would be unbearable.

She knew from the moment she stepped into the office of the Captain of the Guard that Kolya had come for her. He was lounging in a chair with his back to her, a glass of vodka in his hand. With the other hand he was gesturing as he described to the red-faced, fuddled-looking captain the trials of being aide-de-camp to the tsar.

"Glorified errand-boy, that is what I am. Imagine sending a colonel-prince to fetch an insignificant prisoner!" He tossed off the vodka.

The captain hiccuped and agreed that it was shocking. He picked up a document from his desk and gazed at it with eyes that seemed to have trouble focussing.

"Everything is in order, Nikolai Mikhailovich. One more glass before you go?"

Her presence unacknowledged, Rebecca watched as the prince accepted another drink. She became aware that a man in the same uniform as Kolya was standing against the wall behind her. A sudden fear gripped her. If he had brought a soldier with him, would it not be impossible for him to let her go?

She glanced back—and nearly fainted on the spot. It was John! He was gazing rigidly at the wall on the other side of the room, strictly at attention except for his hands, which were clenched into fists.

Rebecca forced herself not to react. For her sake he had come here, under the very noses of the men who were seeking him, and she must not fail him.

Quickly she turned away, just in time to see Kolya rise and shake the captain's hand.

"Remember," he said, "not a word about a certain person's interest in this prisoner. She is merely being transferred elsewhere for interrogation."

The captain nodded. "Of course. Your signature, if you please, Prince." He pushed a document across the desk.

Kolya scrawled something across the bottom of the paper. The captain regarded it with a puzzled frown as John, in response to an order from the prince, stepped forward and grasped Rebecca's wrist.

She could not forebear an exclamation of pain. Though his grip was gentle, her wrists were still raw from the iron shackles. She heard his breathing stop momentarily, and his fingers loosened still more, but he dared not risk letting go, nor did he glance at her. They followed Kolya out of the room.

The moment the door closed behind them, John shifted his hold to her upper arm. She dragged behind, forcing him to pull her along, partly because she felt weak and dizzy, partly to make it seem that she was reluctant to go. There were sentries everywhere.

They reached the courtyard. Rebecca took a deep breath of the cold, crisp air. The gold spire of the Peter-Paul cathedral shone in the moonlight and a million stars twinkled above, but the gatehouse was still ahead. John picked her up, and for a few moments his strong arms held her close and protected before he dumped her unceremoniously in the waiting carriage. He swung up onto the box.

With Kolya riding ahead, waving passes at the guards, the *brichka* rumbled under the arch and she was free.

She stayed huddled on the floor, pulling the bearskin rug she found there about her. The woollen dress she had been wearing when she was arrested had proved sadly inadequate to keep her warm in the damp dungeon. She thought she had grown used to being always cold, but the biting wind off the Neva cut through her.

The *brichka* was moving slowly. Though Rebecca wanted to call out to John, to urge him to hurry, she knew he must have his reasons for sitting so straight and soldierly on the box without a word to her, or even turning his head. She thought she heard Kolya speaking, barely audible above the clop of hooves. The reply came with an English intonation—but it was not John's voice. She thought it sounded familiar.

At that moment the carriage stopped. Someone joined John on the box and he instantly sprang down into the street. Bending low, so that his silhouette would not be seen above the vehicle, John opened the door beside Rebecca.

"Come, quickly," he whispered, and gathered her once more into his arms. The *brichka* started off again after barely a pause.

With a little sigh of content, she rested her head against his shoulder as he stepped back into the shadows.

"I knew you would come."

His only answer as he strode through the night was to bend his head momentarily so that his cheek pressed warm against her hair. She felt a rush of love for him, for his gallantry, his strength, his uncertainties, even for his peccadilloes. She put her arms around his neck and clung to him. She had no idea where he was taking her, what the future held, but for now it was enough to feel his heart beat close to hers.

It did not last for long. They came to some steps leading down the granite embankment and he set her on her feet, then leaned over the railing.

"Rowson?" His voice was low, as was the answering, "Right, m'lord."

His arm around her waist, John helped Rebecca negotiate the slippery stone steps. At the bottom a small skiff awaited them, with a shadowy figure untying its painter from an iron ring set in the wall.

" 'Tis good to see you, Miss Beckie," the servant whispered as John lifted her in and followed her, setting the little boat rocking on the river.

He took a pair of oars. Rowson pushed off with the boathook and set the second pair in the rowlocks. Aided by tide and current the skiff slid swiftly through the smooth water, the only sound a slight gurgle as the oars dipped and lifted. Seated in the stern, wrapped in a cloak she found there, Rebecca watched John's face in the moonlight. He had taken off the black uniform tricorne and the wind ruffled his dark hair. His grin said he was enjoying himself.

She smiled in response, and he winked at her.

A ship loomed ahead. The boat glided alongside, slowing, and Rowson caught hold of a dangling rope ladder. Rebecca knew with absolute certainty that she could not climb it.

John must have read her expression of dismay for he leaned forward and squeezed her hand reassuringly. He held a muttered conversation with Rowson, then took his place steadying their craft while the manservant swarmed up the ladder. A few anxious minutes later, a canvas sling was lowered. John helped her to sit in it, made sure she was gripping the rope securely, and briefly explained how to fend off the ship's side with her feet.

"I shall climb alongside to steady you," he promised.

Abandoned, the rowboat slipped silently away downstream as some invisible agency on the deck above hauled Rebecca upward. It was not the most dignified method of going aboard, but as she swung over the rail and scrambled free of the contraption with the aid of willing hands, she did not care a whit.

Orders were barked in some unrecognizable language. There were sounds of rattling chains and creaking windlasses, the slap of bare feet on wood.

"This way, Miss Beckie, m'lord." Rowson's voice was no longer hushed.

John at her side, his arm once more supporting her, Rebecca followed Rowson below deck. There was a narrow passage with a door on either side. The servant stopped and turned to face them. A slight flush mantled his weather-beaten cheeks.

"This here's my and Annie's cabin." He gestured at one of the doors. "We got Miss Esperanza in wi' us, and Gayo too. T'other's for your lordship and Miss Beckie."

"What the devil?" John exploded, dropping his arm from Rebecca's waist as if it burned him. "There must be another cabin, or Annie and the child can share with Beckie."

" 'Tis right sorry I am, m'lord, but it seems as Prince Nikolai had to up and tell the captain as you're married. These Finns be Lutherans, he said, and right straitlaced. The captain wouldn't take you aboard if he knowed you wasn't man and wife. Start switching things about and there's no knowing what he'll be thinking."

"Damned—dashed—if I care what the man thinks."

"Trouble is, he'll likely tell his friends in Helsinki, and then we s'll be in the briars right and proper."

"He's right, John." Rebecca put her hand on his arm. He looked down at her, his dark eyes softening. She met his gaze steadily. "I trust you. You know that I trust you."

For a startled moment she thought he was going to kiss her. Then he seemed to realize that this was the wrong time and the wrong place, or perhaps he saw her slight withdrawal. In any case, he shrugged and turned back to Rowson.

"I suppose it can't be helped. Fetch Annie, if you please, to help Miss Nuthall retire. She is exhausted. And I trust a bed can be made up for me on the floor?"

Rowson opened the door of his cabin, stuck his head in and said something. Annie came out immediately.

"Hush, now, the child's asleep. Oh, Miss Beckie, I'm that glad to see you. And your lordship too, of course. Just come with me, Miss Beckie, and we'll soon have you tucked up cosy." She led the way into the other cabin.

Rebecca followed, feeling tears of weakness rising in her eyes. The black maid's motherly kindness threatened to overset her fragile composure.

Behind her she heard Rowson speaking soothingly. "There's no reason to fear Miss Beckie'll be compromised, m'lord. Nor Annie nor I'll speak a word, and none o' these here Finns is like to go to London." The door clicked shut on John's reply.

"And if they did there's only one of them speaks a word of English," Annie told Rebecca, "and not much more nor a word, neither. Here, now, let's get that dress off. It'd best be tossed overboard, I daresay."

"I never want to see it again, but it is all I have." She summoned up a wavering smile.

"Bless you, miss, we've almost everything aboard." Annie undid buttons as she spoke. "Lord Cathcart sent that nice Mr. Crane to fetch our bits and pieces from the house, and his lordship's too. Even the blessed parrot, believe it if you will. A right helpful gentleman, Mr. Crane. He came to Peterhof with a carriage and brought us all here, and I heard talk of him driving off with a *brichka* tonight."

"I thought I recognized that voice, when we left the *brichka*." Rebecca shivered as Annie divested her of the dress, wincing as the sleeves pulled over her wrists.

"Heavens above, look at your poor arms!"

"My legs too." She raised the hem of her petticoat to display bloodstained stockings worn in holes around the ankles.

"I knew I'd need Miss Teresa's medicines. That was the one thing Mr. Crane left behind. I'll fetch a spot of warm water to bathe them, miss, and some linen for bandages. Just you pop into this nightgown here, I've had it wrapped around a hot brick, and I'll be back in two shakes of a lamb's tail."

"Bring something to eat, Annie. Anything but cabbage soup."

Half an hour later Annie tucked the bedclothes firmly around Rebecca and bade her good-night. As she straightened she put her hand to her back and sighed. She was nearly eight months pregnant and ought not be setting out on a long voyage, but there was no choice. Rebecca resolved to be as little trouble as possible—after all she had managed without a maid at Lady Parr's. At least she could take charge of Esperanza during the day.

The dim lantern Annie had hung by the door swung with

154

a hypnotic rhythm as the ship cut through the waters of the Gulf of Finland. The swaying motion was familiar, soothing. Rebecca wanted to stay awake till John came, but she was tired, so tired, sinking into blessed blackness . . .

. . . And the pale dawn light crept in at the window of her cell and with it the clank of chains, the snap of the knout, the screams of men being flogged, yet it was she who screamed as her uncle's fist slammed towards her face . . .

"Beckie! Beckie, hush, my darling. You're safe, love, I won't let anyone touch you." John held her tenderly, rocked her against his chest, smoothing her hair with gentle fingers. "Hush now, hush, don't cry, my dearest."

At last her racking sobs calmed. She realized that she was in her thin muslin nightgown, and John wore only a nightshirt. She ought to move, to cover herself. The warm strength of his body against hers comforted her, and yet she felt a strange agitation. His eyes were black, unfathomable pools in the dim light. Drowning in them, she drifted into sleep, cherished in his arms.

In the morning, he had already risen and left the cabin before she woke. She knew she had been dreaming, but what was dream and what was reality she could not tell.

There was a tap on the door as she lay there musing, and she called, "Come in!"

A little blonde head peered round the door and then Esperanza sped across the narrow cabin to fling her arms around Rebecca's neck.

"I did miss you, Aunt Beckie!"

"I missed you too, Chiquita. Let me get up, and while I dress you must tell me what you have been doing."

"I falled in the stream in Uncle John's new garden. Annie was cross." Sitting on the edge of the bed, she chattered merrily, her chubby legs in frilled trowsers swinging beneath her dark red woollen dress.

To Rebecca, she brought a note of normalcy, an everyday conventionality, into a world that had recently been topsy-turvy. With the little girl explaining why she had used her shoe to try to catch a fish, it was impossible to think about chains and dungeons, impossible to brood on whether John's sweet words had been real or only part of a dream.

And when she went to join him at breakfast in the small saloon, it was impossible to be embarrassed with Chiquita tugging on her hand and announcing her:

"Uncle John, look! Aunt Beckie's wearing a red shawl to match my dress. Isn't she pretty?"

After an appeal like that, his answer was not to be taken seriously, though the look in his eyes was more difficult to dismiss.

"Indeed she is, Chiquita. What a lucky man I am to be escorting the two most beautiful ladies in the world."

"Not counting Mama."

"Not counting Mama, of course," he said obligingly, laughing. "Cousin Rebecca, you will be glad to hear that Rowson has it from the first mate, who speaks a little English, that we have a brisk following wind and are making excellent time. The captain expects to reach Helsinki tonight and we shall be put ashore at once."

Rebecca blushed. Naturally it would be a relief not to have to share the cabin with John for another night—so why was her predominant emotion disappointment?

She was not sure whether she hoped or dreaded that he would seek her out for private conversation. If anything, he seemed to make an effort to avoid it. This was not difficult, as she spent most of the day with Esperanza, while Annie sewed the greater part of John's gold into a money-belt. It was too cold on deck for more than brief venture for fresh air, and their accommodations below were strictly limited.

When Esperanza and Annie both retired for an afternoon nap and Rowson had gone to take the dirty nuncheon dishes to the galley, Rebecca did try to thank John for rescuing her.

"I don't want your gratitude," he said almost savagely, getting up from the table and wandering restlessly about the saloon. "Besides, Kolya had a great deal more to do with it than I did."

156

"I am sorry I cannot thank Prince Nikolai. I dare not even write when we reach home, since they sometimes open letters from abroad, do they not? It was chivalrous in him to run such risks for my sake."

"I wish to God I could have done what he did! I was useless, my hands were tied. He could have managed the whole business without me."

"But would he? I think that if you had not been there, he might not even have noticed my absence. Without you nothing would have been done. And you hazarded your life to take me from that place." She shuddered at the memory.

He was behind her in an instant, his hands on her shoulders. "Don't think about it. It is past. Forget it." He straightened as Rowson came in. "I'm going up on deck for a few minutes. If you will finish that picture, I shall cut it up to make a puzzle for Chiquita when I come back."

Mr. Crane had missed the medicine chest, but he had collected Esperanza's coloured chalks. Rebecca added green fronds to the palm-tree in the picture she had attempted of Turkey, where Teresa and Andrew were now wandering. Absentmindedly she drew in a scarlet-breasted robin. Did they have robins in Turkey? No matter, Esperanza would not care.

She could not understand why John seemed to resent her gratitude. His irritation at her wanting to thank Kolya was easier to explain: his old feelings of incompetence had taken on a new life when he had had to look on while the prince played the major part in her rescue. Perhaps she should point out to him that it was not a case of ability or lack thereof. Kolya had simply been in the right position to help.

When he came down again he was lively and amusing, scoffing at her robin, but she knew that he had withdrawn from her. It was to late to try to reassure him. The brief moment of intimacy was over.

= 17 =

THE NORTHERN NIGHTS were long at this time of year, but even so it was nearing dawn when the little group was set ashore with their baggage on the Helsinki quay. The sky was paling in the east, and the captain was anxious to conceal their arrival before awkward questions were asked.

Esperanza, woken from a sound sleep, was crying, her face buried in the folds of Rebecca's cloak. She refused to let John pick her up. Rebecca, by no means recovered from her ordeal, was exhausted and Annie looked to be in not much better case. From Gayo's cage, well wrapped against the cold, came a reproachful mutter.

"What a pity, what a pity," Rebecca thought she heard him say.

They were all relieved to see the tall, blonde first mate approaching along the quay, talking earnestly to another man, shorter but even fairer of hair under his fur cap.

"Risto Hakiinen," the officer introduced his companion. "You go with. He take care. Good luck!" He bowed to Rebecca, shook hands with John, and walked off towards the ship.

Risto Hakiinen seemed to be somewhat nonplussed by the unexpected appearance of five fugitives. Fortunately he spoke good Russian and his grasp of English was somewhat greater than the first mate's. He hurried them from their exposed position on the waterfront into a weathered wooden hut nearby, that appeared to be a watchman's shelter.

The watchman was within, huddled over a small iron

stove, and a samovar was bubbling on an upended barrel. Hakiinen said something to the grizzled old man, who turned and favoured his visitors with a gap-toothed grin.

"Russki," he mumbled, and spat on the floor, then made a gesture of invitation.

"He asks you sit," their guide explained. "I must go, make plans. You wait here safe."

"Our luggage," protested John. "Bags. Outside." They had brought only what little they could carry, of which Gayo's muffled cage formed a large part.

Hakiinen nodded. "Bring safe. Not worry." He slipped out of the shed.

They sat gingerly on a variety of broken crates. The watchman had filled several chipped, stained earthenware mugs with hot tea, and now he offered them to his guests. Rebecca hoped that the boiling water made it safe to accept, for she felt more in need of a dish of tea than of anything else in the world. She would not let Esperanza take the half-nibbled lump of sugar the old man presented her with. The little girl pouted and ran to John, who took her on his lap and kept her amused with a finger-counting game.

Conversation languished. It seemed a very long time before Hakiinen returned, but when they followed him out the sun had not yet risen. A closed carriage was waiting, and Rebecca was glad to see all their baggage tied on behind. Rowson helped her, and then Annie, into the vehicle, then stood waiting. John, with Esperanza in his arms, was talking to Hakiinen.

Rebecca could not make out their low-voiced conversation, but John was frowning. At last he joined them, Rowson jumped in behind him, the Finn climbed up beside the coachman, and the carriage started off.

She laid her hand on his sleeve. "What is it, John? Has he not been able to find anywhere for us to go?"

"On the contrary. It seems Helsinki is full of people who hate their Russian overlords and are willing to take us in. However, he insists that we must each go to a different house. It will be too conspicuous, he claims, to have all of us together. I cannot like it."

"Do you mistrust him?"

"No," he admitted reluctantly. "I believe him sincere. Only I hate to be separated from . . . to split up our group."

"Surely he will not make Chiquita go alone with strangers!"

"No, no! Nothing so drastic."

"Then she shall go with me and we shall do very well, shall we not, Chiquita?"

Apparently she was forgiven for the sugarlump incident, for the child scrambled off John's lap onto hers and gave her a smacking kiss.

"I don't like to leave Annie, and that's a fact, m'lord." Rowson too was dismayed. "S'posing her time were to come?"

Annie patted his hand. "I daresay Finns have babies too. Don't worry 'bout me. Tell you what, love, you can take the parrot for company."

Both Rebecca and John managed to laugh at that. It was a half-hearted sound, but the maid's indomitable spirit deserved a response, and Esperanza looked less frightened.

"How long is it likely to be for?" Rebecca asked John. While Finns undoubtedly reproduced regularly, it would be dreadful for Annie to have to go through her first confinement among strangers, who might not speak any language she knew and had probably never seen an African before.

He shook his head forebodingly. "There are very few ships in the harbour, and none of them English. If something does not come in during the next week or so, we may have to wait all winter."

Rebecca's heart sank. "If it came to that, surely we could insist on being together? Or perhaps it would be best to sail to Germany, or Sweden. Some country where we should not have to hide from the Russians."

John's laugh took her by surprise. He reached out and touched her cheek with a gloved finger. "To think that I was afraid you might fall into hysterics! It may be more difficult to persuade a foreign captain to risk taking us on board, but doubtless it can be done." He patted his middle, where the money-belt thickened his usually trim girth. "It is certainly worth a try. And if not, I shall not let them keep us apart."

The promise in his eyes seemed to mean more than his words, and Rebecca was quite glad of the distraction when the carriage jolted to a halt.

A moment later, Hakiinen opened the door.

"You stay here, milady. Hurry."

Before Rebecca quite realized what was happening, she and Esperanza were standing hand in hand at the door of a neat-looking wooden house, and the carriage was rumbling away down the street. A buxom, grey-haired woman urged them in broken Russian to come in quickly.

"I'm hungry," Esperanza announced in the same language, and marched in. With a final glance after the carriage, Rebecca followed.

Esperanza was soon on the best of terms with their hostess. She did not mind at all when Rebecca, wilting with weariness, retired to bed after breakfast. For the next three days, Rebecca had little to do besides sleep and eat, and she quickly recovered her strength. She managed to put behind her the horrors of her imprisonment, except briefly when the woman insisted on showing her the reason for her willingness to help. One evening she pulled down the shirt of her taciturn son, who lived with her, showing a back ridged and seamed by the scars of a Russian flogging.

Thankful that Esperanza had already gone to bed, Rebecca said faintly, "I understand."

Despite that incident, there was no recurrence of her nightmares. On the contrary, she dreamed of John, and became less and less certain whether he had ever really rocked her in his arms and whispered loving words in her ear.

If he had, she decided regretfully, it had only been to comfort her. After all, he was a duke's son, and she was a mere governess though she had stepped out of her rôle for a while. She must learn to love him from afar, for that she did love him she could no longer deny. She knew he was attracted to her, fond of her, but it was plain that he was aware of the gulf between them. Nothing else could account for his alternating tenderness and withdrawal.

Confined to the house, with nothing to read and nothing to do but odds and ends of mending, she thought long and hard on the subject but always came to the same conclusion. Though John might despise his father's conservatism, his family's consciousness of superiority to the common run of mortals was born and bred in the bone.

Lord John Danville would never stoop to take a wife from the squirarchy. Rebecca reminded herself firmly of her resolve never to take a husband to rule over her.

It was a pity that her heart leaped at the sight of his face when he appeared at the door on the evening of the fourth day, but she would get over it in time.

His exuberant expression was soon explained. "Beckie, they have found us a ship, an English trader. She came in two days ago. They will finish loading her with wood and furs this evening, and she sails with the morning tide. The captain will take us, for a goodly sum," he admitted with a grin, "if we go aboard tonight. He will not wait, though, for fear of being caught in the ice. It happened to him once, I collect. Are you ready to go?"

"I have kept our things packed up, but Chiquita has just fallen asleep, poor child. Give me a few minutes to dress her."

"Hakiinen has gone to fetch Annie and Rowson. We have half an hour or so. I'll come and carry Chiquita down."

Slumped against John's shoulder, Esperanza slept all the way to the harbour. She roused only enough to mutter a drowsy protest when she was tucked up again in the cabin she was to share with Rebecca. The *Rochester Rose*, out of London, had ample accommodations for all and Captain Hardy was only too glad to find travellers willing to pay for their passage at this inhospitable season.

Risto Hakiinen, on the other hand, like Rebecca's hostess indignantly refused John's gold and brushed aside their fervent thanks.

"Is bad for Russia," he said simply, "is good for Finland."

He shook hands with all of them and disappeared into the night. Feeling almost as safe as if they were already on English soil, the fugitives retired to their rest.

In the morning, Rebecca wanted to go on deck. "I have seen nothing of Helsinki," she said, "and there will never be another chance."

"I see no harm," John agreed. "Captain Hardy has all his clearances and even if we are seen there is no reason anyone should have the slightest idea who we are. By the sound of it, they are already raising the anchor."

Esperanza, a seasoned traveller, was not at all interested in seeing the sights. John and Rebecca hurried up to the open air.

Screeching seagulls battled the brisk, bitter wind, swooping after a bucket of scraps thrown overboard. The ship was inching away from the quay. Rebecca hugged her cloak about her and gazed out over the town. There seemed to be a lot of building going on, though most of the houses were still of wood. She turned to look at the harbour mouth.

Across it spread a handful of islands. They bristled with fortifications, cannon trained on the narrow waterways. Rebecca was about to comment when Captain Hardy approached them.

"A fine wind, ma'am, my lord. A good nor'easter is just what we need to get us started. Hey there, what's toward?" He stared past them at the quay.

Rebecca and John swung round. A troop of horsemen in scarlet uniforms was galloping along the quay. They pulled up just short of the edge, one or two horses rearing, and their leader hailed the ship.

"*Postoy!*"

The captain shrugged and leaned over the rail to call, "I don't speak Russian. No speak Russki."

Rebecca clutched John's arm. "They must be after us!"

"Undoubtedly." John's face was grim.

"Don't worry, ma'am," Captain Hardy assured her. "I'm not about to turn back for a bunch of rascally Russkis. *Nicht verstehe!*" he answered in German another demand to stop.

"But what about the guns on the islands?" Rebecca asked him.

"Trouble with putting your defenses on a bunch of islands is it don't make communicating too easy. It may work well when the enemy comes from the sea, but it'll take those fellows longer to get word to them than it'll take us to sail past. Raise sail!" he bellowed at his crew.

As they hastened to obey, the officer on the quay also shouted a command. The troopers swung rifles from their shoulders.

"Get down!" ordered John sharply, forcing Rebecca full length on the deck. He sprawled beside her, half on top of her, sheltering her with his body as a ragged volley of shots rang out.

Bullets whined overhead. One nicked the wood six inches beyond Rebecca's outstretched hand, between her and the prostrate captain.

She heard John grunt, felt him jerk.

"Are you all right?" She tried to sit up, desperate to see if he was hurt.

"Keep down. They have to reload but we may still be in range. Don't move, Beckie."

"Are you all right?" she repeated urgently.

"The sons of bitches winged me. Nothing serious hit. Ouch! Dammit, keep still, woman. They are bound to fire again."

Rebecca lay still, tears streaking silently down her face. He was hurt, and yet he thought only of protecting her.

"Hell and damnation," swore the captain. "We've made just enough sail to keep under way. I daren't raise more till we clear the channel." He began to crawl towards the helmsman, who stood at the wheel with a pipe between his teeth, nonchalantly steering the *Rochester Rose* towards the island fortresses.

The crack of the rifles sounded again, more distant this time. As far as Rebecca could tell, the bullets did not reach the ship. John rolled off her and lay on his back, groaning and clutching his arm.

She knelt beside him. There was a dark patch just below the shoulder on the left sleeve of his greatcoat. It was spreading ominously and he was very pale.

The most important thing was to stop the bleeding. She undid the top buttons of his coat, then ripped the flounce from her petticoat and thrust it down into the sleeve. His neck-cloth was the ideal bandage. He lifted his head, smiling faintly as she pulled it off and bound it as tight as she could about his arm.

"Better get below," he muttered, struggling to raise himself with his good arm.

She helped him sit up, but he was far too big for her to lift to his feet. She glanced round for help. Rowson was hurrying towards them.

"Head going round," said John thickly. "Going to cast up my accounts." He leaned forward and was thoroughly sick.

His forehead was alarmingly clammy under Rebecca's supporting hand, and he sagged heavily against her.

Rowson joined them. "Best go below, Miss Beckie. The captain's sending the carpenter with a stretcher. We'll bring his lordship down to you right and tight."

"Is there a surgeon on board?"

"I didn't think to ask, miss, but I doubt it, this not being a man-o'-war."

He helped her lay John down on the deck. She hated to leave him, lying so still with is eyes closed and his face a ghastly white, but there were preparations to be made to receive him. She smoothed his dark hair, lank with cold sweat, back from his forehead and hurried below.

Hot water, linen for bandages, a well-warmed bed— what else could she do for him? A gunshot wound was far beyond her experience. Teresa's medicine chest was lost, but surely the captain must have a few basic remedies. She prayed the bullet was not still in John's arm.

For the next half hour she was too busy to worry. Rowson and his assistant laid John on the sheet-covered table in the saloon and cut away his sleeve. The bullet had gone straight through the fleshy part of his arm, leaving a ragged exit hole. Though the bleeding was already slowing, he had lost a lot of blood. He seemed scarcely conscious.

Annie kept the frightened Esperanza in her cabin while Rebecca and Rowson washed John's arm. The ship's carpenter claimed to have been apprenticed to an apothecary before going to sea, and on his advice Rebecca bathed the wound in vodka, there being no brandy aboard. She refused, however, to let him bleed John. Popular remedy for all ills it might be, but enough blood had been spilt.

As she put the finishing touches to the bandage, John opened his eyes.

"Cheer up, Beckie, I shan't stick my spoon in the wall." His grin was crooked and when he reached out to her with his good arm he let it drop half way through the gesture. "Dash it, I'm weak as a newborn kitten though."

She laid her hand on his forehead in what appeared, she hoped, to be a professional manner. "Yes, I daresay you will live to be a hundred," she said with attempted lightness. "At least you neither look nor feel like an iceberg now."

"I'd best get his lordship into bed now, Miss Beckie," Rowson said firmly. With the carpenter's aid he carried John into his cabin, and shut the door in Rebecca's face.

Resisting the longing to sink into the nearest chair, she began to clear up. The mess in the small saloon was indescribable and Esperanza could not be kept confined in the even smaller cabin much longer. Annie tired easily these days. She was always willing but it would not be fair to expect her to take sole charge of the active child, nor to nurse John. There was no time for Rebecca to give way to the megrims.

The carpenter came out of John's cabin and carried off the red-stained debris. Rowson followed a few minutes later.

"He's asleep, miss, and comfortable enough for now. I'll make so bold as to tell you you was splendid. Even our Miss Teresa couldn't have managed it better."

"Thank you, Rowson." No praise could have been more welcome to her ears. She wished John was there to hear it.

"And so I told his lordship," Rowson continued.

There was a spring in her step as she went to release and reassure Esperanza and Annie.

She was sitting by John's bed when he awoke. He was as angry as his weakness allowed.

"We are not on a Finnish ship now!" he pointed out. "These people are all going to London, they speak English, and there is bound to be talk. You are not to come into my cabin alone, understand?"

"Yes, my lord." She smiled at him, glad that he was alive to upbraid her, and glad of his care for her reputation.

As the days passed John gradually regained his strength. Once he felt well enough to get up it was impossible to keep him abed all day. He was quite willing to sit quietly in the saloon, his arm in a sling, making up stories for Esperanza or talking with Rebecca about every subject under the sun.

The better she came to know him, the more she loved him and the harder it was not to show it.

The wounds were healing well and she was pleased with his swift recovery. It was a shock, therefore, when she left her cabin one morning to find Rowson awaiting her with a grave face.

"His lordship's a mite feverish, Miss Beckie. Will you come and see him?"

John was hot and uncomfortable and, above all, cross.

"Don't fuss so," he complained. "I'll wager I just have a touch of the grippe."

"Let me see your arm." Before Rebecca took off the light dressing that had replaced the bandage she could see that the area around the wound was red and swollen. She forced herself to stay calm. "I believe I shall ask our friendly apprentice apothecary to take a look."

Her patient glared at her. "He will just want to bleed me."

"Since you are not half dead from lack of blood, perhaps I shall let him this time, if only to keep you quiet. Do lie down, John, and stop looking daggers at me."

He obeyed, laughing at her fierceness. "Very well, ma'am, but I do not promise to allow that carpenter to cup me." He twisted restlessly.

"Fetch him," Rebecca murmured to Rowson. Their eyes met and she saw that he feared the same diagnosis as she did. An infected wound might mean losing an arm—or it might mean death.

The carpenter-apothecary inclined to the latter.

" 'Tis too 'igh up 'is lordship's arm, you see. Belike the poison'll already be up in 'is shoulder. I'll take the arm off anyways, if you like, miss," he offered with gruesome cheerfulness.

John looked at her with fever-bright eyes and wet his lips with the tip of his tongue. "Whatever you say, Beckie."

Rowson was silent.

Rebecca reached for John's good hand and held it tight. She could not make such a decision! But she had to, they were all waiting.

Then she noticed the faint red line running up across John's shoulder to the hollow of his throat. With one gentle finger she traced it. It was too late.

"No. We shall fight it. The captain must put us ashore to find a doctor."

Captain Hardy was very sorry but he had seen too many men die of blood poisoning to be sanguine. The least delay would increase the risk of his ship being caught in the Baltic ice, and all for nothing. He refused.

John's fever mounted until he was delirious. He was in no state to lay down the law. Rebecca helped Rowson bathe him with cool sea-water and slept on the floor beside him at night. While Rowson held his flailing arms she forced him to swallow a bitter decoction of willow-bark provided by the captain, and poured broth and weak tea into him by the gallon. In his rare lucid moments his dark eyes never left her face as she battled for his life.

She reached the edge of exhaustion, passed it and went on.

$=18=$

"Beckie."

The single word that was more of a croak brought Rebecca instantly out of her light sleep.

"John?" She rose to her knees on the thin mattress and, in a gesture that was automatic by now, felt his forehead. It was cool and dry. "John!"

She reached for his wrist, so thin now that the bones seemed too big for it. His pulse was weak but steady.

"Oh John!" Tears of joy rose in her eyes.

"Fetch Rowson," he whispered. "Quick."

She realized why he had awakened her and hurried from the cabin, a smile of pure delight on her lips. The return of modesty was surely a sign that recovery was on the way.

She knocked on Rowson's cabin door and he was with her in an instant.

"He's not . . .?"

"The fever has broken. He needs you urgently."

"Needs . . . ?" Understanding dawned and a beam spread across his face. "Right, miss." He sped to John's cabin.

Rebecca peeked round the door of the room he had left. Esperanza was fast asleep but Annie was easing herself into a sitting position on the bed, her expression fearful in the dim lantern-light.

"What is it, Miss Beckie?"

"He's better." Rebecca sank down on the bed beside her and hugged her. "He's going to be all right." She burst into tears.

Annie held her, soothing her like a child until she was calm. "Now off to your own bed with you, miss, and you get a proper night's sleep for once. There's going to be plenty to do the next couple of days."

The *Rochester Rose* was two days out of London. As the maid predicted, they were busy days though John no longer needed constant watching. He was too weak to talk and slept a great deal, but the way his face brightened when she entered his room persuaded her to spend with him as much time as she could spare. Everything had to be packed into their various trunks and portmanteaux and boxes, which must be carefully labelled so as not to go astray in the confusion of unloading. Then the captain had to be interviewed.

Since the Duke of Stafford's son had unaccountably survived, Captain Hardy was most anxious to do everything in his power to make up for his earlier lack of sympathy. He agreed that the first priority on docking must be to send one of his crew for a couple of carriages. He agreed that men should be detailed to help Miss Nuthall's party ashore. He agreed to stand surety for them so that they would not be delayed by customs officials, to see their trunks through customs, and to have them sent on by carrier to Stafford House.

In fact, Captain Hardy was so agreeable he even offered to send a messenger ahead on horseback to warn the duke's household of their arrival.

As the ship sailed up the Thames estuary, Rebecca sat back, satisfied that everything had been done that could be done to remove John with all possible speed to the safety and comfort of his own home.

At three o'clock on a crisp, smoky November afternoon, the *Rochester Rose* at last reached her berth in the London docks. That was the moment when Annie's pains started.

If anything, their arrangements were expedited by this. Neither the captain nor the customs men wanted a woman in labour on their hands. Sooner than Rebecca had believed possible, the carriages pulled up before Stafford House.

The front door swung open and a swarm of footmen raced down the steps. Their livery, green with red trim, reminded Rebecca of the uniform John had been wearing when he rescued her from the fortress. How strong and sure of himself he had been then. Now he was emaciated, exhausted by the short journey, lying patiently on the carriage seat waiting for help.

The moment the carriage door opened, Esperanza jumped out and darted up the steps shouting, "Gr'uncle Duke, Gr'uncle Duke!"

As Rebecca stepped down into the street to direct the servants, she caught a glimpse of a grey-haired gentleman in the hall, who caught the little girl in his arms. A short plump lady trotted past them and stood at the top of the steps, her hands clasped anxiously. Rowson was emerging from the other carriage, helping Annie down with tender care. A pair of footmen rushed to aid them.

"Canaille!" shrieked Gayo, the sight of the familiar house reminding him of his old vocabulary. "Hello, *hijo de puta*," he addressed the butler. "Slimy son of a sea snake!"

Rebecca supervised another four footmen in lifting John onto an improvised stretcher. She watched as they carried him up to the front door, the elderly lady fussing alongside, then turned back to see that the few pieces of luggage they had brought with them were unloaded.

The last of John's bags was just being borne away and only her own two portmanteaux were left. There was a sudden dearth of servants. She looked round just in time to see the front door of Stafford House close.

The great mansion with its pillars and pediments had embraced its own. There was no room for the outsider.

Dusk was already falling. Rebecca swallowed her hurt, squared her shoulders, and told the coachman to take her to Hill Street. Lady Parr was her cousin, she would take her in.

As the carriage turned the corner from Park Lane into Upper Grosvenor Street, the front door of Stafford House swung open again. The portly butler, his bald head shining in the light of the gas street-lamps, stepped out onto the top step and peered up and down the road. Shrugging his shoulders, he retreated to the shelter of the magnificent marbled hall and gave the porter a sharp dressing down.

"Lucky for you the young lady went off to her own home," he concluded severely, and forgot the matter.

Cousin Adelaide's house was not precisely what Rebecca would have called home. But then, she reflected drearily as she trudged up the well-known stairs, nor was any other place on the face of the globe entitled to that name.

"Lady Parr and Miss Curtis are in the small parlour," the sturdy footman who was leading her up had told her. At least he had not said he would have to see if her ladyship was at home, thus giving her the chance to deny herself. But then Donald had always had a soft spot for Rebecca when she lived here. It did not mean that he was sure of her welcome.

She wondered what sort of person Cousin Adelaide had found to take her place when she departed for Russia.

"Miss Nuthall, my lady," Donald announced, then stood aside and gave Rebecca an encouraging nod.

While Lady Parr's drawing-room was decorated in the elegant, if uncomfortable, Egyptian style, the small parlour was not intended for entertaining company. The olive green curtains were drawn against the dusk, and her ladyship was seated by a roaring fire in one of the heavy brownish-red armchairs she had inherited with the house from her brother. She was reading aloud from her favourite book of sermons. She paused in mid-word, looking up in astonishment as the footman's announcement sank in.

"Rebecca! Heavens above, what are you doing here?"

The faded wisp of a woman sitting opposite, untangling silks, stared in alarm, as if she thought the visitor might be a ghost.

"We arrived today from Russia, Cousin Adelaide. I hope I find you well?"

"Yes indeed, Emma and I go on excellently together. Miss Emma Curtis is my companion. Emma, this is my young cousin whom I told you of."

Miss Curtis seemed unsure whether to stand up and curtsy to her employer's cousin, or merely nod to an ex-employee. Her internal dithering was clearly visible on her face. Rebecca took pity on her.

"Pray do not get up, ma'am, you will spill your work. I am happy to make your acquaintance."

"Delighted . . . that is, so happy . . . I'm sure . . . " She cast a nervous glance at her ladyship then buried her nose in her silks again.

"Sit down, Rebecca," Lady Parr commanded. "You are thinner than ever, I declare, and no wonder, rushing off to foreign parts as you did, without notice."

For some weeks Rebecca had had no leisure to think of her looks, though she had been vaguely aware that her clothes were hanging loosely on her. However, the second part of this speech was of more immediate interest, containing as it did a scarce hidden rebuke for her abrupt departure.

She was too tired to continue fencing. Sinking into a chair, she leaned forward and said, "Cousin Adelaide, I have nowhere to stay in London at present. I must beg your hospitality for a little while."

"The Graylins have dismissed you? I am sorry to hear it. I fear I have no position to offer you, for I am perfectly satisfied with Emma."

Miss Curtis looked at her with timid gratitude.

"The Graylins have not dismissed me!" Rebecca retorted sharply. "However, they are travelling by a different route and are not yet arrived and I do not know when to expect them." She kept to herself the fact that her charge, Esperanza, was already in London. "I have no intention of attempting to usurp Miss Curtis's place. All I ask is your charity to a relation, however distant, in allowing me to stay here until I can make other arrangements."

Lady Parr was not noted for her charity, so perhaps it was her strong sense of propriety which prompted her to agree to this appeal. "I believe the blue bedchamber is made up," she said, ringing the bell. "You will wish to go up and put off your travelling clothes, I make no doubt."

Rebecca stood up and curtsied. "Thank you, Cousin Adelaide. If you do not object, I believe I shall retire. I am a trifle weary."

"Have you dined? I thought not." The urge to issue commands came to the fore. "You shall have a tray in your room, and I trust you will eat every bite. You must put some flesh on those bones."

Tears smarted in Rebecca's eyes as she remembered how John had piled her plate with delicacies. She blinked them away, glad that her cousin was distracted at that moment. Donald had come in answer to the bell, and Lady Parr was giving him orders for the housekeeper, the chambermaid, the cook. On his way out the footman winked at Rebecca. His friendliness gave her courage.

She followed him from the room. The blue chamber was where she had slept when she lived here, which meant that little Miss Curtis had been relegated to the back chamber. There were advantages to being a relative, even a poor one.

She could not stay here forever, though. As she undressed and washed in the hot water promptly sent up from the kitchen, Rebecca tried to begin planning her future. Thoughts kept slipping away from her into a haze of memories.

Fortunately it was not long before the chambermaid brought in a tray laden with cold meats and bread and cheese and apple pie, clearly intended to "put flesh on her bones." A slice of chicken, a few mouthfuls of pie and half a cup of tea (a strange, dark brew after the amber Russian liquid she had grown used to) were all she could manage. She set the tray aside and moments later was fast asleep.

When she woke next morning, she lay drowsily wondering why she felt so peculiar. Of course, it was the absence of motion. She was ashore at last. She had brought John safely home to England and now . . . and now what?

He was not to blame for her predicament. He had been in no state to see that she was invited into Stafford House. In the confusion of the arrival of a sick son and a maidservant about to deliver her first baby, Rebecca had simply been overlooked. They might send for her at any moment to resume her duties in the nursery.

Or they might not. John was by far too much the gentleman to abandon her without thanks, but perhaps he would be glad that she had been inadvertently removed from his immediate vicinity. It was the easiest way to end the growing intimacy between them. No doubt he would call on her when he was fully recovered, to express his gratitude. If she was here still she would reject it, as he had refused hers. It would be much too painful a substitute for the love she craved.

And if she was not here, where would she be? There was no knowing when Teresa would return. Muriel Danville might be glad to employ her in the nursery, but to apply to her was as unthinkable as to go to Stafford House and request reinstatement as Esperanza's governess.

Whatever she did, she must not let John think she was setting her cap at him. Nor, she resolved, would she ever consider going back to her uncle's house.

Only one course seemed possible: to seek a new position.

The prospect was enough to make Rebecca bury her face in her pillows, as if she could escape her fate that way like an ostrich with its head in the sand.

It would not be so terrible, she persuaded herself. She had discovered that she liked children and dealt well with them. Besides, nothing she might encounter as a governess could possibly equal in horror what she had been through in St. Petersburg and aboard the *Rochester Rose*. She sat up and reached for her dressing gown. Lady Parr always had the latest issue of *Ladies' Magazine* with its advertisements for genteel young persons to take charge of children. That was the place to start, and then there were agencies she could apply to.

The dark blue woollen dress she had worn yesterday had been cleaned and neatly pressed while she slept, and was hanging behind the door to air. One other was in the wardrobe, and almost all the rest of her clothes were in her trunk. Captain Hardy had promised to have that trunk delivered to Stafford House last night.

For a moment Rebecca's heart lifted—it was the perfect excuse to call there. Then she chided herself for her indecision. She already had excellent excuses if that was what she wanted, to take charge of Esperanza or simply to ask after John.

It was *not* what she wanted, she reminded herself fiercely. However good her reasons, she would not give anyone cause to hint that she was chasing after John like a shameless hussy.

She dressed quickly and went down to the dining room.

"Morning, miss." Donald was on hand with a fresh pot of tea, and breakfast was already laid out on the table and sideboard. Lady Parr always rose late, so someone in the household had remembered Rebecca's penchant for early rising.

"Good morning, Donald. Just a muffin and marmalade, if you please."

"Cook's doing a poached egg for you this instant, miss. Her ladyship's orders."

He grinned at her, and she could not help responding despite a slight annoyance with Cousin Adelaide's interference. She need not eat it, but she did not want to offend Cook and besides, she did need to put on some weight. John might come. . . .

She cut off that unprofitable train of thought.

"Would you mind running an errand for me this morning, Donald? My trunk must be brought from Stafford House."

"Right you are, miss. I'll be off this minute and fetch it back afore my lady comes down."

"Ask how Lord John goes on."

Rebecca managed to resist the temptation to tell him to inform them of her direction. If he should be asked, or happen to let it drop, it would be none of her doing.

The footman returned within the hour, carried her trunk up to her chamber, and reported to her in the parlour.

"They was wondering what to do with it, miss. That fancy butler arst where you was staying but I didn't tell 'im, seeing as you hadn't and not knowing the sittywation, like."

Swallowing her disappointment she gave him a half crown, glad that Teresa had insisted on paying her wages. At least she was not completely penniless.

"How is Lord John?"

"Not just what you might call in plump currant, they says, nor yet like to slip the wind. Seems the duchess called in every bone-setter in town though it ain't broken bones as ails his lordship by what I heard. The gen'ral 'pinion seems to be as his pa's right and what he needs is plenty o' rest and plenty o' good grub."

Rebecca was relieved to hear the duke's sensible prescription and hoped it would prevail. A desperate longing to be at John's side made her breath catch in her throat. The letter of application she was writing blurred before her eyes.

"Thank you, Donald," she managed to say, then remembered with a rush of guilt that she had not enquired after Annie. "Did anyone happen to mention a new baby in the house?"

"Yes, miss, I heard talk of a newborn boy. A little black thing they says, mother doing well and Lord John to stand godfather."

That news made Rebecca smile. John would be pleased to be godfather to Annie's baby, for his affection for children was as genuine as it was unexpected in a dashing gentleman of the sporting persuasion.

It was one of the things she loved about him.

"Will you go now and then to ask how his lordship goes on? There is no need to tell anyone where you are from; I daresay they will have scores of enquirers."

"Right you are, miss." If Donald was puzzled, he did not show it. There was nothing but sympathy in his good-humoured face.

A dozen times, as the days passed, Rebecca nearly gave in and sent word of her whereabouts. Pride intervened, and the self-respect John had been partly responsible for instilling in her.

Though it did nothing to salve her unhappiness, the response to her applications for a position was flattering. Most of her letters received answers expressing interest, and one of the agencies provided several interviews with prospective employers. She turned down one offer because her would-be employer was a widower, and another because the gentleman of the house was present at the interview and browbeat his wife.

Lady Parr was not pleased to hear this.

"Well upon my word, you are prodigious choosy for a young woman in your situation."

"I could not like them, Cousin Adelaide. There are still a number of possibilities, I assure you."

Her ladyship appeared to be placated, but the next evening she announced that she had written to Mr. Exbridge.

"You ought never to have left your uncle's house," she said with her usual censoriousness. "I am sure he is the properest person to keep you."

Shocked at first into silence, Rebecca made a swift recovery. She discovered that she was no longer afraid of her uncle. She did not want to see him, and would not go back to his house, but the horrors of the past few weeks had reduced him in her eyes to a petty tyrant.

"That will not be necessary, Cousin Adelaide. I have had two more conditional offers, which wait only on a letter of reference to decide. I hope you will be so good as to write me one?"

"Certainly!" Her ladyship was only too eager to do anything to assist if it would rid her house of her young cousin. "Emma, fetch my writing case if you please. However, I cannot testify as to your ability with children. You had best ask Muriel for that."

Rebecca did not want to ask Muriel for a testimonial any more than she wanted to ask her for a job. It was bound to lead to awkward questions, at the least. Yet, in the end, what did it matter?

Nothing could make her more miserable than she already was. To be sure, she had told no one where she was, but she was not so difficult to find if anyone tried.

Yet she had heard not a word from John.

= 19 =

NOT UNTIL A week after the *Rochester Rose* docked did John at last realize that Rebecca was not at Stafford House. Utterly exhausted, he slept most of the time and his waking moments were monopolized by a constant stream of medical men. In the drowsy times in between he thought constantly of Rebecca, but to ask after her was more effort than he was capable of making.

He assumed that it was propriety which kept her from him. After all, she was a young, unmarried female and in a dependent position. She could hardly demand to see him.

On the third day Sir William Knighton, the king's physician, was spared by his royal patient for long enough to look in on the younger son of the Duke of Stafford. Unlike his colleagues, all of whom had prescribed complicated, and different, courses of treatment, Sir William agreed with his grace that what Lord John needed was nothing more than rest and good food.

From that time he quickly began to mend. By the end of the week he was able to sit up in bed. It was then that his valet, Pierce, restored to him by some magic he did not attempt to understand, brought him a request with his nuncheon.

"It's Annie Rowson, my lord. The state you was in you won't remember, like as not, but you did agree to be the baby's godfather. Annie wants to be sure afore she has him christened that your lordship knew what you was doing."

"I had forgot," John admitted, "but now that you mention

it I do recall. You may tell her I shall be honoured to stand godfather, but I want to see him first. Ask her to be so kind as to bring him here, and I should like to see Esperanza too."

Pierce frowned. "Don't want to overdo it, my lord. Miss Esperanza's a lively young lady."

"Just for a few minutes." If Esperanza came, Rebecca would bring her. John leaned back against his pillows, smugly pleased with his stratagem.

Annie, her figure restored to its usual pleasant roundness, carried in a bundle so swathed in shawls only a little brown face could be seen. For a few moments John was so entranced by its tiny perfection that he noticed nothing else. Then he looked up to share his delight with Rebecca, and she was not there.

Filled with bewildered disappointment, he saw that Esperanza was holding the hand of an unknown nursemaid. The little girl stared at him with round eyes.

"Hello, Chiquita. Where is Aunt Beckie?"

She whispered something.

"I cannot hear you. Come here."

She broke away from the maid and scrambled, sobbing, onto his bed. "Aunt Beckie isn't here and you're ill and they said I must whisper and be good and Mama isn't here and I *missed* you."

Waving back the anxious nursemaid, he stroked the blonde hair gently. "I'm getting better every day, and you still have Annie."

"She was ill too, for three whole days! And then she got a baby." She sat up, the tears drying on her pink cheeks. "It's a good baby, mostly, 'cept when it's hungry. It's going to be called Andrew John, after Papa and you."

"If you don't mind, my lord?" put in Annie.

"I should hope my godson will bear my name." John smiled at her, but the tension inside him was sapping his small strength.

Pierce advanced upon the group. "Time to go if we don't want his lordship in queer stirrups again."

Esperanza's mouth drooped.

"Promise you will come and visit me every day?" John begged her.

"Oh yes, Uncle John, and I'll be good but I mustn't have to whisper, do I?" She slid down from the bed.

"No, indeed. My ears are working very well. I shall see you tomorrow. One moment, Annie, I should like a word with you." He waited till Esperanza and the nurse were out of earshot, then demanded, "Where is Miss Nuthall?"

"I don't rightly know, my lord. I've been a bit anxious, but I reckoned she must have told you where she was going."

"I assumed she would stay here. Someone must know! See if you can find out, will you, without creating a big hullabaloo?"

"Yes, my lord." Her dark face creased with worry, she bobbed a curtsy and hurried out, the baby clasped against her shoulder.

John lay back, drained. Where had Rebecca gone? And why? He had been so careful, before his illness, not to press his attentions upon her when she was vulnerable. He did not want her to marry him from gratitude, or because she was dependent on him. Had his love, his deep need for her, shown through despite his care and made her feel trapped?

He drifted into sleep. In his dreams she was once again imprisoned, but this time the bars were there not to keep her in but to shut him out.

When he woke, his valet told him Annie had asked to see him. Before he could send for her his mother paid him a visit, bringing an egg flip she had made for him with her own hands. The duchess was a short, plump woman, dressed in the height of elegance and given to threatening spasms when things did not go her way. John was very fond of her, but she was not the person he wanted to see at present.

He sipped the egg flip. "Delicious, Mama, only you left out the brandy."

"You are roasting me, you naughty boy." She beamed with pleasure. "When you were ill as a little boy I always knew you were growing better when you began to tease. Now drink it up and I shall leave you to rest as Sir William ordered."

As she bustled out, a dreadful thought struck John. Perhaps Rebecca had said or done something his mother considered encroaching—perhaps she had in fact asked to see him. Her grace was shockingly high in the instep and might have insisted on her departure after such a *faux pas*. Yet surely Annie would have heard if anything like that had happened!

"Pierce, fetch Annie, if you please."

"Too many visitors . . . " He caught John's eye. "Right away, my lord. But your lordship knows his grace will drop by before dinner."

"Fetch Annie!"

She hurried in a few minutes later, firmly shutting the door behind her with Pierce on the other side.

"Where is my godson?" John demanded, distracted from his urgent purpose.

"Sleeping in the nursery, my lord. Her grace was kind enough to say I can keep him by me."

"But you have left him all alone. He is so little, will he be all right?"

She smiled indulgently. "I can't be carrying him about all the time, my lord. The nursemaid will keep an eye on him, she's a good girl."

John could not very well ask a servant whether the duchess had thrown his beloved out of the house. He tried in a roundabout way to find out what Annie knew. "Was she hired especially for Esperanza?"

"No, she's a parlour maid really but she helps in the nursery when Lady Danville's children come to stay. She never saw Miss Beckie, my lord, but Mr. Boggs did, out in the street. She never came into the house, from what I hear. He was expecting her to come in, but she went off when he wasn't looking. She did send for her trunk though, next day. It seems a footman came for it, so she must be all right, don't you think? I did wonder if she might have gone back to Lady Parr."

"Of course! They are cousins, or related at all events. Bless you, Annie, I'll wager that is where she is."

John's relief was so great that it did not dawn on him for some time that he still did not know *why* Rebecca had gone.

His first reaction was to send to her and beg her to visit him. Simply to see her dear face, touch her hand, would be enough for now, until he was well enough to press his suit. His pride revolted. She would come, for pity's sake, and he did not want her pity. He would wait until he could go to her, take her in his arms and smother her with kisses, promise to take care of her for the rest of her life.

Yet that was not right either. She must have more choice than a simple alternative between marrying him and staying with the objectionable Lady Parr. John remembered that he had asked his brother to find out about her fortune.

"Pierce!"

"My lord?"

"I must write a letter to Lord Danville at once."

"His lordship is expected next week, my lord. The entire family is coming, I understand, for Christmas."

"It cannot wait so long."

"I shall send for his grace's secretary, my lord."

"Damn it, man, I can write my own letters," John protested, but his usual firm scrawl went off into wavery spiderwebs and he was glad enough in the end to dictate.

Even that effort tired him, and Pierce refused point blank to send for Rowson. John had thought to ask him to make sure Rebecca was indeed safely at Lady Parr's.

"Go to the devil!" he said drowsily and fell asleep.

He woke much revived by the nap and ravenously hungry. Spurning gruel and restorative meat jelly, he demanded a proper meal and received poached plaice and a blanquette of veal. Though roast beef was more what he had had in mind, he was devouring these delicacies when his father came in.

"We shall soon have you hale and hearty again," the duke said with approval. "Knighton said your constitution is excellent. Since you survived the infection, there is no reason you should not recover your full strength."

"I'd not have survived, sir, without the best of care."

"I know it, and I have already rewarded the Rowsons, though they made light of their service."

"They must have mentioned Miss Nuthall's part in my recovery."

"Indeed, they made it plain that you owe your life to that young lady. However, it is difficult to know how I can serve her when she has disappeared. Besides, she is a gentlewoman. One cannot simply offer her money."

"I am glad you acknowledge that she is a gentlewoman, sir. I hope to marry her." John had had no intention of revealing his secret to the duke, but in his weakness his father's sympathy and encouragement overcame his caution.

His grace frowned and patted his shoulder. "You are naturally grateful to the girl," he said. "We shall discuss the matter when you are stronger."

"And I mean to pursue a career in Parliament."

"Later, dear boy, later. Well, I must be off. I shall see you tomorrow."

"With or without your help," John muttered, pushing away his tray. He had overestimated his appetite.

He must obtain a seat in Parliament. He could not ask Rebecca to become the wife of a superfluous fribble. If his grace would not help him he would go to Hugh Iverbrook, or Lord John Russell, or even Brougham, that brilliant but erratic radical.

His breakfast next morning was brought by Rowson.

"That man o' yours is getting above hisself, m'lord. No visitors, says he, so I takes your lordship's tray out o' his hands and tells him we've private business to discuss. I seen Miss Beckie, m'lord."

186

"Where? When? How is she?"

"She's at Lady Parr's right enough. Annie sent me to check yesterday afternoon and I seen her going in. I didn't speak to her, m'lord, nor let her see me, being as Annie wasn't sure just what you was wanting."

"Sir Andrew's training, no doubt. She looked well?"

"A mite pale and thin in the face, and I can't say as how she looked happy."

If John had been able to rush to her side there and then he would have but he could not so he did not. With all the patience he could muster he set himself to regaining his strength as quickly as possible. He moved from his bed to a chaise longue, and then below-stairs to the drawing-room, where one or two of his friends were allowed to visit him—and his mother and her companion drove him to distraction with their cosseting.

In the meantime, he had received an answer from Tom. While Rebecca's lawyer admitted that the will had been badly drawn up (by his deceased partner), he could find in it no legal justification for giving her even her income before she married or reached the age of twenty-five. The best he could do was to stop paying the income to her uncle while she did not reside with him. It would be added to her principal, to be turned over to her when the time came.

Tom added that he had, with difficulty, persuaded the lawyer to tell him the amount of Rebecca's inheritance. It was sufficient for her to live in reasonable comfort on the income if she took a small house in the country. By no means a fortune, but at least an independence.

Much good that did her, thought John savagely, since she could not lay her hands on it. Propriety forbade his offering to support her if she would not marry him. She might as well be penniless.

Though he did not mention Rebecca again to his father, he did insist on discussing his parliamentary ambitions. The first morning he managed to walk below-stairs by himself he knocked on the door of the duke's study. Invited to enter he obeyed, trying to forget that the last time he had been in that room was the day of the duel, the day he had been sent into exile.

If he had never been exiled, he might never have met Rebecca. He hoped that was a good omen.

"Good morning, sir. I am well enough now to remind you of my desire for a seat in Parliament."

His grace, an active member of the government, looked up from the official papers spread on his huge oak desk and smiled. "Sit down, John. Only yesterday I received from Lord Cathcart an excellent report on your conduct in St. Petersburg. I could wish that your duties had not required of you the dissipation I hoped to see you leave behind. Yet perhaps it is the more to your credit that you managed to keep a clear enough head to carry out your mission success-fully. And to judge by the amount of gold found in your luggage, you won at the tables as usual."

"I have lost my taste for dissipation, sir."

The duke grinned. "As to that, time will tell. Besides, you need only look at the late Charles James Fox to see that you need not turn monk to be an effective parliamentary Whig."

"Then you will . . . "

"I happened to meet Holland at dinner last night. I dropped a word in his ear, and I must confess he was near choked with delight that any son of mine should turn Whig. He expects you to call at Holland House to discuss finding a place for you as soon as you have recovered your full strength."

"Thank you, sir. I am already a little acquainted with Lady Holland."

"Then your future is assured," said his grace drily.

The duke's willingness to use his influence in John's favour raised his spirits considerably. However, he still had not found a way to assure Rebecca of a comfortable life if she did not choose to marry him. If only Teresa and Andrew had not disappeared into the unknown—but then none of these problems would have arisen in the first place.

The duchess might find Rebecca a position, but there was no guarantee it would be any better than staying with Lady Parr. John could not bear the thought of her living in a family that treated her as a menial servant.

His brother's household would be better. Muriel had liked Rebecca, as had little Ned and Mary, and for all his pomposity Tom was never less than kind. John was sure they would be willing to offer her a home for his sake, if not her own. Best of all, he would be able to see her now and then, and perhaps in time he could teach her to love him.

By the time John reached this cheering conclusion, it was the day before Tom and Muriel were due to arrive from Lincolnshire, too late to consult them by letter. And Muriel was bound to go and visit her mother the next day.

She was almost certain to meet Rebecca there, before John had seen her. However she felt about him that would be unforgivable, after what they had gone through together.

Therefore John must go to Rebecca tomorrow. He was not yet as strong as he had hoped to be, but his heart lifted at the thought.

He went up to the nursery to join Esperanza for tea. Though he had not yet ventured out of the house, the stairs were no longer the insurmountable obstacle they had seemed only a few days earlier. Perhaps the obstacles between him and Rebecca would also give way before his persistence.

All the same, after Esperanza's usual energetic greeting he was glad to sink into the shabby old wing chair by the fire.

"Let me hold my godson," he begged Annie. The baby gripped one of his fingers firmly in its tiny brown hand and went back to sleep.

The nurserymaid brought up a tray of tea things from the kitchen and was sent to take her own. As a treat, Esperanza was allowed to toast muffins at the fire. Annie made the tea, poured John a cup, and went back to her ironing. The only sounds were the swish of the iron, the crackle of the fire, and the quiet muttering of Gayo on his perch in the corner.

The smell of singed muffin assaulted John's nostrils.

"Dearie me!" said Esperanza. "Uncle John, do you mind if it's a little bit black?"

"Not at all. Don't touch it till it has cooled a bit."

Annie was about to set down her hot iron to come to the rescue when a sudden shriek from the parrot made them all jump.

"Hello, hello, *dushenka!*"

"Miss Teresa!"

Andrew and Teresa were standing in the doorway, looking as cheerful and unruffled as if they had just returned from a drive in the park.

Esperanza hurled herself at her parents. The abandoned muffin went up in flames, Annie scorched a pinafore, the baby woke and began to wail.

Trying to hush his godson, in what he recognized as an inept male fashion, John watched the family reunion. He envied Andrew his wife and daughter, an abstract envy with nothing of jealousy in it. Teresa was his dear cousin and an admirable person; it was Rebecca he wanted at his side for the rest of his life.

Annie rescued the baby from him, or vice versa, as Teresa surfaced from her daughter's embrace. John rose to his feet while Teresa kissed Annie and admired the baby, then she turned to him.

"John, my dear, you are shockingly thin!" She hugged him. "Nothing but skin and bones. Have you been ill?"

"I shall tell you everything later. It's good to see you." He shook Andrew's hand.

Teresa glanced around. "But where is Rebecca?"

"That is part of the story." He shook his head as she appeared about to demand instant elucidation. "I know you better than to think you need to recover from the fatigue of a journey of several thousand miles, but it will wait until you are settled in. You do stay here, do you not?"

"At least until after Christmas," Andrew said with a grin. "I dread the consequences of refusing the duchess's standing invitation. Come and put off your bonnet, Teresa. We shall be with you in half an hour, John, if that suits you."

"In the library," he agreed.

They went off with Esperanza between them, hanging onto a hand on each side. John made his way below-stairs, trying to decide what to tell them about Rebecca. As he could not explain her absence it seemed better not to try. He would just tell them what happened in St. Petersburg and on the way home, and then ask Teresa if she was willing to take Rebecca back as governess to Esperanza. He could not think of anywhere she was more likely to be happy— except, he hoped, in his arms.

Andrew joined him first and poured them each a glass of sherry. While they waited for Teresa, he told John something of their journey from the moment Rowson left them in Russia.

"It sounds as if you positively enjoyed it," John observed.

"We did." Teresa came in at that moment. "It was a splendid adventure. Your experience was less than agreeable, I collect. Tell us." She sat down beside her husband.

As briefly as he could, John described Rebecca's arrest, imprisonment and rescue, and his own injury and long illness. They were horrified.

"That settles it," said Andrew, standing up and moving to the fireplace, where he leaned and stared into the flames for a moment before turning and straightening. "We endangered our friends, our daughter, and our servants to gratify our desire for new experiences. It is time we settled down, my dear."

Teresa laid her hands on her slender middle, and John guessed that she must be with child again. She nodded, a trifle sadly, and said with resignation, "All good things come to an end. I am determined to like Warwickshire."

Andrew laughed. "I am glad to hear it, but I do not mean to retire to my estate and grow corn just yet. I believe I have earned a post in Vienna, or even Paris."

"Oh yes!" Ever impulsive despite her matronly dignity, she jumped up and ran to kiss him. His arm was about her waist when she turned back to John.

"But that does not tell us why Rebecca is not here," she pointed out.

John felt his cheeks grow warm. Teresa and Andrew exchanged a glance and she came to take his hands in hers.

"Have you quarreled?"

"Good heavens, no!" His astonishment overrode his embarrassment; he could not imagine quarreling with Rebecca. "No, it wasn't that. To tell the truth, I haven't the least notion why she isn't here but I shall go tomorrow to find out. Only there is one thing I must know: will you take her back as Esperanza's governess?"

"Of course. For as long as she wants to stay." Teresa looked at Andrew again and he agreed.

John heaved a deep sigh of relief. If Rebecca accepted his hand tomorrow it would not be because she had nowhere else to go but because she loved him.

= 20 =

REBECCA SAT AT the little marquetry table in the parlour window, the only delicate object in a roomful of furniture as heavy as her heart. Though it was past ten, the sun had just risen above the houses on the opposite side of Hill Street. Frost sparkled on the tile roofs. Below, a dray horse clopped steadily along the cobbles, its driver huddled in his greatcoat on the rumbling wagon.

The sunlight fell on the sheet of paper on the table before her. She was writing a letter of acceptance but the words came slowly, her pen often wanted mending, the ink clogged and must be thinned. She was easily distracted, by a maid shaking her mop out of the window or a footman popping up from the area to run an errand like a rabbit emerging from its burrow.

She set down the quill with a sigh. It was an excellent position she had been offered, but it was no use pretending she cared.

Lady Parr had received a letter from Muriel two days ago. No opportunity of reminding the world that her daughter had married the heir to a dukedom was allowed to pass, and failing any other audience Emma Curtis and Rebecca must suffice, so by now Rebecca was thoroughly familiar with the contents.

"Dear Muriel will be arriving in town the day after tomorrow," Cousin Adelaide had announced. "They always spend Christmas with the duke and duchess, usually at Five Oaks, the Kent estate, but this year they will stay in London,

I collect. It seems that though Lord John is much recovered from his shocking ordeal he is still too weak to travel."

Rebecca clenched her fists in her lap, determined not to reveal her eagerness for further news.

"Does Lady Danville bring her son and daughter?" asked Miss Curtis. "I quite long to meet your dear little grandchildren. They must be the best behaved children in the world, I am sure."

"Yes, and that brings me to another matter. Rebecca, I informed Muriel that you are in want of a situation, and she writes that she will be happy to employ you in the nursery. It is excessively obliging of her, I vow, but then Muriel always was a dutiful daughter. So you need look no further."

"Indeed, Miss Nuthall, you are very much beholden to Lady Danville," declared Emma Curtis.

"It is very kind of Cousin Muriel," Rebecca had to agree. At the same time she had resolved not to accept unless she exhausted every other possibility. She liked the family, but living in John's brother's household she would be unable to avoid seeing him now and then, and that would be agony.

The next day she had been offered a position as governess with a family residing near Bath. She had met and liked the mother and two small girls, and she would be well paid. It seemed ideal. Yet here she was, a day later, unable to put pen to paper to accept.

Rebecca's pride was waning. She must see John once before she went away. If she had already arranged her future he could not think she was pursuing him.

She went back to her letter.

As she dipped her pen in the inkstand, a hackney clattered to a halt just below her window. It was too early for genteel visitors, and the carriage was too close to the house for her to see who stepped out. There was a sharp rat-a-tat-tat at the door, and she heard the sound of Donald's voice, followed by his footsteps clumping up the stairs. Lady Parr was forever scolding him for his elephantine tread.

The footman opened the parlour door. "It's a gentleman, miss, says he's your uncle. A Mr. Exbridge."

Rebecca shivered. For a moment a wild, unreasoning terror overwhelmed her, then she forced herself to remember that she was not afraid of him any more. She remembered the cell in the Peter-Paul fortress, and the endless hours wondering whether John was going to die in her arms. It was like looking down a long, dark tunnel, and the little, angry man at the far end was her uncle.

Donald's voice seemed to echo from the tunnel. "Miss? Are you all right? I'll tell him you're not at home."

"No, let him come up," she said calmly. "Only leave the door open a crack and wait just outside, if you please."

There was no sense in taking chances. Nonetheless she was confident, in control of the situation. She was writing when she heard the door open again and Mr. Exbridge snapped, "Rebecca!"

"I shall be with you in just a minute, Uncle. Pray be seated."

She could almost feel the outrage directed between her shoulderblades, but when she turned to him a moment later he was sitting down and there was as much puzzlement on his face as fury.

"A fine greeting this is, Niece, when I have come all the way to London to fetch you home."

"You came all the way to Lincolnshire before, sir, with no better success than you can expect now."

"Ah, but your fine friends are not here to protect you now, my girl. Her ladyship writes that you have lost your position and that she cannot offer you a home." He was sneering now, the confusion gone as he recalled her invidious situation. "So off you go this instant to pack your traps and we'll catch the mail this very evening."

"No, Uncle, I shall not go with you. Indeed, I wonder why you want me. There is no love lost between us, I think."

"The why is my business." He rose and advanced upon her. "I'll have no more of your defiance or you know what's coming to you!"

195

She kept her seat, shaken more by the memory of his violence than by the threat. Another step closer and she would call the footman.

He took it, raising his hand. The door flew back with a crash and John strode into the room.

His fists were clenched and his dark eyes burned in his thin, pale face. His gaze was fixed on Mr. Exbridge, who took a step backward in alarm.

"Beckie?" John glanced at Rebecca.

"I am all right," she said softly, though inside her coiled the fear that he would once again resort to blows.

Perhaps he saw it in her face, for he deliberately relaxed, letting his breath out in a long sigh. He too stepped back, to lean against the wall, watchful.

"I beg your pardon," he drawled, "I fear I interrupt. Pray do not regard my presence."

"My uncle was about to take his leave, my lord. He was kind enough to invite me to return to Buckinghamshire with him, but as I have been offered an excellent position I shall be unable to accept. Donald!"

The footman appeared instantaneously and looked about with suspicion. "Yes, miss?"

"Mr. Exbridge is leaving. Show him out, if you please."

"My pleasure, miss." He grinned. "This way, sir."

The squire glanced uncertainly from the short but solid servant to John, tall and powerful despite his thinness, and then to Rebecca. Her calm dignity and resolute bearing appeared to be the deciding factor.

"I hope you will deign to visit your poor old aunt and uncle one of these days," he said with uneasy joviality. "For old times' sake. Well, good-bye, then."

He put out his hand but Rebecca did not take it. She bowed slightly.

"Good-bye, Uncle. Pray convey my . . . compliments to my aunt."

"My lord." The squire's nod was curt, accompanied by a glower of intense dislike. John did not respond.

Mr. Exbridge made his ignominious retreat. Donald went after him, closing the door with a click distinctly audible in the silence that followed their departure.

"Will you not sit down, my lord?" Rebecca's voice sounded brittle in her own ears. Her nerves were ready to snap.

"Thank you, no. I am no longer an invalid." He moved to the table, leaned on it with both hands, towering over her. He was angry. "How could you agree to meet that man alone? Of all the ill-considered, muttonheaded starts!"

"Do not scowl at me so!"

"Suppose I had not come in just then?"

"I should have sent him to the rightabout. I am not afraid of him any more. Besides, I had Donald wait just outside the door."

"You cannot rely on servants, and someone else's servant at that," he said impatiently. "Marry me, Beckie. Let me take care of you."

Astounded, she gazed up at him, incredulous, then joyful. All too quickly, she returned to earth. From the moment she had met him he had protected her, rescued her from danger and distress. Gallant, chivalrous, he saw marriage as the best way to fulfill the obligation he had taken upon himself. His offer was almost unbearably tempting—but she wanted his love.

Besides, she told herself, turning away, he would come to regret it. His family would object to her undistinguished, though respectable, birth and her lack of fortune. One day, perhaps, he might find a woman to love, someone as lively and intrepid as Teresa. She would become a burden to him.

"Beckie?"

"No." She had sworn never to allow a man power over her. Her uncle's visit reminded her of her vow. "No, I cannot."

He laid one hand gently on her shoulder, trying to turn her towards him. If she looked into his beloved face, if he tried to argue with her, her resolve would fail.

She broke away and ran from the room.

"Damnation!" John swore softly. In his frustration and despair he drove his fist at the little table, pulling back at the last moment. Violence, even violence that would only hurt himself, was no answer. Was that why she had refused him? After all this time was she still unable to trust him not to react with blows?

He sank wearily into the chair she had just vacated, his head in his hands.

All his plans for the future turned to dust and ashes. There was no point in regaining his strength if he was never again to hold her soft slenderness in his arms. He might as well lapse back into a life of dissipation if she was not going to be there to encourage and applaud his efforts. He needed her belief in him, and there was so much he wanted to give her in exchange. Not only material wealth, but all the tenderness and passion, all the devotion that, unexpressed, was tearing him apart.

He glanced around the gloomy parlour. The dark green curtains, the maroon upholstery and faded carpet increased his depression. When he entered the room, full of hope, the sun had been shining on Rebecca's hair. How splendidly she had defied her uncle! Perhaps she was right, she did not need his feeble protection.

Her letter, lying on the table in front of him, caught his eye. Her firm, rounded handwriting was so plain that he took in the meaning of the few lines without intending to pry.

At least he could spare her the unpleasantness of going among strangers. His immediate impulse was to tear the paper to shreds, but again he restrained himself. As soon as he reached home he would ask Teresa to come here and assure Rebecca of a place in her household.

The sooner that was done, the better. He pushed himself to his feet and left the room.

The footman was waiting in the hall. After one look at John's face he held his tongue and opened the front door with alacrity. Remembering the man's readiness to aid Rebecca, John tossed him a sovereign.

"Watch over her."

"Right, m'lord."

His carriage was waiting. A few minutes later he was back at Stafford House, enquiring of the butler as to Teresa's whereabouts.

"I believe Lady Graylin is in the nursery, my lord." Boggs's usually expressionless face was concerned. "Shall I send James to ask her ladyship to step down? Allow me to lend your lordship a hand up the stair."

John shook his head and plodded upward. He must look as fagged out as he felt. When at last he reached the nursery, Teresa's anxious exclamation confirmed it.

"John, you are exhausted! Come and sit down at once."

Sinking into the wing chair by the fire, he summoned up a smile for Esperanza, sitting at the table with her favourite chalks.

"I'll be ever so quiet, Uncle John, so's you can sleep," she promised. "Gayo's not here so there won't be any noise. 'Less the baby cries."

"Where's Gayo?"

"He's gone back to my dressing room. It would only worry Muriel to think that her children might be exposed to his occasional lapses from propriety."

"He said a naughty word this morning," Esperanza announced with considerable satisfaction.

"Hush now." Teresa kissed her daughter and took the chair opposite John. "Do you want to talk?"

"I want to ask a favour." His arms felt heavy and useless, empty. He raised his voice. "Annie, will you let me hold my godson?"

"Of course, my lord."

She was ironing again; the sweet smell of starch filled the room. She put down the iron with care and went to the cradle in the corner. The baby was awake. He cooed and gurgled at his godfather, waving his little arms. A measure of peace entered John's bruised heart.

"What can I do?" Teresa asked quietly.

"Will you go to Rebecca, right away, and tell her you want her? Tell her you *need* her."

"You were going to do that."

"I didn't have a chance." He lowered his voice and glanced at Esperanza, but she was once more absorbed in her drawing. "Oh, I made a real mull of it! Her uncle was there when I arrived and I forgot all my pretty speeches."

"Her uncle? I have never heard her speak of him."

"She had rather forget him. He came to fetch her from Tom's, before you arrived there, and after I sent him away with a flea in his ear she told me something of her life in his house. I expect I ought not to tell you, but I want you to understand her." Repeating what Rebecca had said, and what he himself had seen, of Mr. Exbridge, John found his impotent fury reviving.

The baby, half asleep, stirred and whimpered in his arms. He strove to remain calm.

"That explains a great deal," said Teresa thoughtfully when he finished the story. "I don't quite understand, though, why the man is so eager to have her restored to his custody."

"He lost control of her income when she left. A paltry sum, yet her keep probably cost him no more than half of it. If she had stayed there no doubt he expected to cow her into handing over the principal when it is passed on to her. However, do you not think his real motive might be resentment at losing control over her, rather than the money?"

"Possibly. He cannot be accustomed to defiance. Yes, I daresay you are right. What a dreadful creature! Rebecca must trust you a great deal to have confided such a shocking tale to you."

"I hoped so. I believed so. Yet she was greatly shocked by that wretched duel, and worse so when I knocked Exbridge down, though it was in her defence. For her sake I am learning to control my violent impulses, which are not frequent, I assure you! And I have never struck a woman since—" he smiled bleakly, "—oh, I was six or so. I kicked a parlour maid and got the birching of my life."

"You love Beckie greatly, do you not? Muriel and I knew you were attracted to her before we all left for Russia. Before you did, I suspect."

"I did not realize how I felt until she was arrested. Even Kolya suspected before I did. What a slowtop I was! Then after we rescued her from the fortress, she was under my protection and I could not honourably pay my addresses. You cannot imagine how difficult it was to stand aloof. Later, of course, I was in a sense under her protection. At least, I was in no fit state to offer. And now I am free at last and I made a cake of myself. I did not even manage to tell her that I had arranged a comfortable future for her if she chose not to marry me. She refused me anyway. Do you think she is in love with Kolya? They were on the easiest terms, and he had more to do with saving her than I did."

"Fustian! She was gratified by his flattering attentions, to be sure, but no more than any pretty young lady with her first admirer."

"He thought of marriage. His father warned him off."

"Did he, indeed! Still, it can have been no lasting passion or he would have defied Prince Volkov. You will not hesitate if you encounter opposition, will you?"

"Of course not," John said impatiently, "but that is beside the point since she will not have me."

"Did she give you any reason?"

"No." The strength of animation died out of him. "She ran from me."

"Excellent," said Teresa, to her cousin's surprise and irritation. She stood up, the energetic grace of her movements unaltered in the years since he had first met her. "I had best be off to assure her of a place in our home. And you, my dear, had best stay right where you are and rest. You are burned to the socket. Annie, a footstool for his lordship, if you please. Chiquita, you have been behaving angelically. I shall be back shortly. Be good until I return and I shall take you to Gunter's for an ice."

"Lawks," said Esperanza with an experimental air, "I druther have Aunt Beckie than an ice any day."

Teresa laughed and swept out of the nursery, her vitality somehow leaving John more exhausted than ever.

"You know," he said to Annie as she set in front of him a footstool decorated with worn needlepoint roses, "I always thought I wanted to marry someone just like your mistress."

She shook her head indulgently. "Now Miss Teresa would never have done for you, my lord. Someone quite different'll suit you a whole lot better, mark my words."

Sighing, he raised his booted feet to the stool, settled the baby firmly in the crook of his arm, and rested his head against the back of the chair. His eyelids drooped. If only he were not so tired . . .

$=21=$

THOUGH NOTHING BUT embers remained in the fireplace, the bedchamber was still quite warm, for Lady Parr did not stint on coals. It was misery that chilled Rebecca as she huddled in the chair by the window. The sun had moved round to shine into the far end of the small back garden, its rays pitilessly illuminating the single leafless tree, the empty flower beds, the yellowing patch of lawn.

Rebecca saw herself withering away into a sere, loveless old maid, always taking care of other people's children, never her own. Was she mad to have refused John? Was not her own love enough to build a marriage?

If he came to regret that he had wed her, he would never reproach her. Yet she could never be content, knowing he longed to be free. She weighed the chance of unhappiness with him against the certainty of long, lonely years without him, and could not decide whether she had made the right choice.

Despite her heartache, a gleam of triumph sneaked into her thoughts now and then. She had defied her uncle and won. Admittedly she had had help, but it was help she had requested. She had made preparations before receiving him, instead of waiting submissively. Even if John had not come in, she would have prevailed.

There had been murder in John's eyes. For a moment she had been sure that her uncle was once more to be laid senseless at her feet. He had restrained himself, for her sake, she knew. He was fond of her. Was it enough? Should she have accepted him?

How thin and pale he was still! Under pressure from Cousin Adelaide, Rebecca had put on a little weight since arriving in London, but she could still feel her own ribs through her thick woollen dress. They were a pair of scarecrows, well matched. She smiled mirthlessly.

There was a knock at the door and the parlour maid stuck her head into the room.

"Lady Graylin's come, miss. She's asking for you. In the drawing-room."

Teresa! Rebecca's immediate impulse was to say she was not at home. How on earth was she to explain that she had forsaken Esperanza because a door had been closed too soon?

Suddenly she felt both foolish and guilty. She had been so taken up with her own emotions she had selfishly abandoned her duties because she was slighted, quite possibly by accident. At the very least she owed Teresa her most fervent apologies. She squared her shoulders. If she could face her uncle, she could face even this embarrassing situation.

"Pray tell Lady Graylin I shall be with her in a moment."

Quickly she tidied her hair, once more severely braided. The dress she was wearing—she had scarcely noticed what she put on this morning—was a plain grey worsted morning gown, with high neck and long sleeves, that had served two winters at her uncle's before she even came to London. It would have to do.

She hurried down to the drawing-room. Teresa was standing near the hearth, examining with visible distaste a statue of the Egyptian jackal-god Anubis that graced the mantle.

"I always did dislike that thing excessively," she remarked in a conversational tone, turning as she heard the door open. "My dear Rebecca, how happy I am to see you again."

Rebecca curtsied, trying to stop her mouth quivering. It was impossible to force words past the lump in her throat.

As she rose, she was enveloped in Teresa's verbena-scented embrace and found herself crying on an azure velvet-clad shoulder.

"I'm sorry," she sobbed.

Teresa patted her back and led her to an elegant if uncomfortable sofa with arms in the shape of crocodiles' grinning mouths.

"I cannot imagine where Lady Parr found these things, I vow! I had forgotten this particular monstrosity. Sit down now and tell me everything."

Rebecca blew her nose. Interrupted by hiccups she tried to express her penitence. "It was shockingly wrong in me to have left Esperanza without a word. For weeks John had been my chiefest care. To tell the truth I had almost forgotten she was in my charge."

"Why did you leave? Why not go with the others into my uncle's house?" Teresa sounded more curious than reproachful.

"The door closed. Somehow it was impossible to go up to it and knock and ask to be admitted. It was silly of me to take affront. I daresay it was only a careless servant."

"I am certain of it. Yet how should you have been able to think straight after what you endured in St. Petersburg and on the voyage home? Andrew and I feel very much to blame for your sufferings."

"Oh no, indeed I never thought . . . "

"But we are. Andrew has decided to quit the spy business and try for a respectable post in a more predictable country. On that basis, we hope you will come back to us."

"You are not only asking because you feel responsible for what happened?"

"Fustian! We need you. I am in the family way again, and Chiquita misses you very much. When I offered to take her to Gunter's she said, 'Lawks, I druther have Aunt Beckie than an ice any day.' "

Rebecca could not help smiling. "She is a darling. I could come to you when you leave Stafford House."

"Did John offend you in some way when he was here this morning?" Teresa asked in her usual forthright manner.

"John?" She was startled. "How do you know he was here?"

"He told me. In fact, he asked me to come and assure you that you have a home with us."

"Then you only asked me back for his sake."

"No, I asked you back for my sake and Chiquita's. Which is not to say that I would not do so for John. I am very fond of him."

"And he of you. He admires you prodigiously. You are the sort of woman he should marry, lively, adventurous, beautiful, well-born."

"What a catalogue of virtues!" Teresa turned serious. "Yes, perhaps he does admire me, but I would not suit him as a wife. Andrew has the self-assurance to be able to cope with my starts. I used to think that John was equally confident. It was you who showed me to the contrary. He needs someone who will support, not challenge him, someone who believes in him, someone to whom he can feel protective, yet who is strong enough for him to turn to in his need, as he did to you when he was ill." She paused. "You did not answer my question: has he offended you?"

"No, but how could I accept his offer when he was only being chivalrous? That's what he said, just as you guessed it, 'Let me protect you.' If I were at Stafford House, he might try to persuade me to change my mind."

"If chivalry was his only motive, then you need not fear that he will pursue you. After all, with Andrew and me you will be in no need of protection. But that was only a small part of it. To be sure it was chivalrous in him to arrange for your comfort if you do not choose to marry him, but he proposed because he is desperately in love. He is very unhappy. Do you dislike him so much you cannot bear his attentions?"

"No, oh no! It is not that. I am afraid I should give in if he asked me again."

"And why should you not?" Teresa sounded satisfied.

Rebecca bowed her head. "I am a coward. I grew up seeing my uncle beat his wife, and I swore I would never put myself in a situation where that could happen."

Teresa took her hand. "It must have been very terrible, but not all marriages are like that. You have seen others now, mine, and Muriel's. Do you mean to go through life being afraid?"

"You cannot understand. You rescued Annie from the slave ship, and Muriel from the slaver when he abducted you. How would you know what fear is?"

"Who told you about the abduction? Muriel? What do you think would have happened if I had let her see how terrified I was? Bravery is doing what you can, even when you are frightened, just as you did on the way back from Russia. Besides, you have no reason whatsoever to fear John. He would, and nearly did, give his life for you."

Rebecca was silent. From the moment when he had pulled her from the river, half dead and wholly at his mercy, John had never treated her with anything but the utmost gentleness. She had seen him refrain from violence under extreme provocation, because she was present. She trusted him.

Perhaps it was pride that had raised the issue, in an effort to postpone the capitulation she saw coming.

"Did he tell you that he loves me?" she asked hesitantly.

Teresa's brow wrinkled in an effort to recall precisely what he had said. "Not in so many words, but in a round-about way. I could not be more certain of it."

"Why did he not tell me? And he guessed where I was, why did he not contact me sooner?"

"He is still not in very plump currant. He is angry at himself for his weakness, because he wants to be strong for you. Uncle Stafford says that John is making plans for a career in Parliament, and my guess is that he wanted to arrange everything before he asked for your hand. Not adequate reasons for delay, I daresay, but remember that he has been very ill. Surely you can forgive him."

"I do, of course. But I have just refused him. I cannot run after him now!"

Teresa grinned. She stood up, straightened her elegant hat with its blue-dyed, curling ostrich feathers and pulled on her kid gloves.

"Chiquita is asking for you. Will you come and see her? And Annie is eager to show off the baby."

"Wait, oh please wait." Rebecca was half way to the door even as she spoke. "I shan't keep you above a minute. My pelisse . . . I must put on a bonnet . . . oh dear, this dress . . . "

"I shall not leave without you," Teresa reassured her, but Rebecca did not take the time to change her gown.

Teresa had come in the duke's landaulet, which was always put at her disposal when she was in London. Rebecca sat beside her, her hands clasped nervously, as the groom drove the short distance through the busy streets of Mayfair.

Suppose Teresa had mistaken John's meaning. Suppose he had changed his mind after this morning's meeting, or, worse still, scorned her for chasing after him. As the carriage turned the corner into Park Lane, Rebecca nearly begged the driver to stop and let her out.

It was too late. They pulled up before the imposing façade of Stafford House, the front door was opening, the vast marble entrance hall engulfed her. Meekly she followed Teresa up the grand sweep of the main stairway, then up a lesser stair. To her relief there was no sign of the duke or duchess.

They stopped in front of a door that was slightly ajar.

"Let me go first," said Teresa. "The baby is likely sleeping and Chiquita's greetings are enough to wake the dead. I shall bring her out here to you."

She disappeared, and for a dreadful moment Rebecca thought that she had indeed been brought here only to see the children. Then Chiquita flew into her arms and it was impossible to feel anything but delight in her welcome.

At last the little girl's enthusiasm calmed. Rebecca's bonnet had been knocked askew. Teresa untied the ribbons, took it off, and set it on a nearby table.

"As I thought, the baby is asleep," she said. "Annie is expecting you. Chiquita, let us see if Papa is home from the Foreign Office and would like to go with us to buy an ice." She gave Rebecca a little push towards the door. "Go on."

The nursery was silent. Annie looked up as she entered, set aside her sewing and curtsied, beaming.

"It's a real pleasure to see you again, Miss Beckie," she said in a low voice.

"It is good to see you, too, Annie."

Rebecca kissed the maid, who had gone through so much with her, but her gaze wandered about the room. John was sitting in a chair by the hearth, cradling a baby in his arms. He made no move to greet her, and she realized he was sleeping. His face was pale and tired, defenceless in relaxation.

All her doubts fled.

Walking softly, she went to him and kissed his forehead. He blinked up at her drowsily. She was distantly aware of Annie deftly whipping the baby from his clasp and departing.

Rebecca had had enough of lengthy explanations.

"I love you," she said.

John pulled her down onto his lap and his mouth took hers with a passionate hunger that was as satisfying as it was unexpected. His arms held her captive, straining her against himself as if he would never let her go. It was some considerable time later that he looked down at her with a tender, half teasing smile.

"Dearest Beckie, there is one thing I keep forgetting to tell you. I love you, too."

If you would like to receive details of other Walker Regency Romances, please write to:

Regency Editor
Walker and Company
720 Fifth Avenue
New York, NY 10019